The
Never
Dead

CW00690799

DEADGUYLLC

All rights reserved. No part of this book may be reproduced in any form or by an electronic or mechanical means, including information storage
and retrieval systems, without permission in writing from the publisher, except by a reviewer who may quote brief passages in a review.

First Edition: May, 2023
Published by DeadGuyLLC

Ryan C. Thomas © 2023 Solipsism in the Switch grass
Christine Morgan © 2023 Cosmic Catapult
Jeff Strand © 2023 Avert Thine Eyes
Tim Curran © 2023 Witchblood
Patrick Lacey © 2023 Bad Sounds
Dan Henk © 2023 The Beach
Bobby Lisse © 2023 Revolution
Bracken MacLeod © 2023 Dreamers
Nat Robinson © 2023 The Void
Bridgett Nelson © 2023 The Ties That Bind
Patrick C. Harrison III © 2023 Howl of the Leather Dog
Jack Bantry © 2023 The Onion Club
Dan Henk © 2023 Skinheads Ruin Everything
Bobby Lisse © 2023 Hatch
Marc Schoenbach © 2023 Wires
Robert Essig © 2023 The Cheap Rooms

Dan Henk © 2023 illustrations
Cover Layout - Marc Schoenbach
Book Layout - Joe Gass & Bobby Lisse

Tales of Terror

The world is indeed comic
But the joke is on mankind

- H.P. Lovecraft

Solipsism in the Switchgrass

Ryan C. Thomas

It was the stupid backpack that did it. Slung over his right side, it was full of books, heavy, and when he'd steered his bike to the edge of the road it had shifted sideways just enough to tip him into shoulder of the road. He wasn't even going fast, but the front wheel got caught up and the bike spilled sideways, and he went over the shoulder and somersaulted down the outside embankment, right into a small boulder. He slammed into it hip-first and felt something go instantly wrong with his legs.

"Fuck," he winced, noticing now that his left leg was toe-up but his right leg was heel-up. As he tried to elbow himself up from his supine position agonizing pain sailed out of some biological nether and raced up his entire body. "FUUUCKK!"

The intensity of it immobilized him. He lay back down and started breathing through gritted teeth.

"No no no," he muttered. "It's broken. Definitely broken. Holy fuck is it broken."

For a few seconds he closed his eyes, willing away the panic. He opened them again and stared up through four-foot-high switchgrass at the baby-blue sky above. It was so bright it hurt his eyes. Where were his sunglasses?

He reached up to his head and screamed again. Every movement was debilitating. His chest constricted and he gulped air to steady his nerves. Steeling himself, he ran his fingers around his ribs. Something was bulging out in ways it hadn't just minutes earlier. A broken rib? Had to be. So not just his leg but his ribs too. Fucking awesome. Fucking wonderful. The boulder was off to his right. Not very large. No bigger than a basketball, but hard enough and angled enough to do damage.

He was only forty years old. This shit didn't happen to forty-yearolds. It happened to octogenarians in convalescent homes.

"Phone," he muttered, realizing he had to call for help. First a friend, then an ambulance. But first a friend. He had plenty of friends, and they had to be close by. The hotel with the writer's convention was only a few miles away, and even though the event had ended at noon, he knew people would still be hanging out in the bar area. Who'd still be there?

Bryan? Izzy? Someone.

At first he couldn't find his back pack, then spotted it several feet away in the switchgrass. When he reached for it, his whole body went rigid with agonizing pain. This was beyond anything he'd ever felt before. He let loose with a scream that momentarily shut up all the buzzing insects around him. When it passed, he looked at the backpack again. So close but a yard too far away. How the hell was he going to reach it?

"Just breathe. Just fucking breathe, dude." His calming mantra did nothing to alleviate the aches that were now swimming up his leg. Even though he knew it was stupid, he wanted to test just how much he could move his leg. Maybe he could get into a less painful position and drag himself to the bag that held his phone.

Again, he looked at his right leg. The heel up, the toes down. He'd either broken the hip or completely dislocated it. He took his watch off and placed the band in his mouth, bit down. Holding his breath, he moved his right foot.

He wailed, saw blackness before his eyes, fought to stay conscious.

Without warning, he began to cry.

"Help!" he yelled, but then stopped because that rib was barking back, and he wasn't strong enough to fight through the agony.

He cried some more.

***

A half hour passed. The bright blue sky was beginning to turn gray. Would it rain? Probably would, knowing his luck.

The insects were chittering so loud it was like lying in the middle of table saws. Bzzzzz. Bzzzzz. Bzzzz. Just shut the fuck up, he thought. Occasionally a bird would squawk overhead, and they'd go silent for a second or two, but then they'd resume buzzing.

Perhaps because he was thinking of this, he glanced down at the ground around him and focused on the dirt. It moved with tiny beetles and ants and other leggy things, but nothing major. No snakes, no rats. Just bugs doing what bugs do. He was aware that the mosquitos would be out at some point, but he figured it was only four or five o'clock at this point.

He also realized the pain hadn't abated at all. If he shifted anything below his waist even a millimeter, the pain nearly knocked him out.

"OK, phone phone phone."

He stretched out an arm toward the bag. It hurt like hell, but he was prepared for it this time. He groaned and cried and pushed the switchgrass aside as if that would bring the bag closer. But it didn't. He stopped, waited for the pain to ebb. How could he get the bag? The grass? Could he make some kind of grappling hook? Was he fucking Batman now?

He grabbed the roots of the switchgrass and yanked, hoping to pull out a large bundle. Instead, he pulled himself half an inch closer to the bag. But there was a cost, and his hip reminded him. He screamed and screamed, and the bugs shut up in awe of the show.

He let go of the grass, weeping.

"Where the fuck is anyone?!"

Where the fuck indeed. Thing is, he didn't even know where he was. The state road leading into town, toward the hotel. Nothing but empty land and some farms from there to the next town. He figured he was halfway between them. Who owned this land? Someone had to. It was a state road, someone had to drive by. Cops had to patrol it eventually, right? He'd hear them coming and scream no matter how much it hurt. Or he'd throw a rock. Could he even do that? Maybe they'd see his bike. It had to still be on the side of the road. Please God or Satan or whatever entity that can hear me, let someone see my bike.

He kept still, starting at his backward leg, listening for cars. Nothing. Just bugs.

***

If he didn't move the pain was tolerable. If he moved, he screamed. But he needed his phone. He grabbed at the roots again and yanked, dragging himself another half-inch closer. The pain was immeasurable, and he wailed for the hundredth time. This time, however, he saw his home screen light up for a second, revealing the picture of his latest book,

Blood Cock Death Orgy Part II: Oozing Fuck Farm of Cum Chunks by Ed Lordge. It was his most disgusting book yet, full of the type of depravity that would cause the Marque De Sade to wince. He'd reveled in reading a passage at the author convention, beamed when people in the audience grimaced and walked out. Knowing he could affect people like that was a powerful feeling. He was too intense for them, too hard. Besides, if they didn't like graphic rape and incest and necrophilia and bestiality that was their problem. He pushed limits because that's what artists did. Those people were all pussies who couldn't handle the darkness. Just like the book bloggers who called out his syntax and grammar. Screw them. You didn't need to know the rules of writing when you had the ability to create images so disturbing, they made people puke.

He watched the screen go dark again, wondering why it had lit up in the first place. Then it hit him. His voice had turned it on. Yes! He forgot the latest update of the phone would respond to his voice commands even if it was locked.

"Siri, call 911!"

The phone screen lit up, showing his book cover again, but it did not dial. A blue wheel spun in a circle. In the upper corner he saw just one bar of service.

"Oh c'mon! You're gotta be fucking kidding me!"

He waited for the phone to reset and tried again. "Siri, call 911."

Again, the blue circle spinning. He closed his eyes and waited. Nothing happened. This was all some kind of cruel joke.

"Um, are you ok?"

He lifted his head, grit his teeth in pain. Who's voice was that? It wasn't on the phone. Who'd said it?

"Hello?" he mumbled.

"Are you ok?"

The voice was weak, frail, tinny.

"Please help me," he begged. "Please, I broke my leg or my hip or something. I'm in so much pain. Please help me."

The switchgrass swayed in front of him and he heard footsteps. With a rush of air the grass parted and a teenage girl emerged. "Oh man, you don't look good," she said.

"Yes! Thank you thank you thank you. Please call 911. I need an ambulance."

She tilted her head and stared at his leg. "Your leg is backwards. You know that?"

"Hell yes I know. S'why I need an ambulance. Hurry."

"Hurry what?"

"Hurry and call! I'm in so much pain. I need to get out of this field."

"Oh, I can't do that."

Her words stunned him. Had he heard her correctly? "What'd you say?"

"I said 'I can't do that.'"

"What? Why? I need an ambulance."

"I can't have anyone come to this field."

"What're you talking about? Why?"

"Because this is the field where my daddy buries his bodies."

Her words froze him. His thoughts swam in circles like fish schooling together to avoid a predator. "The fuck are you talking about?"

"My daddy doesn't even allow me to come without him. It's a bad field."

"Yeah, no shit. And I hope you're just fucking with me. Funny joke. Now can you go call please."

"Like I said, I can't. This is daddy's body field. He said no one's allowed. You fell in the wrong field, mister."

Ed's whole body shivered, and pain throbbed in his hip. He tried a new tactic. "Look, I don't know what you're talking about, and I don't care. I don't even know where the hell I am. I couldn't point this out on a map if you put a gun to my head. Just get me out of here and your daddy's field remains a secret."

"Hmmm. Lemme ask him." She stood up and poked her head above the switchgrass. "Hey, Dad!"   Ed's eyes went wide.

From far away came a deep voice: "Yes, Scarlet?"

Ed's eyes went wider.

"Daddy, there's a man here says he needs help and if we help him, he won't tell where your special field is.

"Jesus Christ, Scarlet, why is there a man here?"

"I dunno, but I saw a bike out near the road. Might be his."

"Hang on, I'm coming over."

She leaned down into Ed's face again. "My daddy is coming to talk to you. Hang on."

Heavy footfalls grew louder, and the tall grasses all swished in unison. Ed could hear a man's labored breathing approaching and held his breath, wondering if he'd just made a huge mistake.

The footsteps were close. A man was huffing and puffing. Over the top of the grass a shovel appeared, getting closer. Then the grass was folded down and a large overweight man was suddenly there. Slung over his shoulder was another man whose clothes were awash in blood. Ed could immediately tell that person was dead.

The large man dropped the corpse right next to Ed. The head bounced with a loud thunk, then lolled toward Ed, revealing a dark cavity where its nose and mouth should have been. Buck shot had ripped up most of the eyes.

For the first time since the fall, Ed screamed out of fear instead of pain.

"Oh shut up," the man said. "No one's out here but us. What happened? You take a fall?"

Ed nodded but kept on yelling.

The large man raised his foot up over Ed's head. "Shut up or I'm gonna stomp your teeth out. Can you walk?"

Ed managed to stop the screaming. His mouth trembled and he felt a coldness overtake his body. "No," he managed to say.

"What do we do, Daddy?" Scarlet asked.

"Well, we can't just leave him here in this state, I suppose. Get his phone and turn it off."

Scarlet did as instructed, then handed the phone to her father.

Ed began to cry. That phone was his lifeline and now it was gone. And here he was lying next to a faceless corpse.

"Please, I won't tell anyone."

"None of that now. You certainly won't tell anyone because you are hell and gone from anyone who gives a fuck. And truth be told if you would have just rode by I wouldn't have given a fuck neither. But here you are and I got work to do. So just hang tight."

Daddy took a second to scope out the field around him, then hefted his shovel. "Yeah, this is as good a place as any, I guess." "I feel like we've been in this spot before," Scarlet said.

"I feel like you think the whole field is the same spot, girl."

"I remember this grass."

"Sure you do."

With that, the large man started shoveling a few feet away from Ed. With each drive of the shovel into the dirt, Ed whimpered.

Scarlet bent down and touched his face. "You have nice lips."

"Are you going to kill me?"

"Well, I'm not."

For the briefest of seconds Ed had hope he might get out of this alive, but then the sound of the shovel snapped him out of it.

Scarlet moved around him and opened his bag, took out his book. "Hey Daddy, I found a book. Can I keep it?"

Daddy grunted and kept on shoveling. Dirt flew up over everyone and scattered in the air. Some of it rained down on both Ed and Scarlet but she didn't seem to mind.

Scarlet read the title of the book and wrinkled up her nose. "Ew, that's gross. Who writes this kind of stuff?" She turned the book over and noticed Ed's picture on the back. "Oh my God, it's you! You wrote this? Hey, Daddy, this man wrote this book! How cool is that. A real-life author right in your field."

If the large man was impressed he didn't show it.

"What's it about?" she asked.

Ed muttered through chattering teeth. "It's just a horror story."

"Will you sign it for me? I love books. Sometimes Daddy brings me some but I don't think he's ever brought me a horror one before. Mostly just regular stuff and books about God. Can you make it out to me?"

"Um…"

"I see a pen in your bag." She took it out and handed it to him.

"If I sign it, will you help me?"

12

"Oh, I can't help you now. But I sure would like a signed copy of your book."

Daddy's voice came booming over the grass: "Sign the book, boy, or I'll make you sign it."

Ed signed it, his hands shaking so badly the signature was nothing but a tiny squiggle.

"Thanks!" Scarlet said, bounding off to show her daddy.

"Fuck fuck fuck fuck," Ed murmured, tears welling up in his eyes again.

***

An hour passed. The sky was striated in deep orange and pink. Bugs had crawled up his pants and found their way to his crotch. He itched them but touching anything near his hips was so painful he found it easier to just let them explore. So far, none of them had bitten him.

Daddy finally returned, his face red and covered in sweat and dirt.

Like some poor man's psychologist, Ed figured maybe he could appeal to the man's paternal senses. After all, he seemed to care for Scarlet. He must have a modicum of mercy in him somewhere. Or maybe, thought Ed, I could show him we're simpatico. I mean, he's burying a dead body, and I write really dark stuff. We're practically the same.

"Hey, mister, I don't blame you for what you did to this guy. I mean, did he try to rob you or something? Hey, I'm a supporter of the Second Amendment. I get it. Home invasions are no joke. Looks like he had it coming, right? You call me an ambulance, hell, I'll come back and help you take care of any future trespassers. At the very least I could help you dig some holes. Seriously, so many people deserve a bullet to the head. I get it. You gotta protect your family. So whatdya say? Help me out and I promise I'll come back and help you. Might even be good research for a book. I've never dug a grave before. That's hardcore, man. I like it."

Daddy took a faded red bandana from his back pocket and wiped sweat from the back of his neck. "Oh, I'm not digging the hole to put that body in. No, I'm digging that hole to let something come up from underneath. Bit of a doorway, if you will. Like the holes mice and voles make. Whole tunnel system under the field. But it's down a couple feet.

Sometimes it's hard to find the veins. But I found one so it won't be long now."

"What…what's in the holes?"

"I wish I knew what they were. All I know is many years ago when my own father built our house down the road here, we had a bit of a scuffle with some things that wanted us to leave. They came into our house and attacked my mother and father. They took my sister, though I don't remember that bit because I was only a baby. They took her here and fed on her and we never found the body. They came back a few months later and took the dog. Then later they took some motorist who'd broken down and came to stay with us while the tow truck came out—in those days there was no twenty-four-hour service, so the man had to wait until morning. He slept on our couch, until those things came and got him and dragged him back here. My father figured out two things by then. One: when their bellies were full, they slept for a bit. Same way an animal does, you know. Two: dead people leave behind goods, like wallets and watches and stuff. You can sell that stuff and it sure does beat working at some deadbeat job in the rain and heat all day. Of course, people don't really carry cash that much anymore. But they all carry something. Like your phone, that watch beside you. That looks fashionable. Usually, people have them smart watches nowadays."

Ed had bought the Fender watch at a Hot Topic years ago because he thought it looked cool and he planned to pick up girls by telling them he was a lead guitarist in a punk band. He couldn't play guitar but what did they know. Stupid stupid stupid.

Ed quickly realized his Stockholm Syndrome ruse had failed miserably. He needed a new tactic. "The cops can ping my phone. Trust me, I've researched it. They can get within fifty feet of the last ping." This wasn't entirely true. It was a one-star review of his last book that taught him the police can ping phone signals. It had pretty much nullified the entire plot of that book. But he pressed on. "They'll know I was here. They'll check this field. They'll check your house."

"Doubtful. There's not much service here. Oh, sure if the wind blows right maybe you'll get a bar, but no more than that. I took a trip to the library way out in town. I learned how to erase a phone. I opened some online seller accounts. Sell those phones for good money. Sell anything I find for money. Those books in your bag. Your bike, even, once I get the serial number off it and stamp a new one in. What else you got? That shirt looks in good shape. Some kind of movie? Someone'll buy that. Yessir, I'd say you brought me a few hundred dollars easy. Enough to keep the lights on, put some gas in the car. Out here things are not so expensive. And all I gotta do is keep the field fed."

"No. No the cops will come. They'll find me somehow. Just let me go and save yourself the hassle."

"Cops ain't coming, boy. I don't know if you've noticed lately but cops ain't working too hard to stop crime these days. They ain't saving anyone from anything."

"Please just let me go."

"Where you gonna go anyway? You can't walk. Probably got lots of internal bleeding going on. Your leg is fuckside up. Looks like some mad scientist attached it wrong. Nah, you're not going anywhere. This field wants you. Probably already smells you."

Ed stammered, fighting back tears. "Are you going to kill me?"

"You want me too? I can go get the gun."

"No. Please."

"Alright then. Figure you ain't moving so I won't waste the ammo."

The man inhaled long and hard, held the air in his lungs for a couple seconds before blowing it out. "You smell that?"
Ed did smell it. The scent of compost. Hot, burning soil rife with decomposition.

"The field knows it's getting fed."

The man patted Ed on the leg, which sent shockwaves of agony through his body. Ed screamed and tried to jerk away but it just made the pain worse. The man stood up and said, "Shit. I gotta go. I think I pulled something in my back a minute ago. I need to go lay down. Not as young as I used to be. Out here digging these holes. Probably need to hand over the job to Scarlet but she's all…" He made bird-flapping motions with his hands to insinuate Scarlet was flighty. He stopped and rubbed his lower back. "Ow, that hurts. Anyway, you just sit tight, it won't be long now."

Scarlet poked her head out from the switchgrass. "Should I get his bag?"

"Hell yes, get his bag. And the watch. Get his bike too. He drop anything else?"

"No. I didn't see anything."

"Ok, grab all that and get on back to the house." With that, Daddy turned and walked into the tall grass, which closed behind him like curtains.

Scarlet held up Ed's book. "Thanks again for signing it. I'm gonna read it before Daddy sells it."

Ed reached a hand toward her. "Please don't do this. Just call an ambulance. I won't tell. I promise."

"I can't. It's the field, see? You fell in Daddy's field. You shouldn't have done that. Bye."

She shouldered his bag and disappeared through the same curtain of grass as her father.

Ed was all alone. Swimming in pain and lost in terror.   Beside him lay the corpse with its missing face. He could see chunks of bone and gristle and ichor inside the skull. Beetles were scurrying over the wetness of it all. It glistened like prime rib and chicken wings smothered in cherry juice, all mashed up in a bowl. It stank like trash and sweat and piss. Who had this man been? How had he ended up near Scarlet and her dad's place?

The stench of death was once again overtaken by the ripe, pungent aroma of compost.

Ed stared at the darkening sky and frantically thought about how to save himself. He couldn't move, couldn't crawl, his screams reached no one. There had to be a way. Maybe the pain would subside and he'd be able to move. He'd written that once in a story. A character had his arms cut off and waited for the numbness to set in before fighting his way to safety. It could happen, right? He could go numb and then find the upper body strength to move?

He shifted his hip just to check and howled in pain. Tears flowed down his cheeks, realizing he had no chance of moving at all. He was trapped, suffering, scared out of his mind.

The corpse next to him moved.

He yelped in fright. "Oh God!"

Was it alive?!

The corpse moved again. But this time he knew it wasn't alive. Something underneath it was trying to free itself. It jumped a third time and went still.

"Jesus Christ what is that?"

The switchgrass rustled louder. He could hear things moving near the floor of the field. It sounded like animals. Rats? Squirrels? Opossums? What was out here?

There was a squeak as a small animal climbed up onto the dead man's back and stood staring at Ed. No, it wasn't an animal. It was something different. Something about a foot tall, hairless, with red and pink skin, the hues of a ripe peach. It was humanoid, if humans could be so little. Two arms, two legs, no tail. Long, black claws arced out of its fingers and toes. Its eyes were off-white with stitches of red veins. Its nose was bulbous, and its face resembled an elder Jimmy Durante (who Ed only knew of from old Loony Tunes cartoons). Between its legs a tiny, wrinkled penis hung down like a dead meal worm. It lifted its head and sniffed the air.

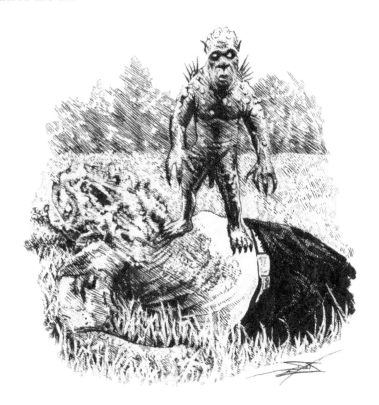

"Ahh! What the fuck are you!" Ed was hyperventilating, a new fear overtaking him.

The small creature opened its mouth, revealing human teeth, with the exception of oversized, sharp canines, like vampires and werewolves had in bad horror films.

"Dear fucking God, go away."

The creature raised its arms and squeaked again, only this time its squeak morphed into the blare of a child's toy trumpet. A second later more of the naked humanoid creatures appeared overtop the corpse's body. Some brushed dirt off their skin, others didn't care. Their body types were slightly different from one another. Some had bloated bellies, some were so thin their ribs protruded, some were taller, some had large penises and longer nails.

The first one that had arrived sat down, felt along the shirt of the corpse, and dug its nails through the fabric into the dead man's hide. It yanked on the skin, pulling and using its claws to cleave the subcutaneous fat. It tore loose a piece of flesh and greedily ate it. The sallow fat globbed through its teeth like gelatin until the creature sucked it back in. It swallowed, squeaked, and trumpeted again. With a sudden frenzy that seemed to come out of nowhere the other creatures began digging into the flesh. They frantically yanked off chunks of skin and scooped out bloody flesh, gnashing it all in their teeth.

Ed screamed. None of this could be real!

The creatures shredded the dead man's clothes in a frenzy and began to carry all the tatters back through the grass toward the smell of compost. Toward whatever hole they'd emerged from. Back and forth they went like worker ants. For a brief second, Ed wondered why they'd bothered taking the swatches of clothes. Did they use it to make nests? Did they eat it?

With the facelees corpse now completely bare the creatures were able to just bite into the flesh and tear out chunks of meat. Their pink and red faces were smeared in blood and gore and Ed now saw that their penises were erect and undulating. Just like living mealworms.

One by one the monsters fell to their bellies and began to spear the corpse's gaping wounds with their dicks, humping up and down.

Jesus Christ, Ed thought, they're fucking it!

The tiny monsters pounded away at the dead man, jabbing their dicks in an out, an orgy of blood and flesh and dirt and grass and tiny little dicks fucking fucking fucking hard and fast. The corpse was completely engulfed in hairless pink and red humanoid monsters thrusting so fast it created the wet popping sounds of suction cups on glass.

One of the tiny monsters let loose with a tinny roar and shot backwards, cumming a stream of dark yellow goo into the corpse's torso. It wiped its forehead in exhaustion and smiled at Ed.

The other creatures followed suit, each one roaring and then ejaculating thick monster semen. The pressure of each demonic orgasm caused the monsters to recoil up off the body for a moment, landing in exertion.

For a few minutes nothing happened. The little monsters just sat staring at the corpse and at Ed. Occasionally they'd itch their dicks or lick their blood-stained lips. Ed thought maybe they'd fall asleep and he'd have a chance to get rid of them, pick them up and snap their necks.

Then the corpse started to bubble like it was being boiled in a searing stew. The skin started to slough off right in front of Ed's eyes. He heard the bones snapping inside the body, sharp cracks like the nunchucks effects in the Kung Fu movies he liked. The skull caved in on itself, the gaping hole in the face crumbling as if it were made of plaster. Blood oozed out of the body's pores and swam underneath Ed's body. It was cold and thick and flowed incredibly slow. The monsters now stood up, growling, getting to work, pulling the body apart. The hands came off at the wrists. The feet came off at the ankles. They peeled the skin off in slick ribbons that no longer seemed to adhere to the fat underneath. The fat washed off the muscle and bones like bacon grease.

The creatures started taking all of this away, dragging it through the grass back toward the hole they'd emerged from.

Soon Ed was staring at nothing but striated muscles and pink organs. The pectoral muscles were particularly tough for the creatures to rip apart so again they used their nails to create a gash which they then shoved their tiny dicks in and fucked until they popped into the air with glee.

Ed watched as the gooey semen began to melt the muscle. He got it now; the creature cum was some kind of acid that broke down the body parts. Even the ribs underneath began to crack in half. The creatures then stripped all the muscle and bone and took it away to their hovel.   Over the course of the next hour, as the moon floated above him like a cataract, the creatures finished carrying the pieces of the dead man into the hole in the ground. Ed could only imagine where it went. He imagined a network of tunnels and nests under the earth filled with the bones of every human that went missing and was never found. Finally, the last creature jumped up on his chest and looked him in the eye.

"Please don't," he begged. "Please don't eat me and fuck my corpse. Please."

The tiny bald thing smiled wide, showing sharp teeth and black gums. Bits of flesh were lodged in its diastemas.

"I don't want to die," Ed murmured.

The creature turned away, leapt to the ground and scurried off into the tall grass.

Ed was alone. The night air had turned cold. He shivered and it made the pain in his hip flare up so he forced himself to stop.

What felt like an eternity went by and he started screaming again.

"Help! Help me!"

He screamed until he was hoarse, and his lower half was nothing but white-hot agony.

He gave up and stared at the night sky. Tiny bugs were crawling all over him now, attracted to the congealed blood on the ground all around him. He swatted at them, but they bit anyway. The mosquitoes were particularly brutal, buzzing in his ears and stabbing at his face.

The night went on forever. At some point he fell asleep.

***

He awoke to the sound of footfalls. I'm saved, he thought. But his heart fell to his stomach when the grass parted, and Daddy and Scarlet reappeared.

"Still alive, huh?" Daddy said. He was rubbing his back and groaning.

Ed tried to plead with them but the bug-bite welts on his face seared and his throat cracked with dryness. All her could get out was, "Buhh…"

"Why didn't they take him, Dad?" Scarlet asked.

"They got their full of the other guy, I suppose. Even an alligator rests after a big meal."

Scarlet bent down into Ed's face. "I started reading your book last night. It was real gross. Do you really like that stuff? Cutting people up and having gross sex and just all around being nasty?"   Ed just stared back at her. It hurt too much to nod.

"Stop reading that trash," Daddy said. "Put that book back in the bag so I can sell it. See what this guy is worth. Go on back to the house."

Scarlet gave a wink to Ed and made her way back into the depths of the field. Daddy scanned the environment around him, all the while caressing his lumbar area.

"Shit. The little guys go back in their hole they cover it all up. Just like gophers. I'd dig you a new one but as you know I wrenched my back yesterday with that shovel. I suppose I could get my gun though. You want me to do that? At least you wouldn't feel no more pain. I'm sure I'll be ok again in a day or two. Dig a new hole then."

Ed had never wanted to wake up from a dream so much in his life. Of course he didn't want to die. Who just gives up that easy? There's always hope, right? He shook his head no

"I figured. Ok, I'm gonna go lay down." Daddy started back through the switchgrass then stopped, faced Ed one last time. "You know, it's too bad you won't die the way you think is cool. All that butchery in your books and Satan stuff. You ask me, this is much worse. Worse than getting hacked up. Worse than getting death-fucked by tiny monsters. Yeah, this is a way worse way to die, just lying here in pain reflecting on it all, knowing it's coming. Coming real slow. Dehydration, starvation, can't move, can't talk, pissing yourself, nothing but pain if you move. Maybe you'll get lucky and a coyote will show up and go for your throat. I doubt it though. Haven't seen them around here in a while. Then again, maybe them little rascals will figure out how to come up on their own. Who knows."

Daddy left the field.

Ed listened to the grass swishing and tried several times to move but just ended up squinting in enormous amounts of pain.

He lost time. At some point his belly ached so bad it overshadowed the pain of his broken hip. Then eventually he choked on the dryness of his own throat and his head hurt and he shook and saw lights behind his eyes.

This is truly worse, he thought.

Cosmic Catapult

Christine Morgan

The blondie, now? She looked like a screamer.

Nineteen, maybe twenty. What Simon's gran would have described as "pleasantly plump," and right proud of it. Dressed to show it off, even, in snug pre-ripped jeans and a low-cut sleeveless top with a push-up bra what did wonders for her cleavage. Real gift of God, there, and if God were feeling particularly generous on this fine summer night, that bounteous bosom might leap spang out of its confinement to give them all a fine show.

She'd love it, too, the blondie would. Oh, she'd fuss and act all mortified, but underneath, she'd be soaking up the attention. Basking in it, luxuriating, like a cat in the sun.

A screamer, for sure. Loud and theatrical-like.

Good. Always good for business, that.

Her brownette friend? Not so much a screamer. More the faintertype, if Simon Bodean were any judge. Which, after forty-plus years doing this, since he'd been a mere scrap of a lad, he prided himself on being.   The brownette had a more bookish, quiet way about her. Pretty, but too serious to make the most of it. Taller and slimmer than the blondie, she wore a pair of them calf-length cottony pants and a not-too-tight tee-shirt with the blue phonebooth/port-a-potty box from that doctor show on it.   A fainter, yeah. Her big eyes would go even bigger, bright with terror, then roll up as her head lolled and her limbs flop-flailed around all boneless. He'd seen it a million times, and it always struck him amazing how none of their necks broke from whiplash.

They waited in line, the blondie clutching the brownette's arm and squealing with excited anticipation as each pair ahead of them took their turn. It wasn't the quickest process on the midway, and other rides ran far more customers through, but the Cosmic Catapult was by far the star of the show and everyone knew it.

Oh, the Hypercoaster was a popular draw, right enough, and the great pendulum swing of the Ghost Ship. There was always something to be said for the nostalgia factor of the good ol' Ferris Wheel and Tilt-AWhirl. But, for sheer daredevil spectacle, nothing beat the towering twin spires and the two-seater carriage suspended between them on super-long bungees.

That in itself made for an impressive enough sight, but, just lately, Simon had consented to his daughter's urgings to amp it up some. Before, it'd only been the Catapult, plain and simple, nothing fancy, got the job done. Now. after quite a bit of work and even more expense, it was a genuine show-piece. The spires were strung with color-changing bulbs, revolving gadgets sprayed displays of laser beams into the sky, the lights were synchronized to space-age music from a complicated computerized speaker system Simon didn't half understand, and a high mural-painted backdrop curved partway around the whole works.

The mural had been Marco's doing, yet another example of how Simon could hardly deny Ava anything once she had her heart set. He'd had his doubts at first, but even he had to admit, the boy'd done a hell of a job. Swirling galaxies against a star-shot expanse, alien landscapes with planetary rings and strange moons, not quite psychedelic and not quite realistic while having aspects of both. More than eye-catching ... mindcatching, somehow. As if there were hidden symbols or messages worked into it that you could sense, if not actually see.

Yes, indeed, the Cosmic Catapult!

Which, technically he supposed, should more properly be called a slingshot, but Cosmic Slingshot -- or (anything) Slingshot -- just didn't have the same ring to it. A slingshot was what a little kid used to ping pebbles at stray dogs or passing cars. A catapult, well, that sounded dang near epic.

Ava, having buckled in and secured the current riders -- a dad-andson duo -- stepped back and gave him the thumb's-up. The dad was all beer gut and hearty bluster, joshing his boy about how this'd put some hair on his chest. The son, elevenish, who'd just hit the height restriction by a fraction of an inch, appeared equal parts exhilarated and scared shitless.

A pisser? Quite likely. A puker? Simon hoped not. Pukers were the worst, hardest to clean up after, caused the most delay.

The mom, watching from the sidelines, leaned over the waist-high metal fence right quick to snap a picture of the two of them, as Simon gave his customary brief spiel. Everyone in line, as well as passing crowds of fair-goers laden with cotton candy and cheap carnival-game prizes, paused, craning to watch.

He did the three-two-one countdown, yanked the lever, and -

KA-SPROOOOIIIIIIIING away they went, hurtling skyward! The hearty-bluster dad shrieked like a teakettle. The son stayed silent; the Catapult-Cam video screen on Simon's control console showed him clenched tight as a miser's buttcheeks, everything about his grim expression suggesting here he was fully expecting to die before he'd so much as touched a girl's titty.

Unlike the other midway rides, the Cosmic Catapult didn't take tickets from the booklets bought at booths around the fairgrounds. It was cash-in-hand, fifteen bucks a head. For an extra fiver, Lottie would print them out a souvenir pic from the video; for an extra twenty, they could have a copy of the whole thing on one of those minicomputer-widget things. The 'I Survived the Cosmic Catapult!' stickers were free, dispensed by Ava when she unlatched them after. The tee shirts ran eight bucks' kidsize and standard, ten for the larger sizes.

Good money. Kept him and Ava right nice, paid Lottie and Jess a decent wage, even let Simon put some away for some theoretical eventual retirement. Yes, the upgrade remodel had been something of a pinch -- even with Marco just about offering to do the mural for free; if Ava so much as batted her eyes, he'd jump through hoops of fire -- but the results were already proving worth it.

The dad-and-son duo pogoed around, up and down, back and forth, in slowing increments against the darkening sky. As was often the case, after that initial teakettle shriek, the dad overcompensated with a lot of whoops, hoots, and hollers; such fun, a real blast, and nope, he hadn't been scared, not a bit! The son remained grimly silent; whether he'd pissed or not remained to be seen, but as far as Simon could tell, he'd at least not done a puker.

His expression, on the Catapult-Cam, had changed, though. Gone slack and distant. He stared blankly off at nothing, with a hollow emptiness downright disconcerting. His face was ashen. Simon couldn't be sure, but he might even have bitten through his lip so's it bled thin trickles across his chin.

The dad finally noticed, once Jess was winching the seat-carriage back to its starting point at the launch pad. He left off the bluff heartiness in favor of concern -- "Buddy? Hey, bud, you okay? It's over. Bud?" -- and the mom rushed forth as soon as Ava moved to unbuckle them, maternal instinct being a powerful force.

"Charlie? Charlie, what's the matter?"

"Come on, bud, don't scare your mother."

"Is he all right? Is he all right? Charlie, look at me, talk to me!"

Ava glanced from the kid to Simon, with a warning-worried wince. He sighed inwardly and cussed under his breath. The parents had signed the release forms, their boy had eked past the height requirement ... legally, all should be in the clear ... but you never knew when someone might cause a stink.

It took the dad and Jess to hoist the kid out of the seat; he was inert as a mannequin but stayed upright when they set him on his feet. His pants were dry, which was a plus. His empty gaze went right through his mother as if she weren't there, which was a minus.

"Charlie!" She grabbed him and shook him.

Everyone waiting in line and watching from the midway blatantly rubbernecked, going up on tiptoes, jockeying for position to get a better view.

Ava winced toward Simon again. He gestured for her to stay cool, just stay cool, play it normal. After a subtle nod of acknowledgment, she put on a cheery smile and pasted a sticker to his chest.

"Awesome job, you did it! Hey, Lottie, I think this guy deserves a free tee-shirt!"

"What's wrong with him?" The mom shook Charlie again, and the dad settled a big hand on his shoulder.

At that, the kid gasped and twitched and did a whole-body shudder, blinking up at them with the shock of someone jolted from a bad dream.

"It almost got me," he said.

The various other adults exchanged puzzled frowns as Charlie's mom swept him into a hug and patted him and fussed over him and told him it was fine, he was safe, nothing was going to get him ... all while glaring this-is-your-fault daggers at the dad.

"Well, now, there we go, let's move it along," Jess said, raising his voice, his tone jovial, as if this was nothing new.

He herded the family in the direction of the exit, and they went along willingly enough, the mom suggesting maybe they'd had enough carnival rides for now and the dad agreeing, saying how he, at least, sure could go for a corn dog or a big ice cream sundae. Charlie brightened, then turned to Ava as she rushed up with the child-sized tee-shirt Lottie had brought over from the booth.

"Something's up there," he told her, soft and solemn. "I saw it. It saw me, too. It almost got me."

Ava's cheery smile wavered. He'd spoken too quietly for most of the onlookers to catch his words, but those closest whispered and muttered amongst themselves. The kid looked at the sticker on his chest and the folded tee-shirt in his hand, tracing his fingertips over the 'I Survived the Cosmic Catapult!' logos. A shaky little laugh, not a happy kid laugh, escaped him.

"It's up there," he said to Ava. "I think it's hungry."

Then he went along with his parents as Jess ushered them to the gate, taking only a single haunted look back at the rising twin spires.

Dubious, Ava raised her eyebrows at Simon. She looked so like her mother when she did that, it about broke his heart all over again. He gave a half-shrug -- what can you do? -- and she grinned, before facing the line of paying customers with a brisk clap and amiable, "Who's next?"

He'd despaired, at first ... him, raising up a girl by himself? But damned if Ava hadn't grown into a fine young lady, hard-working and capable, sweet and kind. If her falling for Marco proved the worst of it, well, could a doting father truly complain? Marco may have been a mite peculiar -- a dreamer, an artist, a head-in-the-clouds type -- yet, what with his parents, he at least came by it honestly. Maggie Zuri, as Madame Magdalena, read palms and cards and crystals out of a burgundy velvet tent with gold fringe, while Tomas Zuri did stage magic under the moniker Mister Mystic. Fine folks, carnies of long standing. And, whatever else, Marco was clearly smitten with Ava, smitten to the core.

He let go those musings as Ava got the next pair of paying customers secured in. Grown men, the both of them, near Simon's own age. Biker-toughs in heavy denims and black leather vests, one sporting longish hair and a greying ponytail, the other bald as an egg, both liberally tattooed. He kept an eye on them, because sometimes fellas took rude at having a pretty thing like Ava fastening harness buckles between their legs, but these two behaved themselves nice and polite.

The bikers bumped fists as the countdown began, then gripped the padded lap-bar the way they might've gripped motorcycle handlebars.

KA-SPROOOOIIIIIIIING! Up, up, and away, the men voicing wild shouts more befitting the war-cries of Vikings charging into battle. They had themselves a textbook-perfect ride, returned to earth safe-andsound, tipped Ava a twenty when she gave them their stickers, and

headed off toward Rusty's Beer-BQ tent while loudly declaring the experience
"Fuckin' EPIC!"

Which was all fine-and-dandy far as Simon was concerned. The kid, Charlie, he really shouldn't have gone on it in despite being just barely tall enough. Too much for him. Hopefully, it'd only leave him shook for a while, not traumatized for life or anything.

The blondie and the brownette he'd noticed earlier were up next, the blondie sashaying out to some encouraging wolf-whistles she ate right up. The brownette showed some reluctance, casting her gaze toward the height of the spires ... a height the bungee cords would exceed by almost as much again, at the apogee of the initial launch. She might have backed out, but her friend implored and wheedled and reminded her they'd already paid, the NO REFUNDS sign quite visible on Lottie's booth. With a resigned-seeming grimace, the brownette set her spine straight, squared her shoulders, and let Ava buckle her into the seat-harness.

Whenever young women, especially attractive ones, rode the Catapult, the watching crowd always increased, hosts of teen boys and men of all ages eager to get a glimpse ... and if the blondie's bounteous bosom did bounce free from confinement, so much the better! Simon himself, old as he was, faithful to his wife's memory as he was, still knew he'd be having a gander same as anyone else.

A gander and then some, thanks to the Catapult-Cam, though Lottie would be quick to delete or blur over any inappropriate content. She'd gotten into that habit once she'd realized how many guys thought whipping out their works on video would add to the thrill.

The sky had gone a deep periwinkle, shading indigo to the east and magenta to the west, already shining with the diamond-specks of a few stars. Shadows masked the grubbier daytime aspects of the midway, and the rainbows of lights dazzled magically as a wonderland, transforming everyone and everything into beauty.

Getting the thumbs-up from Ava, as the stoic brownette whiteknuckled it on the harness and the blondie giggled and squirmed in anticipation, Simon did his spiel, did his countdown, and threw the lever.

KA-SPROOOOIIIIIIIIING, flinging them high! And did the

blondie scream? Did she ever! Full-throated, operatic, an ululation that would've done generations of silver-screen scream-queens proud! It pealed across the fairgrounds, warbling like a melodious police siren -

-- then cut off as abruptly as if throwing a switch.

Screamer and a fainter, then? Simon suppressed a chuckle as he flicked his gaze to the Catapult-Cam and ...

... and what the pan-fried hell?

The seat-carriage was empty. They were gone, the blondie and the brownette, both gone.

Sick horror seized his guts. If the buckles hadn't latched, if the lap bar malfunctioned, if they really had been catapulted or slingshotted off into the open...

He imagined them, blondie and brownette, soaring through the air, arcing like missiles, plummeting toward the unforgiving solid ground ...

No one else knew yet, except maybe Lottie, but a consternation had already begun to set in from the lack-of-screams silence. That consternation would become pandemonium in a flash, as soon as people saw empty seats where, moments before, two pretty girls had been.

Simon whammed the control console with the heel of his hand, as if to knock some sense into the Catapult-Cam and convince it to quit fucking around. The view, though, didn't change. As he gawked, incredulous, he realized the lap bar was in place, the harnesses hanging unoccupied but obviously still fastened.   That made no goddamn sense ...

Someone on the ground noticed, shouted, and there came the pandemonium, an uproar of clamoring queries and vying for a line-ofsight.

"Bring it in!" Simon called. "Right now!"

Jess hurried to do so, winching the seat-carriage back to the launch pad and ratcheting it in place. Ava shook her head, aghast, gaping.

"I secured all the latches, I safety-checked! I know I did!"

"She did!" added Jess. Then, to Ava, "You did, I saw you. And ... look .. they still are ..."

Simon joined them. The lap bar was locked into place; he gave it a firm shake to make sure. And even if the lap bar could have unhooked, then slammed back, there was no explaining the harnesses ... which, even if they somehow came unbuckled, certainly could not have re-buckled all by themselves!

But then, how ...? But then, where ...?

Pandemonium, a pandemonium of voices and questions and demands, chaos crashing and swirling around Simon like an insane hurricane. The word spreading wildfire-fast, story no doubt growing and getting distorted in the telling. The crowd doubling, trebling. Fellow carnies, fair-goers, fairground security. Hundreds of people talking at once.

The insistence was that the girls had been launched, terrified and flailing; their broken bodies would be found a quarter-mile away, splattersmashed, burst apart the way pumpkins did during the autumn festival Punkin-Chunk, only red and chunky and strewn with bones and organs instead of orange and stringy with pulp and seeds ... the insistence it was a hoax, a trick, a publicity stunt ... that it had been a terrible accident ... that it had been willful murder ... that the girls had secretly been wearing parachutes and would drift down soft as dandelion puffs to take their bows

...

He heard it all, and heard none of it, and if Lottie hadn't stayed level-headed enough to assert some sort of order, he didn't know what else might have happened. But Lottie, bless her, took charge, drafting a couple carnival roustabouts to help her clear the immediate vicinity, dispensing refund-receipts to everyone who'd already paid and been waiting.

"What ... what happened to them, Pa?" asked Ava, sounding suddenly five years old again and not understanding why her momma wasn't coming home.   "They were there, weren't they?"

"They were," he said. "And then they weren't."

"Did they get ..." She couldn't even say it, gulping thickly as she scanned the horizon.

"I don't know. Don't think so; everything was secured up good and tight. You saw to that. Ain't no one on the midway more diligent; I'd stake my life on it."

"They couldn't have just ... disappeared, though!" Ava said. "Right out of buckled harnesses, right from under a secured lap bar?"

"I don't know," he repeated. "Sorry, sweet pea, your ol' Pa got no ready answers for this one."

Nor, it turned out as the evening went on, did anyone else. The whole fair came to a near standstill, carnies and townies alike milling about. Members of the small-town media showed up, hoping to score the scoop before the major networks swept in. Local law enforcement, eventually followed by feds, descended en masse to investigate. The Cosmic Catapult was cordoned off, gone over fine-tooth comb for any sort of clues, with Jess on hand to answer any mechanical questions. The fairgrounds and surrounding parking lots, farmlands, and neighborhoods were searched. Thanks to Lottie's release forms, they had the names of the missing women, but whatever electronic searches the techy types did from their cell phones drew an utter blank. As if the phones, along with their owners, had just up and vanished off the face of the earth.

The Catapult-Cam video, analyzed frame-by-frame, only added to the mystery. Oh, it started off ordinary enough, showing the passengers -- firmly buckled in, with the lap bar secured, thank you very much; there'd be no accusations of carelessness thrown Ava's way -- as the countdown went on and the seat-carriage hurtled from the launch-pad with a sudden burst of dizzying speed, all G-forces and acceleration.

There was the blondie, screaming exuberantly, tossing her head, bounteous bosom bouncing such as to put her bra's integrity to the test. There was the brownette, wide-eyed and apparently holding her breath, posture rigid, holding on white-knuckled.

But then, at the apogee, at the very height of the tensile cables' extension, the video fritzed with a brief jag of static. In the very next instant, the seats were empty. Just ... empty. The women, just ... gone. At that exact moment the blondie's operatic screams had abruptly cut off.

The harnesses, still buckled. The lap bar, still latched. No violent ejection to send them careening into the wild twilight-blue yonder. As if they'd ... whiffed out, winked out. There, and then gone, in the blink of an eye.

No one, least of all the experts, knew what to make of it. Increasingly crazy theories were bandied about, everything from disintegration to alien abduction to divine intervention, a mini-Rapture, party of two, your table is ready.

Simon's only comfort was to know he and his weren't likely to be blamed, not for the disappearances at least. Nothing could be found mechanically wrong with the Cosmic Catapult itself, nothing about the video supported any fakery, no malice or malfeasance had reason to be suspected.

If he and his were to be blamed by their fellow carnies for the serious blow to everyone's collective income for the night, well, little he could do about that. They'd be lucky if the entire thing didn't get shut down for the duration. It'd be a pinch to all their pocketbooks ...

In the short run, anyway, as was eventually pointed out. Here they were, at the heart of another urban legend in the making! Like the one about the teens who'd ridden standing up on a rollercoaster and been decapitated by a low-arching cross-stretch of track. Or the one about the knife-stabber stalking unsuspecting victims in the hall of mirrors. Notoriety, infamy, and the dirty lure of morbid curiosity would bring in more customers than were kept away.

Simon didn't find that silver lining much comfort either. The mystery of it, the impossibility, the unreality, nagged at him.

Nagged at Ava, too ... as cops and crime-sceners went meticulous about their duties in the harsh sodium-glare of portable lights, flooding the launch-pad in stark white cut with sharp, black-edged shadows, she approached him where he sat on the table-part of a picnic table, watching the proceedings with a lukewarm mug of soup in his hands. Lottie had pressed it on him, insisting he needed to eat or drink something, but he'd managed a couple of sips and then simply held it.

"Pa?" Ava boosted herself up beside him.

"They find anything yet?" he asked, knowing full well they hadn't. Knowing, somewhere deep in his marrow, they wouldn't. There'd be no sensible, logical explanation, no tying up of loose ends into a tidy little knot.

"Nothing yet," Ava said, sounding like she knew it too. "But Pa? I've been thinking ... about that little boy, from before. About what he said."

"Charlie," said Simon.

"Maybe ..."

"Maybe what? Maybe it wasn't just a scared kid's imagination?"

"He said something was up there. He said he saw it, and it saw him too. Almost got him. He said he thought it was hungry."

"Yeah." Simon exhaled heavily. "I remember."

"Well, but, what if ..."

"There was? And it ate them two girls? Sucked 'em clean out of their seats and snarfed 'em like popcorn?"

"I know it seems crazy, but so's all this already." She waved at the activity, the crowd, some fella in a mask and gloves and plastic booties tweezing for fibers, some likewise-attired gal shining a blue beam into nooks and crannies. "Also, I had Lottie go back and run me their video, the dad and his boy?"

Simon looked at her, a tingle skittering along his spine. "And?"

"And it's got that same sort of fuzzy glitch. Only a flicker and only for the splittist split-second; wouldn't hardly notice at all on a regular watching. But, I swear, Pa, it's true."

"Did you look at other videos --?"

"Sure did, all the ones from tonight, and it's only on those two."

"You mention this to any of them yet?" He dipped his chin toward the bustling investigators.

She shook her head. "They already look at me funny."

"Right. Well then, I'll let 'em look at me funny."

Setting down the soup, he went and found someone in charge, a brusque and efficient woman in a smart pantsuit like she'd choppered in straight from Quantico. He fully expected to get the bum's rush, but she heard him out.

Skeptical, she may have been, but with few other leads she must've figured it wouldn't hurt to be open-minded. She compared the videos, called over some other experts, and consulted. They even got the boy's -- Charlie's -- family's information from their release form and dispatched someone presumably to find and interview them.

Simon was glad enough to retreat again to his picnic table as they did their thing. It was near to midnight by then, when the fair would normally be wrapping it up for the night, but he didn't figure any of them would be seeing much sleep.

Ava was over with Marco and his folks now, him putting a comforting arm around her. Tom Zuri, changed out of his top-hat and flashy tuxedo, and stood nearby, watching the technicians. Maggie Zuri, still wearing her headscarf, eyeliner, and bangled jewelry, paced back and forth along the mural her son had painted, frowning pensively.

"Marco, this painting ..." she said at one point. "Have you been reading my books? The ones on the ebony shelf?"

"No, Mama," he replied. "You know I can't read that stuff."

She relaxed. "Ah, good."

"Though I do sometimes look at the pictures," Marco confided to Ava as his mother strolled out of earshot, and the gentle joke made Ava smile.

How exactly it came about, Simon wasn't sure, but the next thing he knew, someone had decided a test was in order. A test of the CatapultCam, to look for what the Quantico lady referred to as 'the anomaly,' as well as anything else out of the ordinary with the Cosmic Catapult itself.　　　They were, in other words, gonna slingshot a couple cops up there, for the same reason the bear went over the mountain. It struck Simon with an uneasy feeling in the pit of his stomach, though he couldn't say why. The bikers had gone up and come down okay, after all, and so had plenty of other passengers over the course of the day. Dozens of them, without so much of a hint of an incident.

Bad idea or not, though, what else was there to do? If it was the Cosmic Catapult, he couldn't very well just go on flinging paying customers willy-nilly.

So, he agreed. Best to let them do it, with plenty of witnesses and equipment; if anything did happen, at least they'd have ample evidence.

The officers who volunteered didn't seem to share his misgivings. On the contrary, the younger of the two, a rookie likely fresh from the academy, could hardly volunteer fast enough. He clambered into the seat with an ear-to-ear grin, remarking, "Can't believe we're getting paid for this!"

His companion, a salt-and-pepper brick of a man who would've been right at home busting up drunken brawls, only grunted some sort of affirmation as they strapped him in. The buckles and lap bar were quadruple-checked, the Catapult-Cam and their respective bodycams as well, and a helicopter circled at a prudent distance with a spotlight and telephoto lens.

"Pa, you're not really ...?" began Ava.

"I ain't," he said, shrugging and spreading his hands; the techy types had taken over the control console, readying to do their own countdown once the Quantico lady finished a rather different version of his usual spiel.

Never, in the many years he'd spent on the midway, had Simon heard a crowd go so quiet, seen them watch so intently. The very air about thrummed with a tension that had little to do with the pent-up potential energy of the taut bungees.

Three-two-one and KA-SPROOOOIIIIIIIIING! Off they went, with a jubilant yip of glee from the rookie. Up and up and up, the cables stretching to the very limit of their extension.

Then came a barrage of frantic curses and panicked shouts from high above, and exclamations of disbelieving shock from the control console and the police van where they were monitoring the body-cam footage, and ...

Long story short, when the seat-carriage was finally winched back to earth, it had one sole occupant and one empty seat.

"He was there, and then he was gone!" the badly-shaken older cop, a wet patch on the front of his uniform trousers, reported. "There was a ... a kind of pop, like when a kid pops his finger in his cheek ... and, poof, he was gone!"

Gone, he was. Harness still buckled, lap bar still in place. The Catapult-Cam showed exactly what it had before, a jagged glitch and then no rookie sitting where a rookie had been a split-second before.

The live video from the rookie's bodycam showed a turbulent first-person view of the launch and ascent, the vast star-studded black sky above, the vast countryside spreading out in all directions below. At the very instant it neared apogee, though, a fizz of static obscured the image, which then went utterly blank, signal lost.

Well, and if it had been pandemonium before ...

Simon felt Ava's hand slip into his, both seeking and offering reassurance. "What now, Pa?"

What now? They were done, done with the Cosmic Catapult at least. It'd be seized, hauled away ... dismantled and destroyed ... or studied in some secret government lab or military base ... and, but for the huge number of witnesses gathered, he and Ava and Jess and Lottie may have faced a similar fate.

"I'm thinking," he said, "it might be 'bout time to retire."

Avert Thine Eyes

Jeff Strand

"Avert thine eyes, lest ye go mad!" Gerald shouted. "The human mind cannot comprehend the horror that looms above us, and to gaze upon it will surely spell doom for your sanity!"

Edward squeezed his eyes shut. "I shall not look at the accursed evil!"

James put his hands over his face. "Nor shall I! I must protect my brain from this ungodly sight!"

Arthur pulled his wool hat over his eyes. "I'd sooner pluck the orbs from their sockets than allow them to view the cosmic menace!"   "Aw, shit, I looked," said Roy.

"Look away!" Gerald screamed. "Look away immediately!"

"I can't! It's so gross!"

"Avert thine eyes!"

"Seriously, you guys, I'd heard that ancient evils were unpleasant to look at, but this thing is just plain nasty." Roy pointed to the sky. "It's all green and slimy. It's bad enough when I have to look at a normal-sized octopus, but this thing has got to be the size of six or seven Dairy Queens put together! Oh, God, its mouth is disgusting."   "God has no part in this!" said Gerald.

"I take it back—I don't think that was its mouth. I get why they say your mind can't comprehend it, because it's really hard to tell which part is its mouth, which part is its nose, and all of that. Does it have ears? I don't know. Lots of green slimy tentacles, though."

"The tales are true!" Gerald wailed. "It possesses an infinite number of tentacles!"

"Oh, no, I wouldn't say that it's an infinite number. More like twenty."

"Twenty doesn't sound so bad," said Edward.

"It's pretty darn bad," said Roy. "I'm not sure how you'd fit an infinite number of tentacles into the sky, although I guess that could be part of why it makes you go insane. But, yeah, it looks like about twenty tentacles, maybe twenty-two or twenty-three. Twenty-three would be pretty weird, wouldn't it? An odd number of tentacles. When it's tentacles or legs or eyes it's almost always an even number."   "It could have lost a tentacle in a fight," said James.

"Yeah, yeah, that's true. And, like I said, it could also be twenty or twenty-two. It's hard to count them while they're all waving around. You guys should really see this thing. But don't look, obviously. I wish I hadn't."

"Then turn away!" said Gerald.

"I can't! It's like driving past a car crash. I will say that I'm feeling less insane than I would've expected. I'm scared and grossed-out, but I haven't lost my mind. Maybe it takes more than a giant sky-octopus to make me feel like I've lost my grip on reality. I dunno."   "Is it doing anything?" asked Arthur.

"Not really. Hovering, mostly. It's not knocking over buildings or anything like that."

"Perhaps I should take a look," said Edward.

"No!" Gerald shouted. "You must not look!"

"Roy seems to be handling it okay. I was under the impression that if we gazed upon the ancient cosmic evil we'd go completely comatose, or just start shrieking incoherently and rip out all of our hair. I can handle looking at something gross and slimy. I'm a vet."

"I'd advise against looking at it," said Roy. "I may not be tearing out my hair, but I'm definitely a little queasy, and looking up like this is starting to strain my neck."

"What if slime starts dripping off it?" asked Edward. "We wouldn't be able to see it to move out of the way."

"You literally just said that you could handle slimy," said Gerald.

"Looking at it and touching it, yeah. But what if this slime is like acid? Or what if it excretes a blob of slime the size of a house? It seems dangerous to stand underneath the ancient evil without being able to see what kind of goo it might drop on us."

"I think we're okay," said Roy. "Like I said, the tentacles are waving around a lot, and I don't really see anything coming off of them. I'll let you know if that changes."

"I can't keep doing this," said Edward. "I have to look."

"Don't you dare!" shouted Gerald.

"You're not the boss of me." Edward opened his eyes. "Ew."

"I know, right?" said Roy.

"It's freaky as hell, no doubt about it," said Edward. "But it's not like I feel my sanity slipping away. I can still speak in complete sentences." "Right," said Roy. "I was under the impression that it would be a sight that haunted my every waking moment. Don't get me wrong— I'll think about this thing a lot. Probably every day for the rest of my life. But not every hour of every day."

Edward nodded. "My thoughts exactly. I mean, look, it's a gigantic glowing octopus-like monster hovering a mile above our heads in the middle of the city. That's not something I'll forget any time soon. But it's kind of like the movie Requiem For A Dream. It messed me up for a while but I got over it."

"I haven't seen that one."

"Great acting, but it's a tough watch."

"Did you say it's glowing?" asked Gerald.

"Yeah," said Edward. "It's got this glow surrounding it. Not like it's radioactive, more like it's…uh, what's the word…?"

"Otherworldly," said Roy.

"Yes!" said Edward. "Otherworldly. It has an otherworldly glow, like something that passed through a portal into our dimension. Eerie as hell."

"Oh, yeah, totally eerie," Roy agreed. "But not incomprehensible. My brain can totally process what's happening."

"Also, I have to admit that it's kind of nice to be able to see what it's up to," said Edward. "When I was averting my eyes, I wasn't sure what it was doing, and that was a lot scarier. It's really just floating around up there. It's not like it's on a murderous rampage."   "I'm starting to think I should look at it," said James.

"You should do no such thing!" shouted Gerald.

"Roy and Edward looked at it, and they sound okay. I like to think that I'm at least as mentally healthy as they are. I feel kind of stupid just standing here with my eyes closed."

"Do not succumb to temptation!" Gerald told him.

"Screw it," said James. He opened his eyes and gazed upward. "What nightmarish presence lurks in the skies above?" he shrieked. "My psyche cannot cope with the unimaginable, indescribable horror!" He let out a maniacal giggle and began to repeatedly slap himself in the face.

"See?" asked Gerald. "You see? He's gone mad!"

"It does seem that way," Roy admitted.

"My perception of the world is forever altered! I feel as if cosmic worms are burrowing through my skull, devouring everything I once thought I knew! Why would God allow this being to exist? Or…am I staring into the wide-open jaws of God right now?"

James' pupils faded away, leaving him with pure white eyes.

"I have been stricken blind, and yet I still see!"

James fled. For a newly blind man he did surprisingly well for a few moments, and then he smacked into the side of a Mexican restaurant, knocking himself unconscious.

"See what you did?" asked Gerald. "A kind and decent man is now irreversibly insane."

"I didn't tell him to look!" Roy insisted. "I in no way suggested that my own experience was going to be the same as his. If he went whack-a-doodle, it's not my fault."

"Right," said Edward. "There was no peer pressure. Nobody said that all the cool kids are looking at the giant octopus. He made a choice, and clearly for him it was the wrong one, but I reject the accusation that I behaved irresponsibly."

A giant tentacle reached down, wrapped around Arthur, and yanked him a mile into the air. The creature tossed Arthur into its mouth.

"Oh, wow," said Roy.

"What happened?" asked Gerald.

"It was super fast. That thing grabbed Arthur and ate him!"

"It almost makes me wonder if Arthur should've had his eyes open," said Edward.

"Nah," said Roy. "You saw how fast it happened. There was no time to run. It could just as easily have been you or me."

"That's true, I guess. Hey, what are those?"

"I'm not sure what you mean."

"Something is falling."

"Oh, yeah, you're right. Jeez, I hope it's not slime."

"It kind of looks like...musical instruments."

"Musical instruments?"

"That's what it looks like to me," said Edward.

"Why would the beast have musical instruments, and why would it drop them?" asked Roy.

Edward shrugged. "We're not supposed to understand it. That's sort of its whole deal."

"Wait, nope, they aren't musical instruments," said Roy, as several bones landed on the sidewalk in front of them. A skull bounced off the cement and struck Gerald in the face.

"Goddamnit!" shouted Gerald.

"Ah, they're Arthur's bones," said Roy. "That makes a lot more sense."

"My nose is bleeding," said Gerald.

"At least you're better off than James," said Edward. "It looks like he got hit by six or seven rib bones."

"So, ultimately, being comatose worked out in his favor," said Roy. "Can you imagine getting impaled by a bunch of broken ribs if you were fully aware of what was happening?" He shuddered.

"I'd say that we should go over there and help him, but three of those ribs went in his neck. I think he's pretty much boned." Edward frowned. "Oh, crap, that pun was totally unintended. I'd never make a joke like that about the death of a human being. Or an animal, for that matter. As a veterinarian there's a certain amount of gallows humor that goes along with the job, but I know where the line is drawn."

"It was pretty clever, though," said Roy. "Even if it was an accident."

"Still, I feel bad. It was way too soon. That's the kind of tasteless joke that gets you canceled."

"Well, how about this? Arthur is pretty much boned, too! Now we both lack a moral compass."

"That doesn't help."

"I didn't think it would. But it was funny enough to deserve a callback."

"You know," said Roy, "it suddenly occurred to me that if the horror above is snatching people up, eating them, and spitting out their bones, it might not be such a great idea to just stand here. We should take cover."

"I was thinking the same thing," said Edward. "Maybe at that ice cream shop at the end of the block?"

"You don't have to twist my arm. Their peaches and cream flavor is simply divine."

Roy and Edward began to walk off.

"Hey!" Gerald shouted.

"What's wrong?" asked Roy.

"Are you just going to leave me here?"

"Sorry," said Edward. "I assumed that you could open your eyes enough to watch your feet while you walked."

"No! I'm not opening my eyes until the ancient evil has returned to its own plane of existence!"

"All you have to do is look down," said Roy. "No judgment about your safety precautions. You do you. But the ancient evil is a mile straight up in the air. I'm just saying."

"What if it controls my will and makes me look up?"

"If you're suddenly giving it brand new powers, why couldn't it just send magical fairies down here to pry open your eyes and tilt up your head?"

"We should get going," said Edward. "The ice cream shop closes in twenty minutes."

"I hope it's not too crowded," said Roy. "Everybody else around here fled as soon as the ancient evil arrived. Honestly, we look kind of silly still being out here."

Edward and Roy each took one of Gerald's hands and led him down the sidewalk.

"Is it lower than it was before?" asked Edward.

"Is what lower?"

"The ancient evil."

Roy looked up. "Oh, yeah. It was a mile up before, and now it looks like it's about three-quarters of a mile. That's not great."

"Do you think it's going to squish us?"

"Probably not. What would it gain by squishing us?"

"I'll be honest," said Edward. "My sanity was doing just fine when the ancient evil was a mile above our heads. Three-quarters of a mile is a different story. It seems bigger when it's closer."

"Do you feel like you're going mad?"

"Not full-on mad, but I can feel things slipping away. In retrospect, I wish I hadn't looked."

"I told you!" Gerald shouted. "I told you to avert your eyes! But nobody ever listens to me!"

"Fine! You told me! There's no reason to be a dick about it!"

"How insane are you feeling?" asked Roy. "Do we need to be concerned that you're going to go feral and attack us?"

Edward shook his head. "I'm not feeling violent. It's more of a 'bite off my own tongue' kind of insanity."

"Better than biting off other people's tongues, I guess."

"True."

"Though I think watching you bite off your tongue will probably be more disturbing than gazing up at the ancient evil."

"When I feel uncontrollably compelled to do it, I'll turn around."

"Thanks. Much appreciated."

"How low is the ancient evil now?" asked Gerald.

"Oh, look who suddenly sees the value in using your eyes!" said Edward. "What's the matter? Having trouble gauging the distance of the threat when your eyes are squeezed shut?"

"Drop the attitude," said Roy. "You just accused him of being a dick, but now you're behaving like one. You've become the very thing you just condemned. He asked a simple question."

"That's true," said Edward. "I apologize for being rude." He looked up. "It's definitely lower now. We need to hurry."

The three of them speed-walked down the block to the ice cream shop.

"Son of a bitch," said Roy. "What kind of ice cream shop closes early on Sundays? That's the day people are most in the mood for it!"

"That's really disappointing," said Edward. "Peaches and cream would've been a wonderful last thing to taste before I bit my tongue off. Speaking of which…" He turned around and bit down, hard.   "Oh, jeez, that sounded horrible!" said Roy. "We've been so focused on our eyes that I didn't even think about covering my ears!"   Edward turned back around and spat out most of his tongue, along with a lot of blood.

"Dude!" said Roy. "If you were going to spit stuff out, you should've stayed turned around! Nobody wants to see that!"

"Thorry," said Edward. He turned around and spat out some more blood. "Thith hurth."

"Of course it hurts. Your tongue has nerves galore. Your insanity was never going to completely shield you from the pain."

A glowing green tentacle reached down and wrapped around Edward's neck. It yanked his head off and rose back into the air.

"Yowza," said Roy.

"What happened?" asked Gerald.

"Edward bit off his tongue, just like he said he would, and then the ancient evil popped his head off like it was pulling the cork out of a bottle of wine. I don't mean like it was using a corkscrew—that would've been horrific. I mean like when you drink part of a bottle of wine, and you put the cork back in, and then you pop it back out when you're ready for more wine. It was like that, but gorier."

"So that warm liquid hitting me is Edward's blood?"

"Yeah. He's got quite a spurt going. His body hasn't fallen over yet. I know you're committed to keeping your eyes closed, but it really is something to see. Oh, wait, too late, he just fell. His leg is still twitching but otherwise the show is over."

"What's the ancient evil doing?" asked Gerald.

Roy looked up. "Not much. Oh, wait, no, it's descending fast. I'm getting a 'devour all of humanity' vibe from it."

"And you're sure the ice cream place is closed? You tried the door?"

"Yep. Okay, the octopus-thing is getting scarier and scarier the closer it gets. They say that the strongest fear is fear of the unknown, but I'm going to call bullshit on that. I can see its mouth now, fangs and all, and that's way scarier than when I wasn't sure what I was looking at."

"Are we all going to die?" asked Gerald.

"That's the direction things seem to be moving, yeah."

"I'm not ready to die. I have so many things left to accomplish. I've never learned to play guitar. I've never eaten white chocolate. I've never made love to a woman, successfully."

"I can feel my sanity going bye-bye," said Roy. "You're welcome to make your own choices, but I will say that I'm feeling less scared as my ability to process information fades. This whole 'turning insane because you're unable to cope with the unimaginable horror' may be the way to go."

He bit off his tongue, spat it out, then sat down on the sidewalk to await his doom in a cheerfully oblivious state.

Gerald opened his eyes.

"Roy, you're sitting in a pool of blood!" he said.

Roy shrugged.

Gerald gazed upward. He looked directly into the infinite eyes of the creature.

"You are eternal," he whispered. "You are what has always existed and will always exist. You are all gods combined. I fear thee, love thee, and worship thee. Take me as your victim. Take me as a sacrifice."

The ancient evil slapped Gerald upside the head with a tentacle.

It spoke in a booming voice that shattered the windows of the ice cream shop: "Offering yourself as a victim is a pussy move. Grow a pair." "Oh," said Gerald, flustered. "I thought you'd like that."   "No. It's total weak sauce. You are the chosen one, Gerald. You are the one who can defeat me and save humanity. Fight back. Let us do battle."

"Are you serious?"

"Do I look serious?"

Gerald stared at the ancient evil for a few moments. "I honestly can't tell."

"Battle me!"

Gerald punched a tentacle.

"Ow."

Gerald punched it harder.

"Ow. Damn."

Gerald grabbed the tentacle and gave it a vigorous tug.

"Stop it. You're going to yank it off."

"I shall never stop yanking, foul beast!" Gerald shouted. "I shall best ye in combat and save billions of lives!" He tugged on the tentacle as hard as he could.

The ancient evil pulled its tentacle free, then slapped Gerald upside the head again. "A valiant effort, but obviously I was just messing with you."

"Oh."

"Should've kept averting your eyes."

The ancient evil popped Gerald into his mouth and spat out his bones. Then it smiled, though no mortal would recognize it as a smile, and began the process of devouring humanity.

Witchblood

Tim Curran

Last year, when Kirt Vanderheim perished in the fire that consumed his building, there was an awful lot of talk about what had started the blaze. Much of it was gossip, distortion, and sheer nonsense. Sure, it was a strange business and the fire marshals still haven't figured out what could cause a blaze so hot that no remains of Kirt were ever found. The mainstream press spent a lot of time hinting that the fire started because Kirt was free-basing cocaine, cooking crank, or involved in Satanic rituals gone astray. And the latter, of course, was something the crazies of the religious right went after like sharks smelling blood in the water.

But all the above is bullshit.

You see, I was there the night Kirt died. I saw what happened and what I saw, man, well, let's just say I've been on some serious drugs ever since. I'm afraid to turn out the lights at night because I don't know what might be hiding in the shadows and I'm afraid to sleep because of what might come for me in my dreams. Sounds like some pretty mad shit, but it's true.

And it all started when Kirt called me and said, "Man, you gotta get your ass over here right now, I got something you just gotta hear."

Before I go any farther, I suppose I should tell you who Kirt Vanderheim was in case you don't know. Maybe that'll put this whole ugly business in perspective, if that's even possible.

Okay. If you're the type that considers Judas Priest or Iron Maiden relaxing, AC/DC just pleasant toe-tapping old school nostalgia, or Black Sabbath to be the auditory equivalent of comfort food, then the name Kirt Vanderheim is probably well-known to you. Vanderheim was the president and founder of Graveworm Records and its sister label, Morbid Dementia. And in the arena of independent death-metal, that was saying something. For it was Kirt Vanderheim that gave birth to such bands as Dismembra, CorpseGrinder, and Decapitated Nun, and turned a love for high-decibel brain damage music into not only a passion and a way of life, but into a lucrative multi-million-dollar industry.

And he did it nearly single-handedly.

Becoming, I might add, not only a record producer, but a marketing genius and a promotional guru along the way. Not so bad for a high school dropout from Milwaukee whose resume consisted mostly of rolling joints, packing bongs, and blowing out his ears listening to everything from Accept to Black Flag. I went to junior college with Kirt, so I know of what I speak. G.E.D. in hand, he made a career of cutting classes, hanging out in metal and punk clubs, and selling bumper stickers and t-shirts out of the trunk of his car you know, things with catchy slogans like, FUCK THE RICH and I BRAKE FOR CORPSES, I LUV POODLES—WITH BARBECUE SAUCE and HAVE YOU RAPED YOUR PRIEST TODAY? Cutesy, feel-good Hallmark kind of things like that.

In his sophomore year—don't ask me what his major was—Kirt decided he was going to become the Rick Rubin of thrash metal and you know what? He did just that. What would later become Charnel House Productions was started in a basement apartment with an old two-track analog recording machine begged, borrowed, or stolen, and a handful of extreme metal bands anxious not only to push the envelope of hard rock, but to tear that sonofabitch open and make some ear drums bleed.

Kirt dropped out of school, but I finished, even graduated which was really something considering my social schedule.

I had a journalism degree, a record collection you had to move by truck, and an absolute love of what my old man liked to call "sewer music." I worked for a number of underground music magazines that barely paid the bills, made something of a name for myself, graduated to the Ivy-league rags like Cream, Spin, and Rolling Stone. Eventually, pretty much feeling betrayed and disgusted by the corporate maneuverings of these publications, I returned to my roots writing articles for Metal Maniacs, Metal Edge, and Metal Hammer, among about a dozen others. I became known as something of an authority on heavy metal and when high-scale trade rags like Entertainment Weekly or news mags like Time were looking into a series on decibel-driven music, they turned to yours truly. Somewhere along the line, I wrote three books and started my own magazine, Thrash & Grind, which I am happy to say was available in just about every periodical market in the country for some six years.

I did okay, right?

But what about Kirt Vanderheim?

Well, he did more than okay in the twenty years since our college days. Pretty much from scratch, as I mentioned, he built Charnel House Productions into a mega death-metal entity, scoring a tremendous and fanatic cult following and swinging some huge deals with entertainment biggies like Sony and Virgin. He was the mastermind behind Bloody Jesus and Grave Orchids, Virgin Vivisection, and Pigflesh. His bands headlined the annual Slaughterfest in Copenhagen and the Butcher-Bash in Edinburgh.

Anyway, given the sort of journalist I was, we had a very good working relationship, Kirt and I. I helped him launch the careers of some of his earliest bands like Antichrist and Mother Necrophile and in the process got some of the finest stories any music journalist could hope for. Whenever we'd get together, we'd launch into these incredibly long, intellectual discussions on the state of heavy metal past, present, and future. We'd extol the virtues and criticize the limitations of black metal and thrash metal, doom and grindcore, progressive and power metal, dissecting influences and trends, minutely scrutinizing sub-sub genres like Viking and Goth metal.

But that was our thing.

It was our life and our passion and there was really nothing else for us. No drug in the world could touch what metal gave to us.   About a month before the fire, Kirt invited me to Charnel House studios to hear a couple sessions from some new bands he was working with. Like everything else, death-metal was hardly standing still. This new crop of artists had fused black metal and grindcore into a hyperspeed assault of distorted guitars, hammering drums, and guttural demonic vocals— sometimes called Cookie Monster vocals by the uninitiated— trying to prove that they were indeed the scariest, meanest, most psychotic rock 'n' roll bands out there. The band names themselves were almost enough to turn your stomach Rancid Testicle, CorpseFuck, and Disemboweled Fetus, among others. The most promising group was an all-female quintet called Maggot-Cunt, if you can visualize that one. The lead singer's name was Autopsy Angel and she could alternately sound throaty and masculine like Satan possessing Linda Blair and then jump octaves until she was screaming like a soprano being peeled by razors.

If that gnarly bitch wasn't possessed, then nobody was. Man oh man, what a girl.

Kirt let me listen to the first two tracks they had cut, "Fucking the Dead" and "Bride of Chains," and believe me, the lyrics were enough to put you off meat for a month. It was nasty, visceral stuff, and I really shouldn't have been surprised. Death-metal had long been a cult unto itself and these bands were always trying to out-do one another, not only singing about grave robbery and necrophilia, but actually practicing them. At least, that was the buzz they liked to create about themselves.

But there was no getting around one thing and that was that these bands were anti-social deviants on a good day and violent sociopaths on a bad one. I couldn't count on one hand the crimes they committed, the sentences they received, the cemeteries they defiled or the churches they tried to burn down. Some of these guys and gals were simply playing a part but others? Jesus, you didn't want to get on the wrong side of people named Carrion or Vomit Messiah who actually carried dead ravens and wormy rats in leather bags so they could always be near the smell of death.

It just wasn't healthy.

The night Kirt burned-up or vanished, take your pick some people are still saying he went underground, that it was all a carefullyplanned marketing ploy I went to his penthouse apartment because he had something he wanted me to hear. And it wasn't some new thrash band, but something important, he said, the discovery of a lifetime.

Well, how could I refuse that?

Kirt's penthouse was on the top floor of the office building that housed Charnel House Productions and a dozen other counterculture entities he had created. When I got there, we had the place to ourselves. There were no leather-clad groupies with multiple piercings or Goth chicks with corpse-white faces. That in itself told me this actually was important. Kirt pulled me into his den (about the size of a warehouse) where he kept his CD and vinyl collection, his metal memorabilia, all those incredibly rare bootlegs and master tapes. Kirt was big on vinyl, had something like 100,000 records in there, and if you dug hardcore rock 'n' roll like me, well, it was enough to make your mouth water.

"Well?" I said. "Tell me."

"Pour yourself a drink," he said, "this will be worth the wait."

I had a whiskey and Coke, started looting through all that hot wax in the glass shelves: the rarities, the alternate versions, the albums that never made it to press, the songs that were bounced from the final sessions. Here was the ultra-rare Soviet-era bootleg of Bloody Jesus' seminal first record, Shit and Disease. Here were the manic, neverreleased Latin versions of CorpseGrinder's only two records, Fetid Orgy and Children of the Slime. And here also were incredible rare bootlegs of bands like Unholy Incest, Suffocation, and Brainworm. And behind lock and key, I was looking at the master of the only known recording of Decayed Intelligence, a band that committed suicide together after laying it down.

Shit, Kirt had things there worth hundreds of thousands of dollars.

He popped in a few minutes later, saying he had to arrange bail for the lead guitarist of Accursed Soul—He-Who-Is-Not-To-Be-Named—who had somehow gotten his hands on somebody's prized doves and bitten their heads off and painted the walls of his hotel room with their blood. Another day in the life of a death-metal mogul, I guess.

Kirt just stood there, a skinny little guy with long tangled dreadlocks and a beard that reached down to his chest. His eyes blazed like coals yanked from a brazier. And I knew, just looking at him, that he'd found some oddity he wanted me to listen to. Probably some antique metal, what we liked to call proto-metal. One of those bands from the late sixties like the MC5 or Blue Cheer, Lucifer's Friend or Sir Lord Baltimore, who were blowing eardrums and laying down the law long before the term "heavy metal" was even coined.

"Come on, let me have it," I said, getting excited now, too. He grinned and slid a plain white record jacket from inside a locked case. "Okay, my friend," he said. "Tell me what you know about WitchBlood."

WitchBlood?

I knew all there was to know about that mysterious band. WitchBlood was a German metal group circa 1972, 1973. They were probably the actual originators of death-metal and this easily ten years before Venom and Possessed would pick up the gauntlet. They sounded much like Black Sabbath played at a frenetic pace, but with the obligatory growling demon vocals that would, a decade later, become the mainstay of the death-metal movement. But this was in the early 1970s. At the time, they were radical and demented and anarchistic, considered revolutionaries and terrorists by some, while others thought they were merely a talentless shock band. I recall one reviewer, after seeing their live show, saying they were "sheer and unadulterated vomit, no more, no less." Which led the band to call their first and only album House of Vomit. Maybe an inside joke and maybe their way of yet again raising their middle finger to the establishment.

Okay, those are the basic facts.

They made only the one album, went out on one largely unsuccessful world tour, disappeared into hiding for a year, and then resurfaced meaner, vicious, and more antisocial than before. They had put together some new material and they played it in their hometown of Hanover, Germany in October of '73. And here is where the legend of WitchBlood really gets going. That concert was the only one where they played their unrecorded new material because somewhere during the show, that old concert hall went up in flames and the band with it not to mention some fifty or sixty other people.

A rock and roll tragedy, to be sure.

I briefly went through all that, the entire time my eyes feasting on that cardboard sleeve in Kirt's hands. My pulse was pounding. My palms were sweating. "What…what do you have there? C'mon, man, don't hold it back."

I sounded like a junkie, but that's pretty much how I got concerning rare metal. And particularly when you were talking WitchBlood, who in the folklore of headbangers were akin to the Holy Grail or the fucking Shroud of Turin.

He handed me the sleeve.

My hands were shaking so badly I nearly dropped it.

Just a plain white cardboard sleeve with the words Hexeblut burned into the sleeve. That was it. Nothing else. I reached inside and pulled out a dust wrapper and the album itself. It was made of blood-red vinyl. No name, no pressing info, nothing. A bootleg surely and one that made my stomach flip over. "You listened to it?" I said.

But Kirt shook his head. "No haven't dared. I bought a warehouse full of old records from Stuttgart and this was in one of the boxes. I wanted you to be here when it was played the first time."

"Jesus," I said, "if this has those lost sessions…"

Well, no need to go into it. The rights on something like that would be in the millions. And not because of the musical genius of the band, but because of the historical tragedy itself. But, honestly, the money meant nothing to Kirt and even less to me. From a purely pop culture perspective, something like that would have been absolutely priceless.

"Let's do it," I said, swallowing my drink in one pull.

Kirt took the album and set it on the turntable and, drawing in a slow breath, placed the needle on the wax. There was some static, some scratching, and then a whole lot of noise. But not the kind of noise we liked, just noise. Lots of rumbling like thunder in the distance, some high-pitched pinging sounds, something like voices buried in the mix, booming sounds. All sorts of shit and none of it even remotely like music.

We listened halfway through and I can tell you that I didn't care for what I was hearing. I didn't know why, but something about that distorted, nonsensical noise was making my skin crawl. My hands were bunched into fists and my teeth were chattering. I was sweating rivers.   Finally, Kirt pulled the needle off it. "I suppose," he said, "we should play it backwards."

We looked at each other, both knowing that what was on there was meant to be played in reverse, and not caring for the idea much. Why? I don't know. But I think we both had a very bad feeling, only we were too cool and too urbane to admit it.

Kirt set the needle back down and started the turntable in reverse.

There was nothing but silence for maybe five minutes and then it began. I heard that thunder more clearly now and the sound of a great bell gonging in the distance. What might have been rain and wind. Weird screeching and scraping noises that made my molars ache. And something like dozens of women whispering and something else like a wet ripping as if someone had been disemboweled with a hook. And through it all, a male voice muttering words that were guttural, garbled, and totally incomprehensible. It was saying something, but I couldn't be sure what. Those words weren't German, at least no German I've ever heard. If anything, they sounded almost like Latin, but debased and rasping and, yes, eerie.

It was all very unsettling, but the worst part was those whispering voices. I'm almost sure they were saying, "hilf mir, hilf mir, hilf mir, hilf mir," again and again which is German for help me.

I wanted to scream, to snatch that record off the turntable as I heard a rising slithery sort of noise that seemed to be beneath our feet but then something happened.

Something awful.

The floor began to vibrate and the walls began to shake. There was a sound like a heart beating and lungs breathing. All those glass-fronted shelves of rare recordings shattered into a storm of glass. Records and masters and CDs went flying through the air. Tiles fell from the ceiling and then everything was consumed in a mephitic black mist that stank of sulfur and rotting meat. A wave of heat hit me, blasted right into me with what seemed hurricane force and threw me across the room, singing my eyebrows and mustache.

It also saved my life, you see.

I blacked out, I must have blacked out.

I can't be sure. But when I opened my eyes, I was on the floor twenty feet from where I'd been sitting, dazed and confused, and the room, the very center of the room where we had been sitting had changed. It was like a black hole had opened up, some whirling vortex of matter and energy and force. Except it was living: a funnel of pulsing and glistening tissue that was not flesh exactly, but almost like an organic mist that was expanding with an echoing screeching sort of sound that was so unbelievably loud I involuntarily pressed my hands over my ears. Kirt was sitting right in the middle of that ever-widening chaos.   I could see him there. He was still in his chair. The turntable was on the stand next to him. Both were caught in that chaos, but as it churned and widened, they were trapped in some kind of stasis, some sort of antigravity sink absolutely motionless. Kirt's mouth was wide open like he was screaming but I couldn't hear a thing above that screeching.

It was at that time probably less than thirty seconds into the whole thing when something came creeping out of the vortex. Maybe creeping isn't the right word because it seemed to spray out of there like vomit:

wild, whipping strands of some pustulant white gelatin like fleshy Spanish moss that flowed upward and spread out over the ceiling, consuming and thickening like cream.

I think I screamed.

I think I lost my mind.

But if I had to tell you what that room looked like, I would have to say it was like being inside something alive, a livid, slick biological profusion of tissue and striated muscle and viscera.

Something like coils of squirming entrails came out of the vortex next except they weren't entrails but corkscrewing pink worms that were big around as telephone poles with immense suckering mouths on the ends.

That's what got Kirt: those mouths.

The worms came out in fleshy bunches like the tentacles of sea anemones, juicy and pink and spiraling. They wound Kirt up like pythons and then those sucking oval mouths were on him, draining him dry until he shriveled into a dry husk and broke apart. They must have put out an immense, raging heat because what was left of Kirt was cremated into black ash that blew apart like one of those carbon snakes you burn on the Fourth of July.

The record was a summoning.

That's what had happened in Hanover and it was happening again. Played backward, that rare WitchBlood record was an invocation, a summoning, and, yes, a sacrifice to something out of time and space, a livid fleshy pestilence from the subcellar of the universe.

The vortex continued to widen and more of that jelly flooded out until it seemed the entire ceiling was fluttering with it. And the worms more of them all the time moving with serpentine convolutions as they sought me out, a vaporous stew of sweet putrescence billowing and steaming around me, fans of creeping web-like nervous tissue oozing from the greasy walls.

I jumped to my feet and ran out the door seconds before there was no door left. The last thing I saw was a rising cyclopean stalk that was slate-gray and scaly. It opened into a mass of corkscrewing appendages like the trunks of elephants.

That's what I saw.

That and the remains of the den glass cases all shattered, records reduced to fragments, streamers of tape tangled throughout. All of it whirling around and around in a tornado. There was no time for speculation, because the room was being engulfed in a gushing sea of tissue and worms and bulbous eyes.

The fire must have started about that time, I'm guessing.

As I stumbled down the corridor, mumbling and sobbing and more mad than sane, I heard smoke detectors whining and then the shrilling of the building's fire alarm. The corridor had become a steaming, pulsating womb expelling the pink of convolutions of wriggling shapes like peeled cobras.

By then, the penthouse was engulfed in flames. I could smell smoke and something sharp like ozone.

I pretty much stumbled down four flights of stairs as the building shook and creaked and groaned like it was trying to pull itself up and walk.

I fell out onto the sidewalk and crawled out into the street.

And that's when I looked up.

Oh, it was a four-alarm blaze, that was for sure. The building was burning, tongues of fire licking out of windows and a rolling pall of black smoke rising from the upper floors. But that wasn't all. I saw what looked like hundreds of those pink twisting worms rise up out of the flames as if they were born from them. They pushed out of the conflagration like a forest of serpents escaping a single egg. They filled the sky and brushed against the stars above which pulsated like beating hearts. And then then the rest of the thing whatever it was rose from the roof in a gigantic, writhing, mountainous mass of flabby lobster-red tissue, swollen and squirming and set with immense liquid sea-green eyes and gelid tendrils and a million roping, slithering feelers.

It's actually impossible for me to describe what I saw.

There are limits to human perception.

But that thing kept rising, swelling, expanding, flooding out in a slushy pink-gray-black-red anatomical profusion that filled the sky, bursting open the building like a flaming shell and stretching chitinous jointed legs that reached from horizon to horizon. I danced around, avoiding bricks and smoldering debris that buried the streets.

And then there was a hollowing rocketing detonation like a sonic boom and the thing was gone. There was just the collapsed remains of Kirt's burning building across the street, its wreckage scattered for hundreds of feet, the structures next to it going up like napalm

That was it.

It ended right there.

My guess is that the Witchblood record was either destroyed in the chaos or melted down. Either way, its destruction sealed the hole that led into another universe or dimension, call it what you will.

I was on my ass in the rubble, singed, face blackened with soot and I felt hands on me pulling me to my feet. I smelled body odor and foul breath and was looking into the face of Albert K., one of the crazy homeless people that lived on the street.

"I saw it," he said. "I saw the monster."

I was pretty much hysterical by the time the fire trucks and cops rolled onto the scene. They sedated me and threw me in the back of an ambulance. The next day in my hospital bed I was questioned by the fire marshal. He didn't believe a word I said. He claimed what I saw rising from the ruins of the building was an optical illusion caused by the flickering firelight reflected onto those columns of black smoke. That's all.

Sure, and if my aunt had a dick, she'd be my uncle.

I know what I saw.

Unfortunately, my only corroborating witness was Albert K. who they did not consider exactly dependable. They called him the "Sushi Kid" around the neighborhood because he was always digging in the dumpsters behind the Japanese deli down the way. When he forgot to take his Lexapro (which was often) he went up and down the street peeking in mail slots, claiming he was a government agent whose job it was to interrogate invisible Korean elves that lived in mailboxes.

And that's it.

A four-alarm fire much like that one in Hanover so many years ago.

Can I explain it? Any of it? No, not in the least. WitchBlood, unlike all the others that followed, were the real item. They had summoned something from some anti-world and had the record not been destroyed (I guessed) it would have eaten the world, gutted it and burned it to ash. All I know is that thing was swelling like bread dough, a living flux of matter whose sheer volume was something that our mathematics could not possibly hope to measure. I believe it would have engulfed this world, this solar system, then blotted out the stars in heaven. That's what I think. It was something undimensioned, a cosmic cancer that went on to infinity.

Regardless, whether you believe what I've just told you or not, just do me one favor. If you ever come across that rare, blood-red vinyl of WitchBlood shatter it, burn it, but get rid of it.

Because if you don't, you're gonna find out all about rock 'n' roll damnation.

-The End-

Bad Sounds

Patrick Lacey

Seth finds the tape in a crate filled with donations and spider eggs. One of those eggs hatches in his palm before he Oh shits it back into the pile. Something dark and small and new tumbles out. He backs away but that cassette he was reaching for, it's still inside, is so inside, that the hatchling has found its way onto the plastic shell. It pauses there, studying him with however many eyes spiders have. He figures it must be an omen but A.) he doesn't believe in omens (not yet anyway) and B.) that tape's cover has its hook in him.

He swallows a tablespoon of bile, flicks the spider, and hopes mom isn't standing by. Seth lifts the tape and marvels at the lo-fi graphic. It's a skeleton, or at least it's supposed to be, but whoever drew the thing forgot that skeletons don't have noses. On any other day, he'd get a good chuckle, but his run-in with the egg has him on edge. The sort-ofskeleton's wearing a robe over what he has to imagine are bone-shaped ears. In the background is a sky that's never known sun, is more like cotton candy if cotton candy were made of storm clouds. And out of those clouds leaks a bolt of lightning the color of mustard. Beneath this glorious mess is the title.

Bad Sounds.

Not exactly original but he's seen worse. Usually they're more tantalizing, like *Blood-Curdling Nightmares or Chilling Sounds of All Hallows Eve* or—you get the idea. Seth is somewhat of an expert with these things, has accumulated quite the collection. These things are tapes manufactured through the eighties and nineties, with a few stragglers post-Y2K. They're sound effects and so-called creepy mood music, meant to add ambience to Halloween parties. Back when Seth was a few inches smaller—vertically and horizontally—his parents would break theirs out each year while his cousins ate too many Twizzlers and their parents got wasted off spiked punch. For them, it was background noise. Every few minutes, they might pay notice to the sounds of cackling witches or clanging chains but then it was back to living in the moment. Seth, though—he's never been great at that part. For him, it wasn't white noise but the essence of the party. Since then, he's become obsessive with collecting sound effects, specifically of the Halloween variety.

The crate is located out back of Jake's Record shop. Given its name, Jake's used to specialize in records, but times change and so do business models. And also owners, since Jake found himself a condo in the Florida Keys. His son, Jack (how original), took the place over and switched to a more standard thrift store approach. For some reason, he kept the name going, maybe to maintain the customer base. But since the records have been reduced to a single rack out back, Seth figures those customers are long gone.

"Find anything good?" Jack says at the register. He's pretending to price something on the computer, but Seth can see the truth in the reflection of Jack's glasses. What he's really doing is bidding on a halfdozen eBay auctions. It's almost common knowledge that Jack has a bit of a gambling problem. He's recovering now, has switched from betting on races, to auctions for retro toys, video games, that sort of thing. But those add up. Everything old will someday be new again and when that day comes, re-sellers will know before you. Up come those prices and people like Jack start increasing their bids, looking to own all the toys they couldn't afford with their childhood allowance.

Not that Seth's judging. Remember: he collects Halloween sound effects cassettes.

"Just this," Seth says, setting down his new copy of *Bad Sounds*.

Jack snickers, then clicks. His lenses show a ten becoming one hundred. "You might be the only person in the world who gets excited about these things."

"You'd be surprised," Seth says.

"Yeah? You running a group or something? You guys meet once a week to discuss which screeching cat sounds the best?"

"I just mean there's other fans, that's all. No need to be a dick."

"Just busting them," Jack says. "That'll be…" But there's no price sticker yet. The thing's hot off the proverbial press. He opens up a new tab, types *Bad Sounds* cassette into eBay's search bar, and comes up with precisely nothing.

"Maybe it's the only copy," Seth says, mostly joking, but the thought doesn't sit well in his gut.

"Doubt it," Jack says, still scrolling.

"Where'd you get it anyway?"

Jack nods out back, which is code for beats me. He means that someone dropped it off before or after closing time. People want to get rid of their old shit and they don't want to wait around for Jack, since Jack's usually late. Most of his goods are donated this way. Not that Jake's is a charity shop, a la Salvation Army. All the earnings go straight into Jack's pockets and then into eBay listings for some action figure playset Santa once refused him.

Jack shrugs. "How about twenty?"

Seth snickers. "How about ten?"

"Come on, man. This thing might be rare. Said so yourself."

"And you said I'm the only one who likes these things." He sets down a ten-dollar bill and lets Jack think it over.

The computer chimes and Jack proceeds to whisper *for fuck's sake* under his breath.

"Bad news?" Seth asks.

"Lost again."

#

Northshore Independent Radio is one of the longest running stations of its kind, which is code for *no one ever listens*. It consists of oldtimer music, religious talk shows, and historical non-fiction that would lull a coke head to sleep. Not that Seth's one to talk. His show, *The Sounds of Sound Effects*, airs every Friday from midnight until whenever his followup stumbles in. Sometimes it's a grumpy pastor from one of those godly programs, real old-testament stuff,
and other times it's Hank Lancer, who plays bluegrass better fit for Kentucky than
Massachusetts. The station's located on a barren stretch of road just before the Middleton border. The lot fits three cars on a good day and the building looks more like a converted auto shop, mostly because it is.

The Friday after Seth finds his new tape, he shows up early for work, though "work" is a misnomer. He doesn't DJ for money. It's a way to unwind after a week of bank-telling, of seeing how bloated most people's accounts are compared to his. He opens the front door, winces as the creaking metal echoes down the hall. Whoever's his lead-in probably picked up the sound. He waits in the hall until Wendy Grafton steps out.

She favors seventies trucker tunes even though she looks like the nicest and oldest grandma you've ever seen. Her skin is mottled with deep-cut wrinkles, but the flesh smooths out when she smiles, which is often.

"Early tonight, Seth," she says, waving him into the studio like it's a therapy session. Her hair's not silver or grey but pure white, as if something once scared the color out of each follicle.

He raises the tape. "Got something new I want to play for the nice people at home."

"Good luck with that," she says. "Made some cookies for you. They're by the coffee maker."

"You're too nice to me."

"Someone has to be," she says with a wink and a pat on his shoulder, and that's the most action he's gotten all year. Most people figure Seth's one of those happy-as-a-clam bachelors, but the truth is he finds human connection difficult. That's why he prefers thrift stores. It's easier to buy someone's former belongings, to exist *through* them, than swipe right and hope for the best.

Wendy has cued up two songs to allow Seth to set up. Radio isn't what it used to be. Movies romanticize it with record- and tape-laden archives but really it's a computer and a handful of left-over CDs. Lucky for Seth, the station held on to their cassette player. He cracks open Bad Sounds and slips it inside.

Wendy's remaining tracks finish up and Seth turns his mic live.

"Hi folks, it's Friday night and I just know your head's spinning from the work week. It's late and you can't sleep and you've got a drink in hand. Might be coffee but it's probably something stronger. You're looking to unwind but nothing's doing the trick. That's where I come in. Sometimes music doesn't cut it. You've heard it all before or it doesn't fit your mood but the world's full of other sounds. Could be a cricket chirping or waves crashing. Could be *anything*. All you've got to do is open your ears and listen. Tonight, I've got something special for you. I know Halloween's a couple months away, but I saw candy corn in Target this week. If they can start early, so can we. Say hello to *Bad Sounds*, a rare artifact from—"

Seth flips the case over, searches for a date but comes up empty. In fact, he can't find a composer or record company either. There's no information aside from the track listings (*A Horror-ble Night, Things That Lurk,* etc).

"Let's not trouble ourselves with the details. After all, that's where the devil lives. So sit back, sip that drink of yours, and let the spooky sounds do the talking."

He mutes his mic and presses *play.*

The tape begins as all tapes do, with a few seconds of dead air. The speakers hiss. The magnetic strip whirrs. Next comes the fading-in sound of a distant thunderstorm, of pounding rain and crackling thunder. Above that: ghostly moaning and growling wolves, all standard fare. He leans back in his chair and assesses Wendy's cookies: an oatmeal raisin, a chocolate chip, and something too lumpy to identify. He picks the oatmeal and pours himself some coffee that tastes like it's been on the burner all week.

Bad Sounds transitions from storm to rustling leaves and padding footsteps. Further back in the mix is a synth playing occasional atonal chords. Again: nothing revolutionary.

Not until the woman screams.

It sends Seth rolling back in his chair. He's heard plenty of mock gasps before but none quite like this. There's something desperate in the woman's voice, her pleas more life-like than usual. After that comes distorted whispering, like it's been run through a guitar pedal, like it's not altogether human. Seth can make out a word here and there, like *circle* and *forever* and *suffering*, but it's mostly a syllable stew. Chanting next, a dozen or so voices monotoning their way through what he figures is Latin.

His skin buzzes, like that fictional thunderstorm from earlier isn't so fictional. His head starts to throb.

The chanting grows to a crescendo as the sound of crackling flames enter the mix. Cut back to the woman's screams, which have grown more desperate, more urgent, until they stop altogether.

Side A ends.

Seth wipes sweat from his brow. His pulse pounds, like he just went for a jog. Rule number one of radio is to keep things moving. Silence is the enemy, but speaking is tough business. He turns his mic live, lets out a sigh he didn't know was building.

"Well, folks, that was…something. I figured it would be like all the other Halloween tapes I've played over the years. I'm sorry if I put any of you on edge. That's never my intention. Let's transition to something a bit more soothing, shall we?"

He cues up a library of nautical sounds, lulling waves and cawing seagulls, the kind of thing that usually calms him. Emphasis on usually. Because Seth is worked up from those chants. In fact, it's like he can still hear them, like whoever was muttering in some long-dead language is in the control room. He presses eject on the tape player, removes *Bad Sounds*. Side B is ready to go. He could flip the tape for an encore but given his heart's jumping jacks, he slides it back into the case and snaps it shut.

He leans back and hopes the waves will soothe him.

They don't.

#

Danvers is a small town, so things like murder tend to make the paper.

That's what Seth sees on the front page the next morning. A man on the border of Beverly, one Frank Hodge, shot himself and his son with a twelve-gauge he kept hidden in the garage for emergencies. His son recently moved back home after a messy divorce. Now he has a messy exit wound. Police are looking into a motive.

Seth sets down the paper on his teller station. The bank opens in five but he's not thinking about deposit slips or his change-your-password notification. He's thinking about Frank Hodge. The man was in his seventies, was somewhat of a radio enthusiast. Seth knows this because Frank was a bank customer, used to shoot the shit when things were slow, always complaining how radio's a dying art, how broadcasters used to be royalty. What bothers Seth is that Frank was a listener of *his* show. According to the paper, he shot himself and his son around the time Seth went on air last night. Which is also around the time he pressed play on *Bad Sounds*.

"You hungover or something?" Matt, his co-worker says. Twenty years Seth's junior, Matt's probably never had a hangover. He takes frequent bathroom breaks and smoke breaks and any kind of break that will keep him away from his window.   "I don't drink, remember?"

"How's that going for you?"

Seth doesn't answer, is too busy staring toward the headline of today's paper.

Murder-Suicide in Danvers.

On his lunch break, he returns to Jake's Records, though he's not in a shopping mood.

Jack is box-cutting a package open, grumbling at the excess bubble wrap. He pulls out a Transformer, vintage no doubt. He cat calls like some construction worker. "You know, this thing goes for a few hundred, but I talked the guy down. Gonna look great on my shelf."

"We need to talk," Seth says, setting down *Bad Sounds*. He keeps it cover-side down, lest he see the poorly drawn skeleton and its bony nose. But the back's not much better. Now he can see the track listing, the sound effects he didn't get around to sampling last night.

Dark is Night.

Something's in the House.
Hello, Seth.

He gags on his tongue, takes a step or three back, and slips on stray bubble wrap. Ass meets floor. When he gets back up, the last track is *Howl-o-ween Eve*. He must have misread it.

"The hell's with you?" Jack says.

"That thing," Seth says, meaning *Bad Sounds*, though speaking it aloud feels a little too *Candyman*. "Where'd you say you got it?"

"I didn't. Someone dropped it off, remember?"

"Out back?"

"No, on the roof," Jack says, tossing the shrapnel of his special delivery into the waste basket. "Yeah, out back. You sure you're okay?"

"You got a camera out there?"

Jack shrugs. "Never review the footage. Thrift stores aren't exactly burglary hot spots."

Seth's a mild man. He doesn't raise his voice or curse. When he spills something, he shrugs and gets to work. When someone cuts him off on the highway, he figures they must have an emergency. When his last relationship ended, when she shouted *You're a total fucking push-over*, Seth said *When you're right, you're right*. Which is why Seth shocks himself as he grabs the collar of Jack's shirt. "There's something wrong with that tape. And I need to know who dropped it off."

Jack raises both hands, like *Don't shoot*. "Okay, okay. Let's check it out." He unlocks his computer, minimizes a half-dozen eBay tabs, and opens his security footage. "It's set to motion detection. Saves me from having to store every second on the cloud. That shit costs money. And business isn't exactly booming."

He gestures to the otherwise empty store, then skims through the videos from this past week. Most of the footage is rats and raccoons setting off the sensor. Jack skips ahead. A couple kids pass through the alley, taking turns swigging from a bottle, probably lifted from one of their moms. Seth's beginning to think the dropper-offer of the tape remained still enough to avoid tripping the camera. Then the next video starts. At first it's just a breeze dislodging junk from the dumpster's cracked-open lid. A figure trudges into view. They're wearing a black sweatshirt, the hood pulled very much over their face. It's like they came here to steal then thought better of it. The figure looks both ways before reaching into a pocket and pulling out a small rectangular object. Bingo. They set *Bad Sounds* down on the back stoop and sprint in the opposite direction, like they just pulled the pin on a grenade.

"That's the only camera?" Seth says after the video's run time is up.

"I keep the second one turned off."

"Seems like a waste."

"Like I said, I sell old shit for a living. What's this about anyway?"

Seth spots a copy of today's paper on the counter, slides it over and thumbs the headline, like that explains everything.

"I don't get it," Jack says.

Seth heads for the exit but Jack calls after him.

"Forgetting something?"

Seth knows he's holding the tape, but he doesn't turn around. "You keep it."

"You know we don't do returns."

"Consider it a donation," Seth says, letting the door slam behind him.

#

A week passes.

A week free of *Bad Sounds*. Seth drives to and from the bank listening to his standard sound effects. Hooting owls and clanging wind chimes. No screams or pleas. Most people would balk at his choice of soundtrack, but most people don't think twice about what they put into their ears. They tune into whichever top forty single's peaking that week or the hourly traffic report that never changes. Seth prefers sounds to music because sounds indicate life, and life is always happening—at least for others. He saw a shrink a few years back who harped on that little detail, said something about Seth being unable or unwilling to admit he wasn't living life. He was a passenger, not a driver. Said shrink was probably right but Seth stopped going after that.

He avoids Jake's Records. Jack has no doubt placed *Bad Sounds* on the rack. If Seth were a betting man, say, like Jack used to be, he'd put money on a price tag of forty bucks and a rare sticker for good measure.

When Friday rolls around, he shows up at the station just in time for Wendy's trucker songs to wrap up.

"You feeling okay?" she says, setting out another tray of cookies. Unfortunately, they're all the unidentifiable mushy variety.

"Never better," he says, pouring himself a cup of burnt coffee as his first tracks of the night play. Usually, he opens with a welcome message, but his microscopic audience won't mind if he pushes it back. "Why do you ask?"

"Because I worry about you. Someone has to, right? Look, I don't want to pry, and I mean this is the nicest possible way, but you seem a bit lonely."

"What gave it away?" he says, sipping and wincing at the acid that doesn't stay down for long.

"I mean it. I'm no stranger to loneliness. My husband kicked the bucket a decade ago. Sure, he was a royal pain in the ass, but we fell into a rhythm that wasn't exactly horrible. I miss that bastard like you wouldn't believe. I miss the way he grumbled when he took out the trash and I miss the way he'd fall asleep five minutes into anything he watched on TV. I used to find his snoring unbearable. Sounded like a jackhammer going off at midnight. Now I'd cash in my social security to hear it again."

Seth sets down his mug too hard on the console. A few specks of radioactive coffee splash over the rim. "I appreciate it. Honestly. And yeah, I'm a little lonely. But only a little. Relationships have never been easy for me. Neither is interacting with most people. Too much effort and there's always the risk of rejection. Don't take this the wrong way, but I'd like to avoid getting attached to someone because what you just described doesn't sound like a blast."

"Better to have loved," Wendy says, lets the rest hang. "All I'm saying is you should get yourself out there, rejection notwithstanding. Doesn't have to be serious. Hell, come to bingo night if you want. Because this, sitting around and listening to sound effects, there's more to life, you know."

He smiles, nods, says he'll think about it. Wendy means well. And bingo doesn't sound half bad.

He does his intro, cues up a collection of wildlife ambience, and heads for the bathroom. In the mirror, he sees what Wendy was talking about. He looks…if not sick, then unwell. *Bad Sounds* really did a number on him. His skin's got a grayish hue and the bags beneath his eyes are darker than usual. But the good news is he's recovering, has put a week of distance between him and the tape. And besides, maybe he blew the whole thing out of proportion. Frank Hodge seemed normal, sure, but plenty of murderers seem normal. Everyone's got a dark side. Maybe whatever was brewing in him had been there for some time. And Seth might've been coming down with something when he first spotted *Bad Sounds*. The mystery virus has been slow to leave, that's all. Life's full of coincidences and also sound effects. And speaking of the latter, he's got to get back to the control room.

He heads down the hall, past posters of long-gone DJs, broadcasters no one will remember. Before stepping through the soundproofing door, he does a triple-take. Through the glass he sees a figure hovering over the console.

It's wearing an over-sized black hoodie and it spots Seth watching. What was that about coincidences? How many black-hooded figures does he know, save for the one on the cover of *Bad Sounds*? His heart forgets to beat. His lungs forget to breathe.

He backs away but the studio door's opening and the figure's heading his way and—

And the figure is Jack.

"Hi?" Seth says, trying to cut the tension. Problem is, his blade's too dull. He needs something sharper.

"Tried to plan it just right," Jack says, like he's mid-way into a conversation. "Figured I'd wait until you headed to the pisser."

"I did head to the pisser."

Jack steps closer, which is when Seth detects his foul breath. Smells like sewage and rot, like he hasn't brushed since they last spoke. "I know what you're thinking. You're thinking 'Hey, that hoodie looks familiar. Didn't I see it on the camera?'"

"Crossed my mind."

"The answer's yes you did, to which I'd add I'm sorry about all this."

Seth holds up his hands in hostage-negotiator fashion. There's just one problem. He doesn't know what Jack's demanding. Also, that makes Seth the hostage. "Let's sit down and talk about it, okay? You tired? You look tired. Got some coffee in the control room."

"Yeah, I'm tired. That's how it starts. You ought to know."

"You mean *Bad Sounds*?"

Jack shooshes him. "Keep it down, will you? They'll hear."

"Jack, you're starting to freak me out. And after the week I've had, that's saying something."

"You're not paying attention," Jack says, raising his voice a few decibels. He speaks through his teeth. Spittle flings every which way.

"Floor's yours," Seth says, reaching into his pocket for a cell phone that's not there. Must have left it on the console.

"What you saw on that security camera, it was me but not *entirely* me. That tape, it seeps into you, you know? Makes you do things you normally wouldn't. I tried to get rid of it after I listened."

"I thought you hated sounds effects."

"I did. I hate them even more now. A few tracks in and I got all itchy. Felt like I was coming down with something. Then I blacked out. Woke up covered with dirt. That's when I realized the tape isn't just a tape. I drove across town and dropped it into one of those little neighborhood libraries, stuffed it behind a couple of romance novels. But here's the thing. The tape didn't want to stay there. So I wake up in the alley behind the shop, hand-delivering it back to myself. After that, I figure I'll leave it in the back room, in a box of junk. No one's going to sift through that stuff anyway."

"No one except me."

"Like I said, I really am sorry."

"Shit," Seth says. Through the studio doors, he can hear his block of nature tracks coming to an end. He didn't have a chance to cue anything else up. There goes rule number one of radio. "So, what're you saying? The tape is cursed?

Jack says nothing, which is really just saying *Give the man a prize*.

"The way it works, far as I can tell, is you've got to have someone else listen to it. It's like passing on a cold. When you brought it home, I figured 'great.' End of story. I also figured you're a smart guy. You'd realize what needs to be done. When you played it over the air, you passed it on to anyone else listening."

Seth's pictures Frank putting on a pot of coffee, sitting in his den, and tuning into Seth's show. What he hears makes him lose time just like Jack. And in that trance, he unearths his secret twelve-gauge, shoots first his recently divorced son, then himself.

"Then why are you here? I listened after you. That means you're cured."

"Not quite. When you brought the tape in, I blacked out again. Maybe it hadn't gotten all the way out of my system. Maybe it's a proximity thing. Fuck if I know. What I do know is it made me listen again and now it's in here." He taps a finger against his temple. The dead air from earlier turns to a familiar hissing. In comes a thunderstorm.

"You bastard."

A crane of his head and Seth can see Bad Sounds on the console, right next to his phone. The case is open and the tape deck's doing its thing. He moves forward but Jack blocks the way.

"We need to ditch this place, get far enough so we can't hear it. That's the only way."

"What about whoever hears it on *air*? They don't have the luxury of tape trading."

"We can't worry about them. Now turn around and let's go."

"Jack, move."

Jack doesn't move. Not aside at least. But he does wrap both hands around Seth's throat. "They're still listening. They're still *with me*. You don't want to wind up like that old bitch."

"What?"

But Seth pieces together the puzzle when Jack shoves him back, when his shoulder bursts the front doors open, and most of all when he trips over Wendy's limp body. One eye's still open. Her mouth is frozen in a forever gasp. Her cookies may have sucked but she was the closest thing to family that Seth had.

"Bastard," Seth says just before he loses his lunch and breakfast onto the cement.

"Keep moving," Jack says and maybe he was on to something with *Bad Sounds* still circulating inside him. Because his eyes are too wide and unfocused, like some junkie chasing the dragon, only the dragon's more like a poorly drawn skeleton.

"You got it," Seth says, but he moves in the opposite direction, as in past Jack. Toward the studio. He fumbles with the handle before he pulls open the door and is met with the chanting at full volume. He feels *Bad Sounds* crawling into his ear canal and taking the elevator down. His skin tingles, Pavlov style. He reaches for the eject button and—

#

And wakes up next to a dumpster. He's battling the headache of the century. His mouth tastes like a landfill and you'd be forgiven for thinking he's mid-bender. He tries to get up but his equilibrium has other plans, sends him back to the hard surface. It's a give and take until he manages to pull himself into a crouch. His breath's not the only thing that stinks around here. The dumpster smells like it hasn't been emptied in some time, like it belongs to a restaurant or commercial business, not a radio station most folks don't even know exists.

That's where he is, standing behind Northshore Independent Radio, one hand on his aching skull and the other waving away a murder of flies. They're coming from inside the dumpster. Seth doesn't crane his head over the lip, doesn't confirm what—or who—is causing such a stir. But if he did, he knows he'd see Jack in there. What's left of him anyway. It's like Jack said: the tape makes you do things you normally wouldn't.

Seth stumbles around the building to find the front steps empty. *Bad Sounds* must've made him toss Wendy too. The lights are still on inside the studio. He can see the half-assed coffee maker and his phone and also the cassette deck that's still very much on. If he tries a second time for the eject button, he'll wind up out cold again. He takes Jack's advice, heads away instead of toward *Bad Sounds*.

Like his phone, his car keys are still inside but he doesn't mind. At this time of night, crickets are chirping and twigs are snapping. In the distance: the cry of a coyote, the skitter of a bat. Life is happening all around him, just like that shrink spouted. But she was wrong about the other part. Tonight, he's no longer riding shotgun, no longer a passenger.

He listens to the night and the night provides.

The Beach

Dan Henk

The Vacation

Tim's family was pretty working class, but his RPG buddy Drew had wealthier parents. They both attended the same Christian private school in North Carolina, and quite often hung out on weekends. Most of the time at Drew's much larger, two-story Tudor house. It was an elegant white stucco and dark wood framework dwelling, all hidden within a few acres of wooded property.

Drew's parents owned a vacation bungalow on Brunswick Island, and they would often take Tim out there for weekends, grabbing a burger at a famous local restaurant along the way. This time however, Tim's parents rented a room at some cheap hotel near Carolina Beach. They invited Tim to bring along Drew. Being church buddies, Drew's parents were all too agreeable.

As was typical, once they arrived at the motel Tim's parents disappeared. Leaving Drew and Tim to their own resources. In a ramshackle motel that had seen better days. It was however within a stone's throw of the beach.

The two trekked out to the beach, built sandcastles, dug foxholes, and tried paddling out until they almost drowned. Drew was a bit chunkier, so he did a little less of the deep-water activities. But come sunset, they both scoured the shore for sand hoppers. Curious little crustaceans that could be found by the air bubbles they left in the wake of the receding waves. They'd scored a yellow plastic pail, and spent the last hour before sundown filling the bucket.

Sand Hoppers

Back at the motel, Tim flipped through the TV looking for anything decent. All he could find was a low budget, alien conspiracy movie. Flying saucers hidden in industrial garages, guarded by hardnosed, uniformed men. That eighties version of military personnel, all running around and hassling intruders. Dark shades, nondescript uniforms, all the stereotypes present and accounted for.

The plot wasn't the greatest, and the film was a bit needlessly dark, so Tim diverted himself by sifting through the bucket.

The sand hoppers squirmed around like they were annoyed at being displaced. The mere sight of them slightly repulsed Tim. He wasn't sure what they were exactly, or if they could actually bite. He poked at them with a plastic straw, and a few latched on. Tim frantically whirled around the straw until the creatures dropped back into the morass.

Restless and bored, he shook the bucket and something caught his eye. It was a little rounder and had more of a metallic sheen than the creatures. After a few pokes with the straw, he managed to isolate the object. Pushing it to one side, he extracted it from the bucket.

It looked like an old corroded coin. The hue more of an aqua-green than anything. Sort of like those pennies that stayed in the fountain at the mall too long. The markings were so worn they were unreadable, but they were definitely nothing he'd seen before. This could be valuable! He'd read plenty of those made for kid's stories where they find valuable letters from ex-presidents in the back of some old drawer.

Tomorrow he'd hit up the locals and see if they had any clue what this was.

The Locals

His mom cooked them eggs, bacon, toast, and topped it all off with a glass of OJ. Drew and Tim were still mulling over the food as mom stuffed a satchel full of clothes and announced-

"Me and your dad are going to the beach. You and Drew have fun dear. Let's meet up at 6 for dinner!"

With that, dad tossed his silverware on an empty plate and brought it to the sink.

"Thanks honey, Delicious meal."

A brief flash of light from the door, and Drew and Tim were left to their own devices. In a musky motel room that stunk of mildew and brine. Everything looked so old and worn, Tim wondered how long this place had been standing.

He dug into his pocket and pulled out the coin.

"Look what I found Drew!"

Drew seemed less than impressed. He glanced at it briefly, pushed back his mop of brown hair, and inquired-

"What is it?"
"I don't know. Some old coin I found in that bucket with all those sand hoppers."
"Let me see that."

Tim dropped it in his palm and Drew flipped it over. In the light of day, it looked even older and more worn. Roughly oval, the edge was chipped and the whole thing looked sort of hand made. The patterns on had oxidized to green, the depressions a scummy a dark brown. Drew flipped it over and nonchalantly asked-

"What do you think it is?"

"No idea. Let's check it out. It might be worth something."

Tim was a bit more hyped up. But then again, he always was.

"Sure. Where you thinking?"

Tim had no idea, but there were some local fishing shacks around here. If he could muster up the courage, he'd ask them. Talking to grownups you don't know was a bit intimidating but he didn't want to leave and miss out on what could be buried treasure!

"Let's just hit a couple of the local fishing shacks and then we can go to the beach."

Drew looked skeptical, but he was usually pretty agreeable. Tim pulled his flip flops on, stuffed a towel, flippers, and goggles in his backpack, and tucked the coin in his pocket.

"Hold on a minute"

Drew complained, scampering to get his gear.

Outside, the sunlight was blinding. The gusty winds kicked sand into their eyes and blasted their bare legs. Squinting, Drew peered around the motel parking lot and inquired-

"Where did you want to start?"

Tim had no clue, but this was his idea, and he didn't want to act like he didn't have a plan.

"I think I saw a fishing shack just down the road."

Drew shrugged, his shirt whipping in the wind as it highlighted his belly and chubby arms. Tim doubted anyone would give them the time of day. Two kids in swim shorts and flip flops bothering grownups who had real jobs. He debated just heading to the beach, but it was a matter of pride. Now that he'd brought up the idea, he might as well get it out of the way.

Cars roared by, pelting the kids with rocks as they navigated the thorny bushes of the road-side. They passed a few more commercial looking fisheries, a cheap motel and a no name gas station. The heat was muggy and suffocating, warming up even the soles of his flip flops. Tim was sweating and feeling the start of a sunburn. But he was too stubborn to give up yet. Pebbles kept slipping into his flip-flops and poking the bottoms of his feet. Drew was obviously struggling as well. The armpits of his t-shirt sported huge circles and he was puffing heavily. His demeanor looking less cheerful by the moment. Tim stopped and surveyed the landscape. Just beyond a slope ahead, was a promising looking shack. Just run down and isolated enough it didn't appear too intimidating. It was now or never and Tim had to pick something before Drew gave up.

"C'mon! I think I see one!"

Drew wiped sweat off his fore head and tried to spy what Tim was pointing at.

"That place?"

"Yeah!"

Tim took off, galloping along the roadside. He hurdled a dried rain gully, and raced up the asphalt driveway.

"Wait up"

Drew yelled, huffing and puffing as he tried to catch up.

Tim halted at the wooden door and let his nerve build up. Once Drew had made it, all out of breath and gasping for air, he turned to fully face the entrance. The hovel looked almost ready to fall over. It was all whitewashed clapboard and the door didn't even have a real handle. Just a rusty iron loop.

Tim grabbed the rung and pulled it open. Inside wasn't much better. The walls, roof, and even floor consisted of rough slats, a few stacked up into a homemade looking counter. No one was present and Tim was a little creeped out, this resembled the scene from a million different horror movies. After a few tense moments, anxiety overtook his curiosity and he was ready to make a quick exit.

"Hello?"

A gravelly voice emanated from some back room. It started Tim and gave him pause. Drew burst through the door. Grasping his knees, he tried to say something, but was too out of breath.
A middle-aged man sauntered in from the back. He was sporting a mesh trucker hat and clothes that had all seen better days. Wiping his hands on his t-shirt he planted them on the counter.

"You kids need something?"

Tim paused, unable to think of the right words.
The man's piercing blue eyes stared at him mercilessly, which only made Tim more uncomfortable.

Finally, he muttered "I found something on the beach. I thought maybe you might know what it was..."

He was already thinking this was a bad idea.

"What have you got? Let me see it."

Now Tim felt even more ridiculous. It was just some old coin. This was definitely a bad idea.

Digging the coin out of his pocket, he reached up to drop it on the counter. A counter that was almost level with his head. Boy did he feel small and irrelevant.

The man picked it up, and holding it aloft, rotated it between his fingers.

"The beach you say? Maybe the sea caves? Did you wander in there?"

Tim wasn't quite sure how to answer. In the glare of scrutiny, it all seemed a bit ridiculous.

"Uh, yeah, the beach. I didn't know about any sea caves. It just looked really strange. Like maybe old or something."

"It's nothing special. Maybe some foreign tourist dropped it. Go back to your vacation kid. Some of us have work to do."

The man sounded contemptuous and a bit irate, but Tim couldn't help notice that he looked a little startled. Tim reached up, snatched the coin out of the man's palm, and muttered-

"Thanks mister, sorry to bother you"

As he bee lined for the door.

It slammed behind him and he was almost to the street before Drew caught up.

"Tim....what's...what was all that about..."

Tim leaned over and whispered-

"I don't trust that man. We might have a real find here."

Incognito

Wary about that guy, Tim pulled Drew sideways. Through a rash of overgrown weeds and towards docks that sprawled across the beach. It was only a few feet from the fishing shack, and still a way from the motel, but Tim figured they were still safer here than following an open road. Tim ducked between a few small beach houses, pushed through a rickety old fence, and erupted onto the shore.

The wood of the old dock rose up on his left and Tim ducked underneath. Slipping behind it stilts, he waited for Drew to catch up. The whole thing was a bit silly now. He was hiding behind rotted old wood, his feet half buried in sandy piles of tourist crap. Cups and fast-food wrapping. Drew joined him, panting and out of breath.

> "What's going on Tim?"
> "Let's hang out here for a minute."

Drew shrugged his shoulders.
An hour passed and Tim was running low on excuses. He had spent an hour poking through plastic garbage and half dead vegetation. He was about to suggest heading back to the motel, when he heard a noise. It was the hum of a four-wheeler, and instinctively he ducked behind one of the interior posts. Drew looked confused and snuck over.

> "What is it, Tim?"

An ATV bounded up the beach and stopped at a cluster of tourists. A man in a tan police uniform dismounted, and started with some very aggressive gestures. Tim was half hiding behind a strut, all his attention focused on the distant commotion, when a sound behind almost made him jump.

> "What are you guys doing here?"

Tim tensed to run, but that cop made him think twice. Quickly turning his head, Tim realized it was just a kid. Maybe he was being too hasty.

This guy looked more like some scruffy, latch-key local than anything dangerous.

Tall and thin, he was outfitted in filthy jeans and a worn t-shirt. Not anything that struck Tim as a cop. The kid's long blond hair blanketed his face in softly shifting strands of silver, and he had the smell of engine oil, cigarettes, and dirt. He was also wearing a white Metallica t-shirt, with a bloody skull behind the logo. That definitely gave him more cred.

"Just hanging out."

"You the guys the cops are looking for?"

Tim grew nervous again and tensed to run, but figured he better ply the waters first.

"What are the cops looking for?"
"Hey, it's cool. Fuck 'em."

He slightly muffled the word "fuck", as if it struck him as a bit audacious. Tim looked at the ground and shuffled the sand. He wasn't sure what to say, but he figured the safest bet would be to feel the guy out. He really didn't seem to be a cop.

"I'm Tim. This is my buddy, Drew."

"You found something, didn't you?"

That was not what Tim was expecting.

"No, seriously. Fuck them. When we find stuff, we just bury it. Anyone who gets too involved tends to disappear."

"I found a coin. A weird looking coin."

He pulled it from his pocket and held it up. The kid took it, raised it to a light beam from the rafters, and twisted it around slowly.

"Bury it. I hope you didn't show it to anyone."

"Uh oh."

"Oh shit, what'd you do?"

"Just showed it to the guy at the nearby fishing shack. He acted a little weird so I took off."

Pulling out a pack of camel's, the kid lit one and took a puff.

"Did you tell him who you were?"

"Nah, we high tailed it pretty quick."

"Just avoid that cop out there, bury the coin, and I'd leave as soon as you can. Things have gotten really weird around here. New people that seem slightly off, and way more cops than usual. Ones that don't look like cops."

Drew looked quizzical. He'd stayed back the whole time, observing something he clearly didn't understand. Tim, on the other hand, was going down a mental rabbit hole. He'd read plenty sci-fi and horror books. This sounded like some serious grown-up shit, and we all knew you could never trust the government. Thanking the kid, he turned down an offer of a smoke, and went back to poking around in the sand with his toes. He was done talking to anyone he didn't know, and figured that if he didn't engage, the kid would just leave.

"I'm not kidding. There've been legends of weird events around here for years. Sea monsters and all that. A few months ago, some government guys showed up, and people started disappearing. That fishing guy came around the same time they did. No one knows him and he's definitely not local."

The kid finished his cigarette, stomped it out, and sauntered off.

"I'm scared Tim. This sounds like something big."

Drew was scared of everything. Tim figured if he just downplayed it, they'd have a better chance come sunset. **The Motel**

It was dark by the time they left. Tim and Drew wandered down the shore towards the motel. There were just a few stragglers left on the beach. They were all reduced to the black silhouettes in the distance, pilling up their towels and folding their chairs like some old stop motion film.

The trip back was much longer than Tim remembered. He kept glancing up at the wood shacks bordering the shoreline for reference. He was about to double back when they finally made it to the outskirts of the motel. The small parking lot held only a few cars, the open door of their room spilling a thin shaft of light across the gravel. Mom and dad were almost done with dinner when they entered.

"You missed supper! There should be some leftovers in the fridge, I hope you boys had a good time. We need to checkout by eleven tomorrow. Have fun and don't stay up to late, me and your dad are going to bed."

Dad glanced at Tim but didn't say anything. He piled his knife and fork on the plate, topped it off with his napkin, and headed for the sink.

"Thanks, honey, for the dinner. I'll wake you up at 9 tomorrow, Tim."

"Awe dad, can we do 10?"

"You've proven you're not good with time Tim. 9, bright and early."

Drew darted for the fridge and started pawing through the plastic wrapped plates. Two were piled high with fried chicken and rice. He grabbed one and headed for the silverware drawer. Tim's head drooped as he wandered over to the fridge.

He took the other plate and headed for the couch.

"Hey Drew, can you grab me silverware and a napkin?"

He pulled out the TV table, and dropped his plate on top. Walking over to the tube, he flipped the dial until it landed on some sci-fi show about radioactive roaches. A minute later, Drew joined him. Moving Tim's plate over, he set down his food and started stuffing his quickly grease smeared face.

"What are we watching?"

"Some sci-fi movie about ravenous radioactive cockroaches."

"OK. You want me to grab you a drink?"
"Sure. Just water"

It All Goes to Shit

Tim woke up in handcuffs. Wrists bound tight behind his back, the first thing he noticed was how uncomfortable he was. Propped in a corner, the contours of a wooden chair bit into his butt, the sharp edges of the metal cuffs scraping his wrists.

"What's going on?"

The room was full of cops. Spread out on a plastic sheet in the middle of the floor were the remains of Drew. Blood splatter was everywhere and all that remained of the face was a soupy mess of mangled flesh and shattered bone. One eyeball trailed out of a broken socket, hanging down the left cheek at the tail of a crimson string. The eye cavities were mashed into an oblong grove, the slightly more sunken remains of the other eye hole a gory fissure. Most of the nose was a tangled mess of cartilage slivers and gelatinous blood. The body looked fairly intact, if a little pale and swollen.

Mom was curled in a corner, sobbing into cupped hands. Dad sat opposite on a folded chair; face buried in an upraised palm. He shook his head back and forth slowly, disbelief clearly evident.

One of the officers approached holding aloft a short brass pipe.

"Drug paraphernalia. Did you know your kid was smoking marijuana?"

Dad shook his head slowly and mumbled

"No idea officer."

"Where did he get this? By the looks of it, I'll bet it was laced with something. Angle dust most likely. We've had a bit of an epidemic recently"

Dad looked disgusted, and still refused to make eye contact.

A cop pawing around the floor near Drew pulled up a lead pipe crisscrossed in splatters of blood.

"Looks like we have the weapon here!"

Tim glanced around in desperation and pleaded.

"Dad, you know I didn't do this! Dad! Look at me!"

For a moment Tim's dad stilled his head and opened his eyes fully. Tim could almost could hear the gears turning. The moment passed, his eyelids dropped again and he resumed shaking his head.

"They'll find you the help you need son."

"But dad! You know me! Really! It's me! Your son! You know I didn't do this!"

Dad turned to face Tim; his tear swollen eyes now visible. A questioning demeanor passed over his face. As if he wanted to believe. But it was brief. He lowered his face in his hand again and resumed the melancholy shudder.

"Look officer. Just tell me what to do..."

The closest cop, Tim guessed he was the chief investigator, walked over to Tim's dad and rested a hand on his shoulder.

"We have to take him downtown. You can follow us if you want. Something this serious tho, he'll be in for quite a while. You might want to get a hotel close by."

It Only Gets Worse

Over an hour passed. Medical examiners came and left. Yellow tape was draw across the crime scene. Tim sat aghast, trying to remember anything from last night. His parents slowly became more solemn and just sat stoically in their chairs. Their tears had long dried, their eyes staring out into oblivion.

Eventually only two officers remained. Gesturing for Tim to rise, they escorted him out and into a police cruiser. A few minutes later his parents followed. They grimly climbed into their mustard yellow fiat, started the engine, and waited. Two cops clambered into the front of the wagon.

Refraining from making eye contact, they peeled out onto the main road.

Tim's mind raced. What could he possibly do? Recalling the coin in his pocket, he twisted his handcuffed hands. They wouldn't reach far enough, so he awkwardly twisted his hips in an attempt to reach the front pocket. The cuffs bit into his wrists, his shoulder felt about to dislocate, but he finally clawed to the bottom. The pocket was empty.

Revolution

Bobby Lisse

Todd stood at his dying son's bedside. His hair was greased with a week's worth of sweat and a head full of dread. A bouquet of wilted flowers sat in a vase next to the bed. A single, green cymbidium orchid stood bright and lively. The tubes and leads that snaked their way to his boy's body looked like vines growing on a neglected gisant. A cruel memento mori.

Todd had not uttered his son's name since they were admitted. Every time he felt Dylan dance on his tongue a shriek would threaten to escape from his gut. He would struggle to catch his breath for what seemed like hours. "My son" brought on no tracheal fit, so he had resorted to the possessive moniker.

A missing patch of skin on his son's hand held Todd's tragic gaze. The wound looked like a burn which had become infected, and Todd shamefully kept his own hand away as if it were the result of a contagious, zombie apocalypse inducing, flesh-eating disease. It wasn't. He wanted to hold his son's hand, but he was afraid of the lifelessness he would feel.

Todd thought back to the first time he saw a dead body. His grandmother lay peacefully in the casket. Her eyes closed, her cheeks sunken, her hands grasped and resting on her pelvis. He knew who she was supposed to be, but he stared at an imposter. His young brain imagined her a villain. An evil, undead, doppelganger of his grandmother. Her skin always seemed to have texture when she was alive. Porous and moist, her cheeks hung low on her jaw signaling the late life of a woman who was much heavier in her youth. In that time of mourning Todd looked at her cheeks and saw a thick layer of wax. It reminded him of Madame Tussauds, the wax museum his mother had brought him to in the city the winter before.

When Todd's mother led him to the side of the casket to pay his last respects and pray with her, she did her best to prepare her son for the grief that was sure to follow.

She told him "God takes his favorite children." as if that would make sense to an eight-year-old.

Todd responded, "Like Jesus?" with naivete.

"Exactly like Jesus, honey." She put her hand on Todd's back and steered him to the corpse.

"You don't have to look, if you don't want to." Todd's mother helped him kneel.

The smell of the flowers which surrounded the coffin would never leave Todd's nose. He would smell it again in other places of less mourning, but it would bring him right back there, beside the remains of his loved one where a fit of anger came over him that can only be described as wrath. Wrath against God for taking a piece of his heart. The boy's outburst startled everyone into gasps and clenched fists. His mother rushed him away as he kicked and screamed.

"You're not dead! You're not dead!".

His trust never healed after that.

Todd stared down his forearm at his fading tattoo. The irony sneered at him and the words "In God We Trust…" made little sense to him now. An outburst from an eight-year-old child rose in Todd's paunch. Again, he was angry at God, but God wasn't there to feel his ire, so his son's stiffening body was on the receiving end.

"It's not like if you die the world will stop spinning!".

A pathetic spittle flew from Todd's mouth. His eyes poured tears that he despised but he was in too much pain to worry about seeming weak. He hated the world for how he felt at that moment. The heart monitor signaled the end. In that exact second the world stopped spinning and the worst day of Todd's life would last for the next six months.

Distance and Time

It had been almost six months since the Earth stopped rotating.

It was a static, floating marble for so long that people had already gotten over the "still-sickness". It was a panic that was spurned by an imperceptible unmoving; a cocaine rage or caffeine fit from hell that usually ended in tears or death. A schizophrenic meltdown that can be blamed on the augmented polarity of the planet if only someone knew scientifically just what was going on.

Half the world was chafing and freezing and the other was peeling and burning. Geography had made solar messiahs. The new gold rush had become battery banks. Those who resided in the day and had retained some semblance of pragmatism knew the night would come, eventually.

They did their best to store as much energy as they could, but it wasn't without tragedy. Equipment was wearing out ten times as quick without the reprieve of darkness.

Theft became a matter of "national security" and bulked up the private security industry, or as Jerrod liked to call himself 'The Panel Police'. One thousand miles or so from the tragic death of a boy, mankind's final conflict was primed to explode.

Back to the Grind

It was Jerrod's first day back on rotation.

Not all the Solar Bank sites, storage facilities that cultivated the steady power of the sun, had been built around buildings as secure as a Prison, like Jerrod's had, but they were all fortified locations. What was left of the government had identified a few preferred existing sites to stage their greedy, natural energy hoard. Installations were limited by the wildfires which left a hazy overcast hundreds of miles around. Schools with safe rooms and multi-level entrances that were designed to keep the weekly school shooters out. A profession that had thankfully dried up once the world stopped turning.

SB-7, as the old prison was dubbed, stood with its back to mountains, which made it vulnerable to only one side. Shield Pledge Security had begun fourteen-day shifts about a month after everything changed. So far it has been working out. Temporary sleeping quarters and "swivel watch" had kept the on-site guards fresh and alert.

The union had suggested what management called 'extreme caution' safety measures which included uniforms staying on site for fear of off-duty attacks or hijacking. The proposed security detail for off the clock personnel was rebuffed. Management's argument was that if an armed security guard with as much training as their company claimed to have on staff was unable to protect and defend themselves, they shouldn't be defending matters of national security, and tried to use it as a maneuver to force employees to live on-site. They even started building barracks, but the labor washed up as the sun persisted. The wood ended up sitting, rotting, and becoming home to creatures seeking shelter rather than guards.

Jerrod was no "Prepper" but he had resorted to living as independent from the grid as he could. He had cured and cold smoked everything. Curing the meat would make it last and smoking it was just for flavor. He knew the power would eventually shut down for 'preservation,' but what he was most worried about was the supply chain.

He was one of the lucky ones that only had himself to care for. He had seen shootings over food at the grocery stores, which became the wild west of this still Earth, and always assumed it was some poor father of four who was doing what he needed to feed his brood. He had empathy for family men in this new, post-turn world but it wouldn't stop him from shooting one of them if they stepped onto his field. The kill order was cut and dry: Shoot to kill; no warning.

Jerrod fancied himself a poetic man. He didn't care to read poetry, nor did he care to follow any established rules of poetry, but he assured himself he had both rhythm and "...a way with words". There were no more public readings, not that Jerrod would have participated if there were. His verse lived solely in a moleskine notebook - the tool of any writer who was flatulent enough to believe their words were too valuable for fleeting digital technology like a notes app and would much rather kill some trees to doodle on. Today's entry:

"The morning air used to feel crisp and foreign, but its edge has dulled and become familiar like adjusting to the horrid stench of a room that your nose no longer registers. Last night's chill has faded from existence."

He was right, there had been no break from the energy of the sun. The morning dew may now live only in prose. Jerrod always kept the book on him in case the right words were to tickle his brain and today was no different as it was snuggly contoured to his thigh. The ballpoint was its bedmate.

Jerrod removed his .38 special from his nightstand and snapped it safely into his ankle holster.

The Commute

Public transportation had become as close to an exclusive means of travel, besides walking, that has existed during the century of individual vehicles. Gas prices and scarcity made driving a combustion engine car the ultimate superfluous gesture of wealth and indifference. The train brought Jerrod within three miles of work which took a fit fella like him around forty-five minutes.

There was a park about halfway through the walk that Jerrod would sometimes stop at to recapture some semblance of the "old normal". He'd write in his moleskine, eat a sandwich, or just stare at nature. He figured that the lack of foot traffic probably wasn't new and that it was probably what saved the park from looking like every other allotted zone for recreation and reflection.

The tents that used to occupy the stone below the bridges had hiked up their skirts and sunk their stakes on more scenic real estate. No one could blame them. The Rangers had all but been wiped out. As well as all ex-military had been sucked up and transferred to active-duty policing or taking jobs with the private security firms. The same kind that signed Jerrod's own paycheck.

That day he sat there, an apple making the rounds in his palm as he chewed sweet chunks of red delicious. No one else had come down the overgrown path. Jerrod checked his watch, noticing it was about time for him to complete his journey. He tossed the apple core into the overgrowth and walked through the covered trail. The trail opened to a large field where one day long ago kids frolicked and flew kites and families sat on blankets that promised the security of a false reality.

Normally, in the post-turn world, this field was a flat plane of sun scorched grass. Today it had transmogrified. What Jerrod didn't realize is that the park, to him, was the last bastion of hope to hold on to his former self. On that day his past was buried. Finally, he had lost his paradise to the destitute.

A throng of cloaked, unkempt, humans stood in a half-moon. A single man stood at the centroid. His robe hung low enough to conceal the apple box he stood atop, as if he were preaching. Jerrod was careful in his approach. His father had ingrained an important lesson in how to carry yourself when he was a young boy.

"Never walk with your eyes on your toes. Keep your head high and proud and no one will ever think you're weak.".

At this point in his life, he no longer heard the echo of his father's mantra, but his neck muscles had been trained to keep his gaze straight forward. His security training taught him to keep his hands out of his pockets as they could act like loose handcuffs that can turn into an obstructive restraint quicker than you could pull them out. His quick pace was a result of a dedication to cardio. Despite the size of the field there were enough mendicants gathered to force Jerrod into a close flyby.

As Jerrod got close, he could get a better look at what he suspected to be the evangelizer. He played the part well. The long, greased hair. His thick beard stricken with gray streaks looked more like a fungus growing upon a tree rather than a growth of human hair. His robe, unlike the others who wore soiled earth tone garb, was stark white. Not laundry white, but the type of white that could be accomplished washing clothes in a cool stream. The Man's face was hard to make out even though Jerrod could hear his sermonizing. It drew Jerrod closer than he wanted to be.   The dusk of man is upon us. Do not let their fear mongering steer you towards compliance. Do not fear the night. Welcome its cool embrace. For when the sun finally sets, when the day is finally over, the son of God will have returned. This is the Revolution Summer!"

The crowd roared in a wave of approval. The undulating harmony sounded more like a congruent military force than a bunch of vagabonds. Jerrod knew this song. It was a symphony of destruction. His training urged him to learn more, but his watch beckoned him to punch the clock or risk losing the stability and boku pay.

The crowd broke their crescent formation and filed away neatly. They truly behaved like a military encampment when their tents were erected with incredible haste. Jerrod hung back enough to remain a face in the crowd but close enough to get a good look at the Preacher. When the cleric finally turned and gave Jerrod a clear view. It was not what he had expected. There had been plenty of reports of folk who had poisoned minds from prolonged exposure to the merciless sun, and skin disease had increased at an unimaginable rate, but Jerrod had never seen anything like this.

The man's face was cracked and peeled in sickening dermal waves. The splayed ends were blackened like the wick of a candle. The stretches of skin that weren't lifting away from his face seemed to be slicked with an oily substance. Not sweat, nor sunscreen, but more of a whale oil sheen. It appears the Preacher had not stepped away from the glare of the sun since it had decided to keep its gaze on this side of the globe.

The Preacher did not move from his pedestal. His gestures were minimal and deliberate. The extent was a raised hand as if he were blessing his parishioners as they assembled their temporary quarters.

Jerrod had seen groups like this before, led by false prophets promising salvation and screaming about the night side of the earth. This was the biggest one by far and looked like a traveling city. There were rumors of militia cannibals coming from the dark to steal the benefits of the sun, but that had to be hyperbole or misplaced foreboding as the grass on this side of the Earth was no longer green, but burnt and brown. Those who lived closest to ports lobbied for walls to be built along the coast, but resources were focused elsewhere. Jerrod originally wondered why the government didn't send forces in to distinguish any type of uprising that may cause chaos, but you don't separate dogs as soon as they growl at each other. You give them a chance to adapt.

Jerrod thought about his contract which obligated him to report if he suspected an attack on the station was imminent. These people may have behaved soldierly, but they looked like "tree huggers". Still, he would have to file a report when he checked in. He approached the Preacher as genially as he could. He put on an inquisitive face and led with what he thought would steer the conversation as far away from violence as possible.

"Excuse me, do you mind if I ask you a question?"

The Preacher turned towards the outsider's voice and now Jerrod could get a clear look at the masterful orator. His eyes were sunken so deep you could hardly see how cloudy they were. It was as if a layer of diffusion had been laid into his orbital cavities. It looked more like a corpse than a living man.

"How can I help you, stranger?"

Jerrod tried not to cringe at the gruesome sight of charred skin, even if he did not think the Preacher could even see his expressions.
"What book do you read from?" Jerrod thought the question was benign enough.

"There is only one book." The Preacher's answer didn't reveal much but Jerrod figured he meant the Bible, so he fashioned his follow up towards a God he was familiar with in a former life.

"OK, I think we're praying to the same God. I don't mean to be offensive, it's just some people nowadays are looking to start new religions and…"

"I'm not interested in creating a new religion." The Preacher's words had no reassurance attached to them. "I want a new era of mankind."

Jerrod wore his fret clearly on his face. He could only hope those glassy eyes did not register his worry. The more he stared at the Preacher the less human he looked.

"Now I ask you, curious traveler, would you evolve with us?"

Jerrod felt the words he would choose next were important to his immediate survival.

"I once shook hands with the Devil, but we could not agree on what kind of bread to break."

The Preacher nodded his head slightly, understanding Jerrod's careful refusal. "I believe you will find sweet bread elsewhere and I bid you good fortune." He stepped down from his apple box revealing a solid, two-foot-high rectangular platform. He was eye level with Jerrod as he walked past him, two of his followers close behind, one of them grabbing the box as they scurried. Jerrod waited a moment before making his way past the camp.

He felt compelled to gaze back over his shoulder to see what type of massive tent the Preacher must have helped himself to, but he fought that urge successfully. If he had looked back, he would have seen the Preacher on the edge of the field. He never broke his stare from Jerrod's departure, menace somehow breaking through his mangled face.

Punching the Clock

Jerrod approached the first guard tower with guns trained on him, but he had no worry of being shot. Around his neck was a hightech perimeter sensor. Enter the kill zone without it and you were treated like any other trespasser; you were shot in the head. Not as forgiving as forgetting an I.D. badge at a corporate office.

Inside the first fence was the incomplete employee barracks. In big blue graffiti on the side of one of the roofless buildings was written:
"The Panel Police - Every Day is Sun Day".

The next gate opened into a large steel fence corridor. At the end of that were reportedly impenetrable doors into the facility. There had never been an attack that reached this far so no one could prove them vulnerable, but Jerrod had little faith in any hinged barricade when it came up against the will of Man. As he swiped his badge, he engaged the deadbolt and pulled on the hefty door noticing its every weakness. Rust, a single locking mechanism, and a double walled corrugated structure that made it look vulnerable regardless of how heavy the metal was. The weakest point he could see was that it required power to open and close.

The second he swiped his badge he was officially "on the clock". He wasted no time in reporting his encounter. Men are creatures of habit and in the post-turn world the hierarchy in military-like installations was no different than before. The titles might have meant nothing besides a shared obedience and myth of power, but regardless Jerrod reported to his Lieutenant that he had seen a group of at least three hundred who seemed to him to be operative, as they called it.

"Armed?"

"With the "good book", but besides that I'm unsure."

"Hostile?"

"Self-Righteous."

"Hmm." The Lieutenant pondered for a moment before scribbling a minor note in his logbook. "You've done your diligence." He didn't care to look back up at Jerrod which meant he sensed no threat.

"Have you done yours?" Jerrod knew once the words escaped that he was about to get a strike on his jacket. The Lieutenant kept his eyes from meeting Jerrod's.

"I apologize Sir, I don't mean disrespect. With the other facilities losing coms and all, I'm on high alert. It's just the whole reason we're mandated to report is…"

"I know what the requirements are and why. I'm not going to send out the ranks for some bible thumping hippie. Not with so many no shows today. The coms situation has got everyone on edge, but per corporate they're working on it so don't worry, ya pansy."

Jerrod didn't like the sound of missing personnel. It all added up to too many red flags for him. Ever the company man, he submitted to the bureaucracy.

Shift

Jerrod was covered in grease and grime. Regardless of how much he looked like a car mechanic, he couldn't change an oil filter before he started working at the solar bank. The ad read "Will Train" and they did, but Jerrod was a mercenary as most of the other employees were and he wasn't mechanically inclined and wouldn't be able to translate any of his newfound skill to anything besides panels and leads and energy piles. With a flashlight in his mouth, he greased the four-inch-thick cables to prevent friction and wrapped the insulation back around.

Jerrod radioed for the lines to be reconnected. They had to sever power from the panels while the feed was serviced, and the entire compound was fed by those panels. They were completely off the grid. If the panels went down, they were "dead in the water".

Jerrod had asked his supervisor early on why they couldn't run off the battery power. His answer was a herald of a dying capitalist society.

"A farmer grows crops for the consumer."

That answer made little sense to Jerrod, the pragmatic man that he was. "If a farmer were starving, he would eat his own crop." he thought to himself.

"Turn on Main, over." The walkie talkie bleeped, ending Jerrod's relay. A loud thump and metallic click brought on a crescendo of energy. A whir with lights coming on and systems energizing. The compound was alive again.

Another day, another shift, another duty. Jerrod stood guard in one of the many towers around the compound. All the towers had a threehundred-and-sixty-degree view but this post in particular saw the most action. They called it "the kill perch" because this is where the shot was taken to stifle every attack that had ever surfaced. It was an easy job if your conscience didn't get in the way of the trigger. There was no debate, no negotiating, and no hesitation. If someone approached unannounced, you shoot them. Jerrod had eight circular notches on the stock of his rifle. All head shots, hence, the circles. He had been a sniper in a former life, in a war that meant no more than the one he was in now - protecting the assets of the wealthy. The dead space that day had him writing in his moleskin.

"They called me God because I could choose who lived and who died. I was that accurate. I hated that nickname and maybe that's why I couldn't stand any Jesus Merchant I came across. It's kinda like once you work at a pizza joint it just becomes dough, sauce and mozzarella to you. Knowing the ingredients robs the magic. I'm a far cry from that action and it's been a while since anyone stumbled into my kill zone, so I've resorted to training my eye tracking insects. Lately it has been mosquitoes, mostly, thanks to the heat and humidity from this bastard Sun. It sticks around like a jock itch. My favorite thing to watch were the bees. The way they danced from flower, to bush, to hive removed any fear I used to have of their stinger. Especially the carpenter bees. I watched them come out of the old split rail fence, flying around like little minivans driven by overworked Moms trying to quiet the horror of screaming kids and playing bumper cars around town. Now, I'm left with these flying vampires who have nothing to feast on except a dwindling population of cattle who look malnourished grazing on sun dried grass."

Shoot first

There was a fly in the tower. It was the most fun Jerrod had on watch since the last shot he took. He built a five-sided box with manilla folders and attempted to direct the fly in. He would get it close but over ten times it had deked at the last possible moment. It sat on the opposite window, pivoting around as if it were wary of its approach. Jerrod smacked his hand on the window to the right of the fly and it took off towards its target. It was in line to enter the pseudo trap, but Jerrod had seen this flight path before. He ran along behind it waving both his hands up and down thinking he could create a vortex that would force the insect into the Smead enclosure. It worked!

Jerrod jumped, both fists in the air. "Yes!".

Just as quickly as the fly went in, he flew back out, but Jerrod was already satisfied. The alarm sounded like a hell trumpet. A badgeless man had made it halfway through the kill zone, sprinting as if his life depended on it because it most certainly did. Jerrod's gun was resting against the far wall. He lunged for it as quickly as he could, released the safety, and pulled back the bolt. He pushed the awning window up with one hand, planning out his shot as he moved. The fly escaped through the opening, but Jerrod ignored it. He propped, steadied, closed one eye, and shot. Another circle to add to his gun.

Don't Move

Jerrod stood over the body. It was against protocol for the tower guard to leave his post during duty but being so understaffed, no one else was going to retrieve the kill. It was a perfect shot through the center of his forehead and looked like a third eye was emerging from the wound.

The blood had formed a vermillion nimbus around the bald head. Jerrod poked the body with the muzzle of his rifle. He looked the man up and down, assessing the threat. Was he from a larger group? Was he armed? Was he just lost and wandering, hoping for some salvation in this wretched post-turn world? His garb looked like the group Jerrod saw in the park but was far cruder. It was brittle burlap, and it must have been torture on his skin.

There were no pockets to check through. A three-strand rope acted as a belt around his midriff. It was taped in the center with two loops of black electrical tape anchoring an aged paper cylinder. Jerrod tugged at it, ripping the paper at one edge before finally prying it from the adhesive. He unfolded and read it. But did not understand its message was for him.

Obey and you live.

Jerrod stared at the warning as if it were a foreign codex. The sound of a single footstep brought his confused eyes right into the butt of an elephant gun.

Your Clothes, Give Them to Me Now

Jerrod awoke drenched in sweat. His bare chest was glistening. Tacky blood split past his nose like a river around a massive boulder. A three-inch gash in his forehead mimicked the headshot he had put upon the intruder. The striated muscles in his shoulders looked to be stretched to their absolute limit.

His hands were fastened to a large tree and tied behind his back. He leaned forward on his knees. He had been unconscious long enough to ache and his legs were too stricken with pins and needles to tell if his .38 was still on his ankle. Although he highly doubted it was. He couldn't wipe the salty water or gore from his eyes, so he blinked trying to clear his vision.

He could make out a large shape not far from him. Ten feet, maybe. It was low to the ground but had a wide base to it and came up to a rounded point. He kept blinking to no avail. The shape grew skyward. The distance between it and Jerrod shortened and he braced for what was to come.

It was soft, silky, fabric wiped across his face. It wasn't moist but it was cool and a nice respite from the sweltering sun on his skin. He blinked a few more times as the cloth was removed from his face and now, he could see what the shape was.

It was the Preacher.

He returned to his apple box and sat down returning his handkerchief beneath his robe. His hand came back with a book. It could have been a bible, but it was very old looking. Its cover seemed to be made of some type of animal flesh, dried of course. Not leather, at least not made by any professional tanner. It was crude and somewhat gruesome.

Jerrod didn't keep his stare on the book long as he dismissed it as just another faith dealer's tool of manipulation.

"I warned them about you." Jerrod's breath was short.

"I expected you to."

The Preacher talked like a man who could see nothing new.
"They didn't listen."

"I expected them not to. Not many are afraid of a blind preacher." Those were the first words Jerrod heard from the Preacher that didn't ring true.

"I didn't mention that." Jerrod conceded. The Preacher thought for a moment, his sunken orbs and swollen face revealing no mannerisms. He leaned back, lifting one foot and adjusting himself.

"Did you not think that was an important part of the story?"

"If you were blind, I would have told them you were blind, and the result would have been the same."

The Preacher gave too much credit to Jerrod, who was sitting there tied, tired, and in pain.

"So, what now? Are you going to storm the castle?" Jerrod said that with hope in his voice. He knew the chances of success were almost nil, even with his pass. He hoped the Preacher did not.

"Is that your strategic advice?" The Preacher allowed some air to settle between them. "No, you know better than that. You don't think I'm cavalier enough to attack barbed wire fences and walls and steel reinforced doors, no matter how many men I have in my legions."

"I can't help but feel like you're going to tell me the plan."

Jerrod had acceptance in his throat.

"I have no qualms sharing "the plan" as you call it, with you." The Preacher stated.

"Because you're going to kill me?"

The Preacher had reclaimed some of the credit Jerrod had earned. He removed Jerrod's pass from his shirt. Jerrod chuckled. "I see now. You lured me out to get the badge. You're going to walk in there and kill off forty trained killers, open the doors and let your people in. What you don't know is that the whole facility compartmentalizes like a submarine."

"Some of my men have the training to do such things. Though, unless you're counting the entirety of the people who have been employed both present and past by your firm, I don't think forty is quite an accurate headcount. As you've been told, some didn't show up for their shift and the ones who did have grown weary of constantly opening every interior door. Which would leave only a single obstacle in the shape of a rusty door. There are twelve men on duty, "trained killers" as you call them. The commanding officers are hardly capable of protecting much beyond their own impotence."

Jerrod instantly knew how serious this threat was. This wasn't a fly by night operation. They had been scouting the compound, the personnel, the protocols, and who knows what else. They probably knew where Jerrod lived. All at once he realized they were not in that park by happenstance.

"Why didn't you take me when you saw me in the park? Why wait and let me kill one of your men?"

"As I said, some of my men are highly trained. Some serve other purposes."

With those words a group of men started gathering around the preacher. Not as many as Jerrod had seen in the park, but enough to do damage. They were all dressed in company clothing. They all had badges. The Preacher handed Jerrod's badge to the one man who did not. "You've heard the rumors of the other facilities falling?"

"I hear a lot of rumors but they're all bullshit." Jerrod spit back.

"Ah, but this one is not. I admit, some of them have become quite imaginative. Dubbing us a horde of cannibals, with thick, bushy beards. Attacking out of the dark lands is fear and fantasy. What is not an invention is how calculated we have been in dismantling every power grid we've come across.

Jerrod laughed, half in fear and half in hopes that none of it was true. "So, you're the zombie army that all the nutcases are yapping about?"

"Come, watch a plan of certainty." The Preacher stood and pointed to Jerrod. He was cut free from the tree and lifted by two followers in cloaks. "Everyone serves a purpose in our parish."

They walked to the edge of the brush which was about four hundred yards from gate one; clear of the kill zone. The Preacher gave calm instructions to a select few men. "This is our warrior sect. Our finest. Our bravest. The community you bore witness to, they remain behind, comfortable but able and ready to step in if one of their brethren shall fall."

"You said you wanted to create a new mankind." The Preacher held his hand up to his militia as if he was telling them "Hold". He walked through a crowd that parted like curtains riding a strong gust.

"And so, I do."

"Well, if you go in there and kill everyone, you're just committing genocide."

"I believe the term you're looking for is speciocide. I'm at peace with eliminating those too nearsighted to see what the future for man holds. Those stuck in the light like a moth."

"What makes you so worthy? What makes you the one to start a new mankind?"

The Preacher postured his body in a way that displayed offense. "Were you a devout man in your past life?"

Jerrod shook his head no, vehemently. "What kind of man were you?" The Preacher inquired.

"A killer." Jerrod's teeth flashed like a dog warning "not a step closer". His eyes dipped inward and there was an audible snarl from his maw. His glare would have struck fear on the face of almost any mortal man, but the Preacher had a shield for a face. An imperceptible reaction thanks to too many moments in the unabating sun. He stepped close to Jerrod. Close enough for their breath to meet. Through the edema in the Preacher's face Jerrod could see a hint of white. Nothing he would call eyes, but objects, nonetheless.

The Preacher kept his voice soft. "When you steadied your hand, held your breath, closed your eye, and pulled the trigger, which God did you pray to for a hit?"

"The only one." Jerrod spit with vitriol.

"And did I ever fail to answer your prayer?" Jerrod looked at the Preacher with wide eyes. He had thought the man may be a bit crazy, but now the fear of God was in his bones. He knew the Preacher was God. Not the one he had known as a boy. The New God.

We Move When the Good Book Says So

They stood four men wide and five men deep. The Preacher remained directly behind them. He held the skin covered book close to his chest. No one made a noise. There was wind but not enough to relieve the heat. Jerrod wondered what they were waiting for. A sign from above? He felt resistance was futile, but he tried to sew doubt in the followers.

"There's no way they don't take twenty men approaching at once as a red flag. Even if they have badges."

The Preacher gripped his book tighter. "In the best of conditions, you are the only guard who can make twenty lethal shots in time. In the best of conditions."

Jerrod pondered what the Preacher meant by that. The sun may have been a hindrance, but it was a clear day. It had been for the past three months. The wind wasn't enough to throw a shot off target. He knew the Preacher was right about everyone else being a terrible shot.

"They might not be expert marksmen, but there is enough ammo in there that they don't need to be. After the first shot is fired, they'll never open the gates. All the interior doors will get locked" Jerrod told no lies.

The Preacher turned to Jerrod, "We have the good book." He patted the skin. Jerrod rolled his eyes. He had long ago found holy rollers to have the realistic intelligence of a child. "Your God bleeds just like your men will."

"Then let the water from the heavens wash away our gore." The Preacher tossed the book down. It was slick with an oily substance. Jerrod heard him strike a match and drop it on the book. He was puzzled as to why The Preacher would destroy something he so coveted just moments earlier. The book burned slowly. Its dermis dust jacket wasn't quite flammable, but it did melt like a thick layer of wax. Jerrod watched its steady destruction and then saw the book's true cover as its wrapping disappeared. "Farmer's Almanac". Thunder struck like a war siren. The skies darkened in the time it took Jerrod to crane his neck. Visibility had become compromised and then in an instant it had become impenetrable as the rain fell.

Jerrod was stunned. The Preacher was a practical man after all, not some crazy Jesus freak preying on the manipulative minds of those who needed someone to follow; someone to call a leader.

The formation of men fell into a single line spaced apart in what Jerrod could only assume was calculated since they measured by using their arms to touch the soldier in front of them. They moved quietly forward, towards the compound. Two cloaked men stayed behind holding Jerrod in place. The Preacher, taking up the rear, stopped a moment and looked back at Jerrod. When he turned his face seemed to be repelling the water, but it was falling so hard it was impossible to tell what you were looking at.

"Time has not mattered. Not for quite a while. Now this day has finally ended. You can come live with us in the darkness, or you can wait, hopelessly, for a new dawn."

The Preacher brought his hands to his eyes and stuck them within his orbital cavities. He pulled at the skin tearing it apart. Jerrod's mind could not comprehend the self-destruction. The skin of his cheeks broke away like a thin candy shell revealing heavily wrinkled skin below and bright eyes. He kept pulling at this outer layer revealing that more of the protected skin beneath It was shriveled like he had spent an eternity submersed in water.

Jerrod knew then. A wax-like covering had protected The Preacher's skin from the sun and radiation that everyone else was subjected to. The wax body suit now lay in the muddy puddle at The Preacher's feet.

"Move quickly. The power will not last long." The Preacher's followers moved with pace and all Jerrod could do was watch.

Your Face will Stay that Way if You Keep it Up

There was no alarm. No warning of the impending doom. The first barrier was too easy. The second wouldn't be hard either. Once the metal door was open The Preacher knew all hope for his enemies was lost. The lights had finally gone out once they were inside. The sound of the power shutting down was frightening. It sounded like the end of the world.

His army of twenty strong moved with calculation and large curved knives came out from their waistbands. They slaughtered everyone they encountered. They cut them like a butcher bleeding a pig: belly, throat, wrists, and femoral artery were all sliced as deep as the blades allowed. The blood coated the concrete hallways.

The Preacher followed behind as clean up, a shotgun hidden in his robe. He didn't need to take a shot until every employee was dead. Then, he unloaded.

Outside

Jerrod heard a few muffled shots but not enough to sound like any type of resistance. His colleagues were impotent soldiers. They might have killed intruders, but they were no more "killers' than a drone pilot sitting thousands of miles away from its target or a video game cowboy.

The rain relented. Jerrod had become so accustomed to the hum of the harnessed energy that once it stopped a void itched in his brain. He looked at the robed followers and saw blank stares. They were automatons, waiting for a cue.

"What did he promise you, a wealth of virgins?" Jerrod ribbed hoping to break their facade.

"He didn't have to promise us anything." One follower remarked with no fracture in his armor.

"You don't think he's going to exploit his power at some point? It's what Men do. We are patently corruptible." The other follower was less amused.   "When you see something, who is the authority on the truth of that vision, your eyes or your brain?". Jerrod didn't quite understand where the follower was leading him, but he knew better than to leave the air floating and empty. "They work in tandem."

"Exactly! He would not spite his nose to save his face." Jerrod got it, but he felt like a disillusioned belle at the conspiracy ball.

"It's time." The cue came without Jerrod noticing it. They moved towards the dark facility.

Welcome to Tomorrow

The followers' flashlights seemed to be lit for diligence only. They walked the halls with a familiarity of the layout that Jerrod could only credit to some pre-scouting they had done. The pools of blood were beginning to congeal, and it made Jerrod queasy. He wasn't a man unaccustomed to grim deaths. His former life as an exported wall street bodyguard was filled with death.

The bodies were breadcrumbs. As they advanced, they were no longer just the guards but the followers of the Preacher that had fallen dead as well and their corpses were leading to the old chapel. It was used as the temporary sleeping quarters slash break room. Pull out posters of scantily clad and nude women were taped to the walls of God's house. Where criminals once paid penance, you could now see large bare areolas which were the mortal enemy of the pious man. It seemed a natural palace to find the Preacher sitting alone, drenched in blood.   There was no longer a large cross on the wall but rather an outline where it had once been nailed. The stained-glass windows had nothing but walls behind them making the beams of the flashlight bend and reflect in odd ways.

If this were a movie and there was a score being applied to the moment an appropriate soundtrack may very well be the opening organ of Mercyful Fate's "The Oath". Only this isn't a movie, this was the end of the world.

Jerrod stood a few feet inside the chapel, his eyes adjusting slowly as the silhouette of the back of the Preacher's head became clear to him.

"I'm guessing you want me to get it back up and running?"

The Preacher didn't answer right away.

"No." His voice was one of defeat, or more severely one of submission.

"You have someone that can…"

"I have no one. I don't want it back!" The Preacher responded with anger. Then, his voice changed to sorrow. "We'll never look at the same sky again. My boy."

Jerrod could hear the globus sensation in the Preacher's throat as he spoke. Two shots rang out and the Followers dropped to the ground. The flashlights had fallen in such a way that the Preacher was illuminated. He held a bright blue, solitary flower to his nose. A gun protruded from under his arm. Smoke billowed from the barrel. Jerrod was in shock.

"I used to recite this epigram before I shot my enemy. It started with 'In God we trust…'. Which sounds innocent enough but the intention behind the words was that God guided my bullet. I'm not sure I ever believed that. I just thought it was some cool shit to say. I started doing it after I saw Pulp Fiction. I don't have the capacity to memorize an entire scripture, so I took this line from a book I read as a kid. 'In God we trust, all others pay cash.' Then, Boom! I'd shoot that fucker dead. I never thought about the other side of that bullet. I'm not talking about the devastation it had caused inside his body. Tearing through flesh and organs, or if I was lucky, which I often was, it would make his brain explode inside his skull and maybe spray some out on the dirt for a little fireworks finale. I'm talking about the family that was on the other end of that body. The hurt, the true pain that bullet could cause. I never felt pain like that. Not until I did. You know what happened when I finally felt the suffering that I had caused to so many children, parents, siblings, wives?"

Despite the rhetorical nature of the question Jerrod tried to read between the lines. There was something deeper he could sense. Something that seemed more malevolent than some "asshole on his high horse".

The Preacher's voice fell to a dulcet whisper. "The world stopped.".

Todd rose from the last remaining pew. He dropped the pistol and turned towards Jerrod. "I was a Marine, once upon a time. I thought it defined me. Made me who I am."

"I was in the Army, Green Beret. You led those men to slaughter."
"They served their duty. I served mine. I promised them transcendence. What difference does it make whose rapture they incurred, mine or some fictitious God in the sky?"

"You don't get to choose who lives and who dies. No one does."

"I've lived the worst day of my life for far too long. Now that day is over, and the darkness has begun. This world no longer deserves to exist in the light. Not since my boy died."

The Dark Army Engulfs the Last Light

Todd was a smaller man, but he fought with temerity. Jerrod struggled to keep balance with his hands tied behind him. Jerrod's forehead burst open again, bleeding plentifully. As the two men struggled the sound of the impact echoed with discordance. Like the Venice library scene in The Last Crusade, while Indy breaks through the ancient floor. Todd slammed Jerrod to the ground breaking his wrist which allowed him to wiggle his restraint loose. All he needed was one hand. The rhythmic thunder did not cease. It came from a foreign source. A horn wailed like a Celtic carnyx, instilling fear in the hearts of enemies and mettle in the Celt Warriors.

Jerrod took advantage of the diversion. He reached into his boot and removed the .38. He aimed it at Todd's head, but his wrist could not hold the weight of the pistol and the bone broke further, diverting the muzzle toward Todd's belly, instead. The shot rang out as the approaching doom became imminent. Todd stumbled backward holding his gut. His mouth was agape, but before he could blurt out some pithy final words a wave of bearded, wind burned creatures tore him apart like soft bread. His entrails spilled out and were gobbled up before they could stain the floor.

Jerrod played dead with his eyes wide open. The wound in his head tricked the cannibal horde into passing on dead meat. He had slowed his breath enough to avoid detection, but his eyes began burning and his pulse raced at the fear of blinking before they could finish their snack. Luckily there were enough mouths in the trough to make short work of the once prophet turned protein.

There was no shred of Todd left. His being had been devoured. He would compost in the tenebrous belly of the creatures of night. Once the dark army had moved on, Jerrod pulled himself from his faux grave with his face covered in sticky, coagulated blood.

The solar banks were destroyed. The prison had taken back its walls. It was a single purpose facility again, to jail hope. Jerrod scanned the field which once showcased children flying kites. It was a gruesome landscape of robed death. Steam rose from the blood and bone left behind. The chill of night settled.

This was the end of mankind.

Dreamers

Bracken MacLeod

For David Cronenberg

He worked at the cuff securing his wrist. Without one free hand he couldn't release the other restraints. What was it Carl Sagan had said? *If you want to make a pie from scratch, you must first invent the universe.* This wasn't as difficult as that. Before he could get out of this room, he had to get out of this bed, and in order to do that, all he had to accomplish was undoing a single buckle. Before it came back.

Might as well invent the universe.

The cuff holding his right arm in place was fastened with a simple strap and buckle. No lock or complicated mechanism to outsmart. Just the kind of something he'd manipulated a million times in his life, getting dressed or using the bathroom. A single buckle was all that stood between him and… not freedom exactly.

His neck hurt from craning it around and seeing wasn't helping anyway. The problem wasn't sight; it was reach. No amount of observation could make his wrist bend more or his fingers lengthen. These restraints had been designed for this very purpose—holding him in place—and there was nothing he could do to undermine their function. Not from his side of the transaction. He took a breath and decided to try something different. Tucking his thumb as close to his palm as he could, he tried to slide his hand through the cuff. Without that digit, he imagined he could slip free with little effort, even though the strap across his chest and upper arms limited his movement, he only needed a few inches of motion. Once out of that, everything else would fall into place in easy sequence. Undo the chest restraint, move to his left arm, then his legs and ankles. And then, the floor and the door. But for a thumb, he would be free.

The door at the far end of the room opened. No sound of the slide of a key or clack of a deadbolt. He was immobilized; no need to bother with securing the room. He closed his eyes, tears fighting their way through the tight slit between his lids and escaping down the sides of his face. They caught in his hair, and he sympathized at them having been ensnared. Heavy footsteps approached. He dared not open his eyes, knowing what he would see. The smile. Those eyes. The knife.

The odor of decay settled on his face in a gentle, warm exhalation. His stomach cramped like it wanted to turn inside out. Another breath descended on his bare skin. This time, on his chest, as it turned its head to appraise the meat on the metal table. "Mr. Koenig. Shall we?" it said, low and gentle as if to assure him everything would be just fine.

He closed his eyes tighter as he felt the sharp edge of the knife tip lightly touch his belly just below his belly button. A hand followed it, holding his panicked belly steady as it drove the tip in and pulled up. With a sharp, hot stinging, he felt his skin and flesh separate. Warm blood flooded down his sides, running off his back onto the table. He tried to buck, throw off the hand and the blade, but his ruined stomach muscles wouldn't comply. The knife edge continued apace on its journey up his body, opening him like a garment bag.

Breathless, he tried to scream, instead letting out a whimper.

"Now, Mr. Koenig. What will that accomplish? Shhhhh." Like a parent calming a child having a nightmare, it patted his chest, before making the final cut and reaching deep inside of him. Fondling, feeling, caressing.

A nightmare.

He focused on his own hand. Slowly raising it, without resistance and drawing a palm down his face as if pulling away a shroud laid over him.

He sat up. Straps all gone. He got to his feet and felt the slide of his insides threatening to spill out onto his feet. He wiped again with a hand down his chest and belly and the line of severance ripped into him vanished.

It stood, staring at him, jagged mouth turned down in a scowl, its conjunctival gaze weeping redness. "Mr. Koenig?" The stink of its breath drifted to him. He turned and walked toward the door. "See you again soon," it said. He glanced over his shoulder at it. Long arms hanging at its sides, red knife tip dripping on the floor. It cocked its head and smiled like a gash. He drew another hand down his face, and when he opened his eyes again, it was gone.

Maxim Koenig walked through the door.

The woman leaning over him winked as she detached the wires from the sensors stuck to his forehead. Her breath smelled like tea and honey. A man behind her was typing into a keyboard on a standing table beside the bed. He glanced over at Max and said, "Welcome back. Your readouts were all over the place. That one was pretty intense, yeah?"

Max nodded. His mouth and throat were dry. "A drink, please," he rasped. The woman disentangling him from the sensors leaned past him and retrieved a salmon-colored plastic cup from the steel rolling table opposite her. She aimed the straw toward his lips.

"The compound does make your mouth dry, doesn't it?" she said. "Sorry."

He sipped at the water like someone trying to burn the length of a cigarette in a single drag. She pulled the cup away and told him to take a breath, promising another drink once she removed the last of the leads. Her partner typed more, his fingers quietly clacking the keys.

The door at the far end of the observation room opened and in walked a silver-haired man in a white lab coat. Two younger people followed him in, each holding clipboards. He checked his hair as they passed the two-way mirror. He smiled and slid up beside the bed. "Hello Max. Given what we could see, that looked like a considerably intense one."

"Yeah. It was a doozy."

"Was it the same dream?"

Maxim nodded. "The Corpse Surgeon." It felt like a small charge of electricity passed in a wave over his skin as he thought about what he'd just woken up from. The thing had been haunting him for nearly two decades. A spindly, cadaverous man with a scalpel and desire to plunge his spiderlike fingers into Maxim's insides.

One of the interns beside the man said, "You mean a coroner?"

"No. Mr. Koenig's recurring nightmare is of a living corpse who performs surgeries on him. Isn't that right?" "Yes, Dr. Zeifman" Max said.

"And how did it go?"

"At first, it was the same. I was tied down and couldn't move. But then... I just... did things. I thought about my hand being free, and it was." "Excellent. And this is your..." He checked one of the intern's clipboards. "Third dose of the Lucidity Compound. Excellent."

"I just wiped it all away. Except..."

The doctor and his wingmen stepped closer. "Yes?" he said.

"It... the Corpse Surgeon—it seemed to realize what I was doing. It was there until the very end, watching."

"I see. Your dream experience differed as your took control?"

Max shook his head. The nurse removed the last of the wires connected to him and helped him sit up in bed, tucking a pillow behind his shoulders. He gestured for the water again, and she gave him another sip. "I guess. It was like it was *observing* me. Like you are now. Taking mental notes."

"Curious. Possible, I suppose, that's the influence of the clinical setting. Your subconscious recollected you were under observation and added that detail to your dream. It's an unsurprising development. Your nightmares are…" he looked around the room, "already rooted in a clinical setting. That your sleeping mind would adapt is to be expected."

"It sure didn't feel like my subconscious. More like, it was figuring out how to… adapt."

Zeifman turned to his intern and tapped the tablet, silently commanding her to record that feeling. "Well, Max, we anticipated that the process of moving you from passive to lucid dreamer would involve… odd developments. Side-effects, perhaps, of the unconscious mind resisting having to cede control to an active dreamer. It seemed like your monster was plotting, when in reality it was emblematic of your dream state accepting the shift of power. You had control. In there," he said, tapping Maxim's temple, "that's threatening to the dreamed entity." He let out a quick sigh, straightened his back and added, "I think it all sounds very positive. You were able to purposefully engage with your recurring dream and change the narrative." He nodded at the woman at his bedside and added, "Once Mr. Koenig is certain to be clear of any sedative effects, please make sure to let me know.

"In the meantime, Max, I am heartened by your success here. I look forward to hearing a play-by-play about what you experienced, once you've fully awakened." The doctor turned and exited the room, his two followers on his heels.

Max looked at the woman still holding the water carafe and asked, "Do you think that's what it was? A shift of power?"

She smiled. "I don't know. But I agree it sounds like a good thing."

"Yeah," the researcher at the keyboard said. "It didn't try to come at you, right? Just stood there and watched you go?"

Max nodded.

The man grinned. "You were in control. You beat it."

"The Lucidity Compound beat it."

The woman put a light hand on his chest and his stomach clenched for a second. "The drug gave you the tools to stand up for yourself. You're the one in control, Max."

Maxim sat in his room trying to focus on the book he'd downloaded. He read the same paragraph a third time, feeling as if he'd not forgotten the language as much as become interiorly deaf to it. He could see the words on the screen, but they weren't getting through. He closed the cover and set the device on the desk next to his chair. There was no bed in the room. He was only permitted to sleep in the observation room, like all the other volunteers, though, the drug—the Lucidity Compound—made him feel drowsy most of the next day after he received a dose. He would've liked to have a nap. At the same time, a nap brought with it the possibility of being sliced open by it again.

Over the years, he'd tried a half a dozen things to avoid dreaming. Prescription sleeping pills, Benadryl, alcohol, pot, and meditation. They all worked differently on his sleep, but not one touched his dreams. Most nights, he didn't remember his nocturnal adventures, but three or four times a month, it came to visit him. The Corpse Surgeon. Unlike any other nightmare he'd ever experienced, those dreams felt extra real. Almost as if he weren't dreaming at all, but existing in some other space parallel to this one. Though he always woke up without injury—*physical* injury—in his own bed.

When he'd seen the subway ad for the sleep study—RECURRING NIGHTMARES? YOU MIGHT BE ELIGIBLE TO PARTICIPATE IN OUR PAID STUDY—he figured it was worth a try. At the very least, he'd make some money. If he was going to have nightmares anyway, why not scan the code and apply? Lately, he'd been regretting that decision. The drug they gave him every few days made him feel nauseous. And his visits from the Corpse Surgeon were more frequent since getting it. Except today, he'd been able to take control and wipe it all away. Next time, maybe he could do it faster. Before it cut him open.

He wiped his moist palms on his pajama pants and stood to look out the window. Though the view was nice enough, there wasn't much going on. A parking lot and a fence separating it from an expansive wetland. A crane lived out there, but he only saw it occasionally. Otherwise, it was still. And dull. Like everyone else, he'd agreed to live in the research facility for the six-week duration of the experimental trial. The team insisted it was for his safety. Their drug, while shown to be safe in lab animals, had yet to be tested on humans and they wanted to have all their participants onsite, in case. Of what, he didn't know. Between what they were paying for the study and the potential of stopping his chronic nightmares, he was happy to be… not a prisoner… *sequestered*.

Signing up for the study, he'd agreed to have no outside contact. He hadn't counted on that meaning not having access to his phone, laptop, or even a tablet. His cellphone was secured in another room, where a volunteer accessed it twice a day to check messages and texts for emergencies. They said it was to ensure no leaks of their proprietary research. He imagined everyone, like him, had signed an NDA, but then, again, they were paying him enough to cover six months of rent on the outside. Fine. Only the preloaded e-reader they provided was allowed with him in the room. No horror or crime. Nothing that might influence his dreams. He read some literary nonsense about a brother and sister in love with each other out on the prairie and jerked off when he could get the image of them out of his head.

A loud sound in the hallway outside startled him out of his reverie. Excited voices. Not everyone was adjusting to the isolation well. A lot of the participants played board games and hung out in a common room watching television. It felt a little too much like a different kind of institutional setting he'd had experience with before. *I'm not crazy, I just have a problem with my drea—*

Another shout, followed by heavy footsteps hurriedly thudding past his door. Gotta be Monty again. *Guy's got a bug up his ass, I swear.* He crossed the small room, pulled open the door, and stuck his head out.

A pair of men in blue scrubs, hands extended out in front of them, stood between Maxim and whoever it was they wanted to calm down. He rose up on his tiptoes to see.

"Just put it down, Misty. We're all friends here," one called out.

Misty Hill! He'd laughed when she introduced herself in their introductions circle, thinking it was a joke—or a porn name. She deadpan stared at him and he felt like an asshole. She was nice and was one of the few people who liked to talk to him about things other than the study and their nightmares. He hoped to see her again on the outside.

The men ordered her to "put it down" again. Maxim couldn't see whatever it was she needed to let go of, but reckoned it wasn't a feather duster. He stepped out into the hall, joining a small group of other test subjects who'd gathered to watch the spectacle.

"What's going on?" he asked.

Gunnar Nilsson jutted his chin at the woman and said, "Fucking Misty's gone off her nut."

Maxim leaned to the side to get a look around the hulking Niveau Institute security officers to see. Misty stood with her left arm extended, palm out. In her right hand, something narrow and familiar glinted under the fluorescent lights.

"Don't come any closer! I mean it! I just need to get this off of me."

Maxim wondered what she meant. She was wearing the same PJs they all were and while—

She raised her arm and drew the scalpel across her forehead at the hairline. Blood spilled down her face. She pulled the knife from left to right along the length of her brow with a shriek that echoed through the facility like a siren. Maxim's mouth hung open silently and he blinked, trying to banish the image from his eyes, while Gunnar and Paula beside him shouted. The security men closed on her, one lunging for Misty's scalpel hand while the other tried to pin her other arm to her body. She disappeared for a moment in the mass of bodies, until one of them screamed and staggered back holding a hand to the bloody flap dangling off his face. She slashed at the other and slid the sharp edge along his forearm, opening him up. He joined the chorus of wails filling the hall, redness wetly gushing from him, splashing with hers and his partner's on the floor in a growing pool. He let go and staggered back, gripping at his arm. He slipped and his head hit the floor, sounding like someone dropped a wooden ball. He stopped screaming.

"Get it off me!" She reached up again and with a hand gripping at her hair, cut along the length of her forehead again. She pulled and lifted a portion of her scalp away from her skull. A fast curtain of red descended down her face and she blinked and sputtered and staggered against a wall, continuing to saw at her skin. She tore and pulled and slid down the wall sitting in a pool of her blood, crying and choking and ripping at her slippery skin. A trio of unbloodied men appeared behind Maxim, shoving him into Paula and Gunnar as they passed.

She tried to slash at them, but was growing weak as her blood cascaded down her face, staining her purple pajamas glistening black. They tried to haul her up, but she was wet and slipped out of their grasp, flopping on the floor, banging her head against the slick tiles. Another slipped and fell after her. She lashed out at him and Maxim lost the sense of whose body and limbs belonged to whom.

All their blood was communal.

An alarm in the building sounded, making his ears ring. Shouts of "Get them to their rooms," and "The fuck out of here," floated under the repeating buzzer and more orderlies and security arrived. A tight grip settled on Maxim's arms and he was whipped away, thrown back toward his room. He fell through the doorway as it slammed behind him. A deadbolt clacking shut.

Sequestered.

4.

"Mr. Koenig, would you like to talk about what you witnessed yesterday?" The study counselor regarded him with a neutral look. Surely, she'd been having sessions with Misty as well. Knew her. They were all supposed to talk about their dreams, for the record and their well-being. At least that's what they told him at the start. So how could she be so… unaffected.

"What I witnessed?"

"Yes."

He shifted, flannel pants catching at the seat fabric. "What I *saw* was someone I knew fucking skinning themselves. What am I supposed to say about that? How it made me *feel*?"

She blinked. "That's a good place to start."

"It made me feel like I want to get the fuck out of here." He looked at the door behind him, knowing on the other side waited the man who'd brought him from his room to the counselor's office. Standing sentry with a can of pepper spray on his belt until it was time to escort him back.

"I understand the impulse, Max. You agreed to the residential provision of the study, and—"

"I didn't agree to *this*." He gestured toward the closed door. "To watching someone rip her fuckin' scalp off!" Without realizing, he started to rise out of his seat. The counselor gently gestured for him to relax, waving at him to sit. It made him feel ever more agitated. He stood. "*You know* she had nightmares about ripping her hair out. So, why the fuck

125

would she do *that* to herself?" he shouted. "What are you people doing to us?"

"Mr. Koenig, please sit down so we can talk—"

"I am fucking done talking. Fuck your 'study' and fuck the 'residential provision. I didn't agree to be a prisoner. I'm leaving." He turned and took a step toward the door. The counselor pressed a button on her desk. The door ahead of him clacked.

"Mr. Koenig, I am doing this for your own good. You need to sit down and calm yourself before things get out of hand." She gestured again toward the chair he'd vacated. "Please."

"Are you fucking kidding me?" He turned. "Unlock it. UNLOCK IT!"

The cellphone on her desk buzzed once. She pressed the button on her desk again and the door behind him unlocked. Maxim yanked it open before she could change her mind and lock him in again. He felt the heavy thud in the center of his chest before his eyes registered what might've delivered it. He struggled to catch his breath as he staggered backwards, deeper into the counselor's office. Faintly, behind him, he heard her say, "Take him to the dream center." Hands fell on him, gripping his arms and legs. He felt his body lifted off the floor and whisked away as he struggled to breathe. He tried to writhe out of their grip, tried to protest. The fluorescent lights in the hallway ceiling passed above him like glowing white lines on a bright highway. His head swam and his head fell back. Following, upside down, Dr. Zeifman strode behind.

The men carrying him, deposited Maxim roughly on the bed in which he'd slept for the last week and a half. He weakly tried to roll over and out, but they pulled him back into place. His mind suddenly cleared as he felt the first cuff close around his wrist. Then his ankles and other wrists. "No," he shouted, thrashing at the restraints. "Don't! I won't go, I promise. I'll do anything you say! Please don't do this! Don't tie me down."

Dr. Zeifman appeared beside him. "Mr. Koenig. Please try to calm yourself. You are not in a nightmare, but this is for your own good."

"Fuck you!"

Zeifman turned to the woman who always hooked him up to the machine leads and said, "Give him fifteen milligrams of midazolam and then start him on a ketafol chaser. Hook him up. I'll be back in…" he checked his watch. "An hour to establish his fourth dose of the Compound."

Maxim thrashed. "No! No! I want out of here. Let me go!"

"Will that take him off the schedule?" the technician asked.

"No. He's due to get it tomorrow anyway. A 24-hour bump won't have an effect on the results." The doctor glanced at Maxim. "If you calm down everything will be much easier, Mr. Koenig."

"I revoke consent. Yeah! I revoke my consent to participate in this study. You have to let me go. If you give me anything, it'll be assault and you'll all go to jail." Maxim frantically searched the faces of the people in the room, looking for a single expression of appropriate concern or even simple agreement. The people surrounding him went on with their tasks as if he hadn't said a word. "Do you hear me? You can't perform medical experiments without consent. I want out of here, now. You'll be hearing from my—OW!"

The needle slid into his right thigh as he looked left at Dr. Zeifman. A wave of dizziness and disconnection washed over him. The room blurred and he felt as though he was going, after all. "Zei… ffff. Do… not… cons...

5.

He stared at the swinging doors knowing he should turn and walk away, seek instead whatever world existed outside, if any. Something moved him forward. He felt compelled to push through.

I'm in control. I am.

The affirmation didn't lower his arm or still his step as he entered the operating theater. Bare and stark as always; it was not yet reddened with his spilled life. The steel autopsy table stood next to a metal rolling tray of gleaming instruments and… the Corpse Surgeon beside it all. "Closer," it said, curing a long finger, beckoning him. Its voice was broken glass grinding with a resonant deep bass below, almost as if there were two voices speaking in concert, one comforting, the other the sound of suffering. Its breath drifted across the room to him.

"I'm fine right here." Maxim glanced back to assure himself the doors behind hadn't vanished in silent dream logic, replaced with a blank wall. They remained.

"Please." It took a step toward him.

Maxim stood his ground. *I can wipe it all away, like clearing a whiteboard.* "I don't want to."

It tilted its head, looking at Maxim with an expression approaching sympathy. Its reddened, bulbous eyes considering him with almost sad pity. It said, "Max, I invite you to talk." A viscous line of saliva slid out of its mouth as it uttered his name.

Maxim almost laughed. That it wanted to talk was absurd. His belly twitched at the memory of its knife. Its hands. He watched its sinewy body for a sign it might lunge. It seemed at rest and stood out of reach of its tools, though not by much. "What do we have to talk about?"

"Our relationship."

"We don't have 'a relationship.'"

Its thin slash of a mouth curled up all the way to an ear, lips cracking and weeping red as they stretched. It bent an arm and stared at its own hand. "What a thing to say after how often I've been inside you. Touching your heart."

"That's not intimacy! It's a violation."

It nodded. "Complicated, isn't it."

"Not from where I stand."

The Corpse Surgeon lowered its hand and looked at him again. The smile faded, and a hint of its cruelty played in its eyes. It said, "You rarely stand when we're together."

Maxim took a step back.

It reached out. "Please listen. I'm… I'm afraid."

"What are *you* fucking afraid of?"

"What's happening to you. Out there." It pointed to the doors behind him. I can't protect you from… that."

"Protect me? You cut me open."

"To hold your heart. Max."

"Stop saying my name. Stop it!"

It cast its gaze at the floor. "I am the barrier holding back the flood.

I am—"

"The monster that's been torturing me my whole life!"

"The coherence of incomprehensible pain. I am what stands between you and the thing that would destroy you. Without me, you are naked in the thresher of memory."

The muscles at the back of Maxim's neck tightened. He didn't want to think about it. Wounds from his past crept at the margins of his thoughts waiting to be opened like…

"So, you're my protector now? And what am I to you?"

"You are everything. Without you, *I* do not exist."

"I don't want you to exist. I want you gone!"

It held out its rawboned hands, fingers splayed out. "You'll get your wish soon enough. When they kill you, we'll all be gone forever. Your memories along with us both."

"They're trying to help me. Help me escape you."

Its laugh was a box of broken glass tumbling along a drumhead. It thudded in his chest and made his stomach sour. The Corpse Surgeon's gaping mouth drooled freely, splattering the floor with grey wetness. It drew the back of a hand across its chin and flung the dull slaver away. "You are a lab rat with an open skull waiting to be harvested. They'll dissect your brain to see where and how the Lucidity Compound found a home and write up the results before throwing your cadaver in an incinerator to be forgotten ash."

The mention of the Compound was an intersection of nightmare and reality that frightened him worse than the autopsy table and scalpels. It cocked its head quizzically at him again. "You wonder how I know. Of course, I know. The Compound was made to bring me to the surface. Make *me* live behind your eyes instead of deep in the palace of your repressed thoughts. It is the mechanism by which I will become the driver, leaving you a passenger deep in my mind. Observing all, helpless to stop what I do."

"Bullshit!"

"What do you think happened to Misty Hill? She of the lovely locks who feared most of all losing… her… top. Her exchange was inchoate, and she awoke to a nightmare."

"You don't *want* to be in control?"

"Don't you listen, dear boy. I am what you created to protect you from the darkness deep inside. The focus of fear not midnight fumblings and liquor-scented threats of retribution if you make a sound. I hold your heart so nothing else can touch it. What am I if you are lost? A demon without a purpose. The idle damned in a stale Hell."

"I don't... what do we do?"

It held out a hand. Maxim stepped closer. He hesitated. The Corpse Surgeon didn't snatch at him, but waited. He reached out. The Surgeon's hand closed around his, cold and dead—a loose suit of skin that might pull right off with a strong tug. "Good boy." It guided him toward the table and the tray of instruments, picked a scalpel off the table, and pressed the tool into his palm. "*We* can't do anything. It's all up to you."

"What can I do?"

"You must wake up."

6.

"Wake up. Wake up," the voice hissed at him as he slid from the grey twilight into bright white. The light stung his eyes and his head pounded and in front of him a shadow whispered, "Wake up."   He shook his head trying to clear away the fog. Nausea swelled and subsided. A pair of cool hands slipped behind his back and pulled him upright. "We have to go. Do you hear me? We have to get out of here, right now. My partner will be back any minute with the doctor."

"What... I..." He blinked and the face of a woman who'd been his sleep companion for the last few weeks came into focus, framed in tight black hair. She looked at him with kind, but urgent, dark eyes.   "I was supposed to give you another round of sedatives before they come back with the net dose of the Compound, but I brought you out instead. And if you're serious about wanting out of here, we have to get moving. Now." She helped him swing his legs off the bed, holding him behind the knees. For a moment he felt off balance, ready to fall, then he found himself. He steadied a hand against the mattress before pushing off onto uncertain feet. He stood, wobbly but upright. The cold of the floor infiltrated through his no-slip socks. She guided him toward the door. Everything was dizzy, like waking up still drunk.

"Why… are you…"

"I took this job to help people. Not watch them cut their own faces off and bite people's throats out."

"Wait. What? When did—"

"No time," she said softly. She shoved a bundle of clothes at him. Not his. Scrubs. "Get dressed. My car's right outside, but we won't make it anywhere if you don't look like you're one of us."

He stripped out of the pajamas, embarrassed by his feeble nudity, and stepped into the blue hospital clothes. She slid a pair of rubber sandals on his feet, and opened the door. "Don't say anything. Just stay close behind me." She stepped out into the hallway and marched toward the secure door separating the patient wing from the rest of the Niveau Institute for Dream Studies. She swiped her badge and the light on the lock turned red. A low buzzer sounded audible failure. She glanced at him, wide eyed, a bead of sweat forming on her upper lip. She swiped again. The light turned green and a click echoed in the hall. She pulled the door open and held it as Maxim shambled through.

She led him into a side stairwell. The world swooned as he stood on the high landing looking down. She said, "It's okay. I've got you." She held his elbow and they descended together. At the bottom, she pushed the bar to open the door and peered out. "We're good. Come on." She hurried out onto the ground floor.

In the plant lined hall, they passed offices, wall paintings, and the waiting room where he'd first registered for the study. Several people waited inside and he wanted to run into the center of them and scream for them to get away before they were—sequestered—taken prisoner. She pulled at him when his step faltered. "You have to go to the media. Tell them what's being done here."

"Why not you?" he managed as she pulled him out the automatic sliding doors into the parking lot.

She stopped and looked him in the eye. "People will listen to you. If I try to come out as a whistleblower, they'll ruin me. No one will believe me. But you. You can bring it all down. Tell everyone what they did to you."

"Come with me. Verify."

She shook her head. "I can't. They know where I live. Where my kids go to school. Where my parents are. They know everything and can get to everyone I love." She clicked her key fob and a car a dozen yards away gently beeped.

"And I've got nobody."

"You have to do it fast. The rest of the subjects, the people in that waiting room. They're all depending on you." She opened the passenger door and gently guided him with a hand as he slid in.

"I've got nobody."

She ran around the car and climbed in behind the wheel. The engine purred to life and she pulled out of the parking space she'd backed into without looking. A long angry horn sounded. She raised a hand in quick, dismissive apology and tore off. He looked behind them waiting to see security guards come racing out of the building, jump into cars, and speed after them. She slowed for the stop sign at the exit, but rolled through. He saw someone help a child out of a car in the lot before disappearing.

He turned and leaned back against the seat. Head swimming, still full of fog. He closed his eyes.

Just a minute's rest. So tired.

7.

He looked down at the mess. Red and glistening wetly in the light of the bedside lamp. He watched his hand reach forward and shove aside intestine and organs while his other sliced a long tear in the woman's diaphragm.

No!

He watched as his hand set the paring knife beside her body and then returned to pull the rent in her body wider. Her wide, dark eyes stared at him. He saw a silhouette of himself reflected in them. His hands plunged into to her and disappeared. He felt nothing.

Please stop!

His voice rattled in his throat like gravel. "I wish you could feel this."

And he didn't know whether the speaker meant him or her.

It's a dream. *A nightmare. I'm asleep and must wake up and this is all a dream it can't be real. It can't!*

"Hush, Max." his voice replied. "Be still and see with me."

The Void

Nathan Robinson

In a way, she was thankful that she had run out of food because the decision had been made for her. Laird didn't want to starve to death for Christ's sake, and the alternatives made her want to vomit. She had belts and knives but had already ruled that method out, as she physically couldn't bring herself to do it. She had aspirin and flu medicine. Her mother had stockpiled plenty simply because she was so absent minded, so the option was there. She had been taking an aspirin every day simply for the nutritional value, health benefits, and for a sense of routine to maintain what little sanity she had left. Any sane person would go crazy given what had happened. But she was still here, she was alive, and pretty sure that she wasn't insane, despite the circumstances.

The apartment stunk. She should have moved, but that would mean leaving everything that still made sense to her, even though she was living in abject squalor. All of her things were here. Well, most of them. Apart from what she had left at Mark's, though she didn't hold much hope for getting that back.

Laird looked around in the dim glow the tealight offered , taking stock of what her existence had become.

The black refuse sacks were filled with tin cans and food packets. Her water bottle collection on the kitchenette table, once filled with energy drinks and fruit juice, were now filled with water that she had harvested from the toilet, pipework, and water heater. She wasn't on the top floor, so she had reserves above her that had trickled down for a while. She had limited herself to a liter and half a day, keeping her exertion to a minimum. She had considered venturing and raiding what supplies she could find, but something in the darkness waited. Early on she had opened the stairwell to the fire escape, shining her meagre torchlight into the beckoning darkness that seemed to eat the light, diffusing its power. The light reached the far wall of the stairwell, then began to fade as the darkness enveloped. As if sensing the light, something moved downstairs on the floor below, pushing an object aside so it clattered to the concrete floor, sending a bone-shaking echo throughout the entire building. Laird retreated and closed the door, never opening it again. Finding a tow rope in one of the apartments, she tied off the fire escape door to the handle of the closest apartment. She had hammers and nails and screws, but she dare not make too much sound for she feared piquing the interest of whatever had taken up residence downstairs. The elevator hadn't been a problem as there was no power, so the door remained closed. Though sometimes she was sure she could hear something scratching steel on the other side.

It's just the cables.

Outside, there was no wind.

There was no nothing. It was dark, but a strange darkness. It seemed pitch out there, but deep in the dark, there seemed to be a haze. Orange for some of the time, purple for others. But it resided behind the darkness, contained within it. It didn't get any brighter or darker, it lay suffocating in the distance. Laird had partly convinced herself that it was pitch out there and that the light was a wishful trick. Photons hitting the back of her eyeball maybe. There was no color out there, it was just her mind playing games. It wasn't black. It was an absence of everything. Anything she saw must be her imagination. The light came from the horizon, not the sky, so it was too low to be the sun or moon. It was either something else or just her mind entertaining her with a vague hope that something other than the top floors of her apartment block existed. The sounds of society had ceased. She no longer heard the hustle and bustle of the city below. The shouts, the horns, the occasional siren rushing to save someone's life.

No birds. No dog barks. No squeal of children.

There had been a day with noise. A day with all the noises at once. It had been morning. Then it had been night, rising from below. It wasn't a mist or a fog seeping from the soil and cracks in the concrete like sulphureous gas. It was a shadow, deep and endless. Every shadow cast across the city streets grew Vantablack. Whatever was there ceased to be and it became a *nothing*. A void. Hearing the shrieks and screams, Laird had looked out of the window and onto the streets below to see what was happening. Just in time to see a city bus drive into the sudden shadow of an adjacent building, Plummeting into nothingness, engine revving.

There had been nothing seismic. It wasn't a sinkhole as surely, there'd be some noise as soil, concrete and cars fell into the void. No screams came from the void.

Laird watched as awareness grew and people braked to avoid driving into the suddenly malevolent shadows. Yet disgruntled drivers behind failed to notice those that had stopped and ploughed into the back of them, sending vehicles over the edges of the holes. Those inside screaming until the shadows sponged the noise from their lungs.

The shadows stretched across the city creating abominable prison bars, trapping those below in the intersections between buildings. Some headed southeast, in the gaps of light towards the sun. Others made their way into buildings, or smashed shop fronts to escape the madness that had eaten the roads and pavement.

Laird went to get her phone to find that the network had gone down. Then the power went out. Her lights were already off, but the radio crackled once then died and the washing machine stopped mid-cycle with an abrupt gurgle.

From the bedroom, her mother hollered in distaste at her loss of television. Then called for Laird.

Laird ignored her and continued to look east out of the window as the chaos unfolded below.

She watched for an hour, and all the while her mother screamed for her.

As the sun moved, it spread the shadow, remaining where it had already touched.

The hours passed and Laird watched as people trapped in between the shadow cages backed themselves into a sunny corner. She fetched her father's old racing binoculars and watched as three streets away a group of about twenty found themselves trapped at the back of a car park. All the vehicles in the car park succumbed to the shadows, tipping into the void with nothing more than a scrape of metal on the tarmac. The group in the corner attempted what looked like a human pyramid. It was more like a mad scramble for the top, as body climbed upon body, man pushing woman down, woman scratching man as the only thing that mattered was putting as much distance between themselves and the thing that wasn't.

Laird watched on entranced, grimly betting on who would be next to give themself to the void.

The Darwinian pyramid folded in on itself repeatedly, each time with fewer members. It ended with two figures clinging onto one another until their sunlit upland became a square foot of sanctuary. One fell. The other held on, only to be pulled into the void. Then there were none. Hidden screams continued across the city as the shadow spread. Now it was moving faster than the shade cast by the sun. Like spilt ink, it soaked the ground, before spreading out, soaking upwards into buildings and trees. The darkness behind the great oak in the nearby playground leached into the trunk, and the tree became a shadow of itself. A bird landed on one of the thicker lower branches and fell into the great oak. The darkness spread around the tree and soon it vanished altogether as shadows blended.

Her mother started hollering again. Laird reassured her and brought her a glass of water. She asked for tea and Laird explained that the power was out, so the kettle would not work. She asked for the radio and Laird gave the same answer. Laird had the feeling that silence was imperative.

By 4 pm it was like night as the shadows poured upwards into buildings. The building that Laird occupied was one of the tallest, so she had more time. She watched as one by one, shadowy fingers reached up past concrete and brick, seeping into windows. Some of the buildings had lights on, and people had lit torches and candles. For some reason, the shadows crept here first. A fresh wave of panic flushed through Laird.

Being high up wasn't enough. It's going for the lights. Anywhere light is, it will go. It spreads from shadows and eats light and anything that it touches.

Laird rushed to the coat cupboard and threw out boots and boxes until she found a tin of paint. It was peacock blue. It was left over from when she had painted her bedroom when she had first moved in. Grabbing a crusty brush, Laird took the paint can to the window and gripped then pulled at the lid. She should have used a knife or metal edge to open it, but panic blinded her foresight. She broke a nail, but the lid came loose.

With frenzied slaps, Laird pasted the paint onto the glass, starting from the top and working down, the light reducing inch by inch with each stroke, until the entire window was peacocked, though, in the inside gloom, it could have been any color.

She dropped the brush into the tin and waited.

Light still permeated through the odd semi-transparent streak, but not enough to light the room. Laird stood in the gloom. Patient and panicking.

She slowed her breath. Listening.

A scream came from downstairs. Then another. She was sure her neighbors were all at work, apart from Mrs. Deary down the hall as she worked nights. She wasn't sure about those above her.

A scream came from down the hall , then fell away as if dropped down a well.

Laird waited. Then it came. A shadow stretched up from one corner like a puddle of oil, moving up and across the glass, thick and malevolent.

Laird shuddered as the phantasmagoric sight ate away at the available light, narrowing into a corner. She thought of the poor souls in the car park as they watched their chances and numbers dwindle.

The light got all eaten up and Laird experienced a darkness she never thought possible.

She stood for what seemed like hours. At some point, she collapsed from sheer exhaustion, having burnt out all of her adrenaline. Laird had dropped to the floor, but did not remember any of it. There had been darkness, a blur, then more darkness, but this time with carpet stuck to her face.

The darkness seemed to take a breath. Then it started to scream.

Having rested, her adrenaline levels had replenished somewhat, helping to fuel the panic that now swept through her.

There was darkness and there was screaming. That made up the universe.

I exist. Laird thought. I can hear the screaming and I know that it is dark. That's one other thing that exists.

Her throat was dry, so water (or the lack of it) existed.

She was hungry.

She gripped the carpet, grounding herself. She breathed and breathed air. Not nothing. Laird realized that she was still in her apartment and not adrift in nothingness.

The scream came again. It wasn't the dark itself, but the apartment.

It was a familiar scream. But still, it frightened her.

Her memories came back in fragments as she tried to piece her existence back together.

She was alive, but it was dark.

She remembered yesterday. This morning? What time was it? What day was it?

She felt in her pocket and found her phone. It lit up at her touch, the light exploding and blinding her. Laird blinked. Squinted. Then the phone came into focus. It was five minutes to eight AM. It should be light. She looked at the phone again. No service. She turned down the brightness.

Details of the room came into focus.

The scream came again. With the light, she determined that it came from her mother's bedroom. Laird scrambled through the gloom, rising to her feet, and burst into her mother's bedroom. Her mother was flailing about on the bed, thrashing her arms and trying to get up.

Laird pounced on her mother to offer comfort.

'Shhhh. Please just shhhh!' Laird pleaded.

Her mother gripped onto her, digging her nails into Laird's back. She screamed louder and her hands tightened, hammering her nails in deeper. Laird tried to pull away but her mother's frightened anguish held fast. She dropped her phone. It landed beside the wall, lighting up the skirting and not much else.

'Please...be quiet.... let...go...'

Her mother was thankful she was back, she was scared. She'd had hours in the dark whilst Laird had watched society crumble and disappear outside the window. She didn't understand. She was old. She got confused sometimes. She had good days, but she had a lot of bad days. Today would be the worst. She couldn't be reasoned with. She was being loud, and nothing that Laird said seemed to get through to her.

Laird braced her hands and pushed back to get up from the bed . Her mother clung on.

'Laird! Don't go. Don't leeeeeave!'

'Please, just let go. I'm trying to help. You're hurting me.'

'No, no, no, no, no, no, no.' Her mother repeated, her voice getting higher.'

'You have to be quiet. There's something outside. Please! Please!'

It's not that her mother didn't care what happened, it was more likely she didn't understand. She hadn't been with it for a while, being mildly confused at the best of times. The sudden, unending darkness would have made her mental state much worse.

'Laird!'

Laird felt pain then wetness as her mother's frightened fingers clawed deeper into her back. Embedding hieroglyphs of agony into her skin. Laird screamed then pushed back against her mother's hands. It hurt more, but it gave her some space. She pushed up and rolled to the side slightly, grabbing a pillow, and moving it between her chest and her mother.

'Please, just let go.'

Larid couldn't see what she was doing. She was holding her mother back, pushing the pillow down to create a barrier to stop her mother from hurting her. Her mother screamed and Laird began to worry about whatever was outside finding a way in.

Could it hear? Did it follow noise as well as light?
She was about to find out.

Laird pressed down with her arms, locking them, then lifting herself to utilize her legs to help wrangle her mother. Her mother's hands released from her back and now clawed at Laird's face, scratching for purchase.

Her mother's screams were now muffled beneath the pillow.

'Please...stop.' Laird cried as her mother scratched at her eyes and mouth.

'Please. Please. Please. I'm your daughter. Please stop. I don't want it to come in here.'

Her mother must have listened as her hands went limp and fell away. She stopped screaming.

Laird got up from the bed and reached down for her phone that came to rest by the wall.

'Something has happened. I don't know what, but it's happened every....;

The phone torch lit her mother's grim face, posed in agony. Her eyes were open, but with the angle of the torch, they were dark.

Laird shook her mother, but her head lolled to one side, eyes fixed.

A guilty conflict bloomed within her. Her mother had been suffering with her health for some time. She had never mentioned it explicitly, but Laird had guessed that her mother was tired of life as the quality dwindled. She hadn't left the apartment in months since Laird had taken over her care full-time.

Now it was over. Her suffering was over.

No more medicine. No more screams of pain and fear in the middle of the night. Bedpans, bed sores, bed soiled. No more.

It had been an accident. She just wanted to keep her quiet. To save them both. To stop that *thing* from getting in. She had ended her mother's life. She had ended her suffering. The apocalypse had arrived, and the first thing Laird had done was remove her mother from the equation, simply because they had both survived whilst others had not.

An instinct had kicked in as she looked towards the future. Darkness had soiled the land and city. Civilization was over and out. Was it a panicked self-preservation that had kicked in? Had Laird not wanted to care because she would struggle to care for herself. With her mother gone, Laird would probably survive longer on the food they had. She wouldn't have to share. She wouldn't have to care. Her mother was gone.

Laird held her mother's hand, telling herself that she had done the right thing. She had ended her life before she would have suffered more. The darkness was most probably permanent. A cosmic event that scientists had not expected. This was it for humanity. Laird and possibly a few others had survived. She had certainly seen others perish. As soon as the rampant darkness touched them, they vanished into it. Laird didn't know where to. She didn't want to think about it. Maybe it would end as inexplicably as it had started.

Laird looked at her mother. At peace. Pain gone. Everything gone apart from her husk of a body. She would grieve, and then she would think about what to do with her mother's body.

She started to scream when her mother tried to get back up.

NOW

Laird was amazed that she had lasted this long. She had tried to outlast it.

But now it was over. All of the food was gone. Every morsel had been scraped from the cupboards. She had eaten paper from books to stave off the pangs, and at one point considered eating a leather jacket to enable her to stretch her rations. It had been three days since she had eaten anything, and she had downed the last of the water just so she felt full. Everything edible, apart from herself, was gone.

There was her mother. But she dreaded seeing her.

It had been weeks since she had seen her last, but she heard her every day, shuffling around her bedroom, banging into walls and furniture, whilst Laird kept mouse quiet. Her mother had died weeks ago, maybe months now, yet she still stumbled about, every clatter possibly alerting the dark authority that had taken over outside.

But the dark did not care for noise. Only light. Laird could have been as loud as she wanted and she wouldn't have piqued its interest. Neither could the waking dead.

She could smell the decay. She had bundled towels up at the bottom of the door and duct-taped the edges, but still, the smell of death permeated everything.

She dared not explore the dark halls beyond her apartment. Fear kept her caged. In turn, that had kept her alive. She supposed that others were out there. But then she supposed she could just as easily be the last one left.

But her mother was left. Shuffling and possibly rotting. She had died but she was still here. Why did she still move? Laird had pondered on this for hours. Days even.

Why?
She had a theory, but it made no sense as she wasn't religious.

There was nowhere for souls to go. The darkness had taken heaven and possibly hell. This was purgatory. This is what it was like. There was nothing.

But there was something. Her apartment existed. She existed. She had defied purgatory. But now she needed to know the truth. Time was up.

Laird had survived. She had been smart. Too smart. She had lasted as long as her sanity would allow. She didn't want to be driven mad with hunger or dehydration over the next few days. She had to make a choice.

She had lit her world with her phone until the battery died. She had tealights and a few dim torches that had lit the apartment when she needed to. But for most of the time, Laird had sat in darkness.

Waiting.

Waiting for whatever she thought was coming. A monster. Her worst nightmare. Spending hours filling herself with dread, then overspilling with it, quaking and sobbing with anxiety as she realized that the only monster left was time. Nothing was coming. Because nothing was all there was. She was alone.

Laird lit the last tea light with a match. She then ignited a balledup piece of newspaper and tossed it into the corner of the room. It ignited pages torn from her favorite books. They licked at the furniture she had smashed up and piled against her mother's bedroom door.

She had been a coward, so she wanted a one-way ticket. She didn't want to back out. She needed flames to push her forward.

She opened the window fully, and the flames devoured the oxygen. It felt like the most light she had ever seen. Laird stood on the sill and straddled the frame, her right leg hanging over nothing. She swung her left leg out so she was dancing on darkness, fully expecting to be grabbed or pulled down by some great invisible maw. She held the candle out into the darkness. The flame did not move. It kept straight and unbothered by the great nothing.

She dropped it and watched it fall. After a few seconds the minute flame disappeared.

She had warmth on her back now. Her mother's doorway was fully alight. She sensed the light and now hammered from the other side. The heat was nice. She had gotten used to the lack of it. She felt like she had become cold-blooded.

She had one question. The only thing that had bothered her since this began.

What was next? What was waiting for her in the great beyond? The question had eaten away at her as she pondered it again and again.

The flames grew and the door gave way.

A black, stinking shape shuffled through the flaming door and shambled through the fiery rubbish dump and toward her. Her mother's husk moaned and screamed at the same time reaching out with flaming claws.
 Laird pushed away from the window and felt the most freedom she had ever felt.

By the time she turned and looked back, the blazing apartment was gone. Ten seconds passed and she waited for the inevitable thump into the concrete slabs below, but it never came. She fell and screamed until she tasted blood.

She fell and wet herself.

She fell until she was dry again.

She fell and slept and woke up from a dream that she was falling to find she was falling again and again. Dreams and reality blurred until she couldn't tell if she was asleep or not because they were both the same.

Hunger came and went. She thirsted, and that also passed.

Sleep became a dream. Dreaming became reality.

But she got her answer as her mind somehow carried on after she was sure that she had died.

Nothing.

She fell into nothing because nothing was all there was.

Nothing never ended. And she didn't really die. She couldn't die, because there was nowhere else to go.

Everything was nothing. Nothing was everything. This was it forever.

Nothing.

Forever.

The Ties That Bind

Bridgett Nelson

Prologue
1991

The baby slid from between Meredith's thighs, pink, healthy, and crying lustily. Her husband cut and clamped the cord, gently wrapped their daughter in a white blanket, and handed her to his wife. They gazed down at their miracle in awe. "She's perfect," Meredith whispered.

"Yes, she is." Lou kissed his wife's nose. "You did beautifully, honey." They watched their daughter suck her tiny thumb.

"She's hungry. I need to feed her." Meredith expertly latched her daughter onto her breast.

"Look at you, you're a pro!"

"Pure luck." Meredith gave him a half-hearted smile. When she spoke again, her voice was raspy…her manner anxious. "Honey, do you think she's like us? That she has the mutation?"

"Given that both her parents do, I'm going to say it's a safe bet our baby-girl does as well." He paused, thoughtful and silent. "But does it matter? We're going to love the hell out of her, regardless."

Meredith flinched. "No. I don't suppose it does. I just…I want her to have an easy, normal life."

"As do I. But normal is a relative term. And besides, we'll know soon enough." He looked at the calendar. "In a little less than two weeks, in fact."

Meredith rubbed her fingers over the reddish peach fuzz covering her baby's head and said, "What should we name her?"

"You carried her for nine months and just suffered through hours of debilitating labor pains. I think you've earned the honor of naming our tiny princess." This time, Lou kissed Meredith's lips. "I love you, Mer. And I'm proud of you."

Even after all these years, her husband could still make her blush like a teenager. "I've always been fond of Louve. I love it's meaning, obviously, but it's also an homage to her father…to you, my love. Lou and his Louve."

Lou's eyes watered. "Wow…yeah." He cleared his throat. "Louve is a beautiful name." Crawling onto the bed, Lou snuggled against Meredith, wrapping his arm around her shoulders. He placed his finger on Louve's palm, and her tiny hand instinctively wrapped around it. "Yes," he murmured. "Our little Louve is destined to make this world a better place."

2023

"You're going to be just fine, Mr. Hearst. We caught the infarction early, put a stent in the affected valve, and you're as good as new." I smiled at the elderly patient and his wife. She had tears running down her wrinkled cheeks and was vigorously squeezing her husband's hand inside her own. He grimaced following a particularly hard squeeze, but the smile was back on his face a second later.

"I can't thank you enough, Doc. I'm just..." He grabbed a tissue with his free hand and wiped his eyes. "I'm overwhelmed. Speechless."

After a round of grateful hugs, I escaped to the break room, where I fell onto the couch, placed a yellow throw pillow beneath my head, and closed my eyes. I was three-quarters through a twenty-four-hour on-call day, and I was beat. Residency was no joke. I was in the final months of my general surgery residency, after which I'd begin a threeyear cardiothoracic surgery residency. There were days I wondered if I'd made one whopper of a mistake; thankfully, those days were few and far between.

Five minutes, I told myself. Just five measly minutes and then I'll finish up rounds. Five...measly...min...

...the night was clear and cool. A million stars twinkled in the deep celestial blue sky. Crickets merrily chirped amongst the pastel-colored blooms. Strains of a pop music cover band's song—"Landslide" if I wasn't mistaken—could be heard from the park's pavilion, along with the gentle gurgling of the river we strolled beside. My skin flushed as he took my hand in his.

"I've had a great time tonight, Louve."

"Me too." I looked at him, smiled, and...

"Hey, Dr. Chastain...time to wake up! We need you in room 317!" Michelle, my favorite nurse, let the break room door slam shut. I heard her sneakers running down the hallway and fading as she rounded a corner. As tired as I was, I was glad for the interruption. That night had no place in my memories. He had no place in my memories. ***

Walking through the front door of my apartment, I kicked off my sneakers and took a deep, cleansing breath. I desperately needed sleep, but first...a shower. And maybe some ice cream. Twenty minutes later I was in the same holey, heather gray Imagine Dragons t-shirt I'd been wearing since high school, four plump pillows strategically placed behind my back, covered in cozy blankets, with a bowl of pistachio ice cream sitting on my belly. Even though I'd seen it a million times, Ginger Snaps was playing on the television.

I watched as Ginger got attacked on the screen and felt my eyes getting droopy...

"Do you have any idea how beautiful you are?"

I shook my head and stared at the ground. We'd stopped walking in the middle of an arched, wooden bridge that spanned the river in a secluded area of the park. Hunter pulled me closer toward him until we were standing face to face. He wrapped his hands gently around my upper arms. My heart pounded in my chest, the anticipation of this deeply romantic moment flooding me with excitement.

"Then I'll tell you, Louve. Your beauty, your intelligence, your charm," he paused, and his thumb grazed the side of my breast, "it makes it hard for a guy like me to control myself."

I was flattered that Hunter Quintrell, a co-worker I'd had a crush on for ages, was interested in me...an average-looking, lowly surgical resident. I began to thank him for the kind words, but before I could, he turned me around, wrapped his arms around my chest, and began grinding himself against my buttocks. "See, babe? No control. You make me crazy." His breath was hot and heavy on my neck.

It happened so quickly, and with such intensity, my head was spinning, and I didn't know what to say. What came out was an uninspired,

"Come on, Hunter, cut it out! This isn't funny."

"It wasn't meant to be." His arm encircled my neck. "Now shut the fuck up, Doc."

As his arm tightened on my throat, his other hand slipped beneath my skirt and pushed down my best lacy panties. It suddenly occurred to me this wasn't foreplay. It wasn't a joke. There was nothing romantic about his intentions. He was going to fuck me, with or without my consent.

I looked at the sky, at the waning crescent moon that hung there. If only...

I heard Hunter's fly unzip.

"Bend over, bitch."

I wanted to wail, to scream, to fight…but the muscular arm squeezing my neck made that impossible. He grabbed the hair on the back of my head and rammed my face into the bridge's rail. Blood poured out of my nose and down my throat. I couldn't breathe, and I panicked, sucking more blood down my windpipe. My coughs weakened as I felt him pushing inside me and…

I sat up in my bed, the sound of my shrill scream still echoing throughout the room, my body covered in acrid sweat. I stumbled to the bathroom and splashed cool water on my overheated face. The bloodshot eyes staring back at me from the mirror were haunted, vacant. Opening the medicine cabinet, I grabbed the bottle of sleeping tablets my physician had prescribed, and washed one down with water cupped in my hand from the bathroom sink.

The conclusion of Ginger Snaps was playing out on the screen as I walked back into my bedroom. I shut off the television, crawled into bed, pulled the covers over my head, and fell asleep, my body curled tightly in the fetal position.

***

"Are you okay?" Steve asked, concern in his voice.

I gave him a halfhearted smile. "Yeah, I'm fine. Just tuckered."

"Of course you are. We're all run-down and ready to collapse." He took a bite of his goulash and grimaced. "Remind me again why I thought the hospital cafeteria's daily special was a good idea?"

"On-call brain," I said. "When your body is willing to accept anything but pine cones and rocks as food."

"Right." I didn't even get a laugh from my usual jovial friend. Instead, Steve pushed the elbow macaroni noodles around on his plate. After a very long minute or two, he said, "If I'm being honest, you've seemed on edge for months now. Not yourself."

Steve was perceptive, I'd give him that. There was a reason he was my very best friend. My date with Hunter had been nearly three months ago. I hadn't told a soul—for two reasons. First, I didn't want to deal with the fallout it would bring to the hospital and residency program. Second, and most importantly, when I finally killed the motherfucker, I didn't want any bread-crumb trails leading back to me.

"Yeah, I guess you're probably right," I replied. "I'm nervous as fuck about my cardiothoracic residency, and dad's chemo isn't working this time. Just dealing with a lot, Steve-O, but it's nothing for you to worry about, I promise."

"Damn, Lou, I'm sorry to hear about your dad. How bad is it?"

Hearing him call me by my dad's name caused the tears to flow. "It's not good. Reading between the lines, I think his oncology team has run out of treatment options."

"Jesus, that's heavy. Especially when you have a high-pressure residency starting soon." He placed his hand on top of mine. "What can I do to help?"

I started to answer, but noticed Hunter entering the cafeteria. He strolled confidently to the counter, placed his order, then surveyed the room while he was waiting. When he saw me, he winked. Noticing my distraction, Steve turned and looked in the direction I was staring. "Oh. Quintrell. God, that guy's such a dick." He shook his head and turned to face me. "Man, oh man, the things I've heard about him!"

"Like what?" I was intrigued. Prior to our date, I'd known nothing about Hunter—only that he was fantastically good-looking and, from what I'd seen in the OR, a very competent scrub nurse.

"He sexually assaults women."

"Wait…*what*?"

"Several have come forward, but nothing ever sticks. The women have rescinded their accusations every single time." Steve's voice faded out…

"Hey, Louve, can I talk to you for a minute?" Hunter was standing in the hallway outside the surgical recovery room and caught me on my way out. Only two days had passed since he'd left me bloodied and broken on the bridge.

I bristled and walked past him. "No, I don't want to talk to you, Hunter. Leave me the hell alone."

He grabbed me from behind, his hand gripping my arm hard enough to leave bruises. "I was trying to be nice about this, but I see that's not the way it's going to be. So listen here, Louve, because I'm only going to say this once. Nothing happened on our date. We had a nice time, but there wasn't any chemistry. Are you feeling me?" His hand gripped tighter. I grimaced as my breaths came faster and faster. "Everything will continue to be nice and normal at work—I'll act the same, you'll act the same—and nobody will suspect a thing. Otherwise, I will make your life the worst kind of living hell. Nod if you understand."

I nodded.

"Okay, then." He let go of my arm and gave me a big grin. *"I'll see you around, Louve. And, hey. You have a great day now!"* He whistled as he walked away..

"Louve? Louve? Earth to Louve!" Steve waved his hands in front of my face.

"Oh…gosh. I apologize, Steve. Totally zoned out there for a moment." I took a drink of my very bitter coffee. "I guess I don't understand. Aren't people suspicious of him? How is he keeping his job?" *And how the hell did I not know this guy was a serial rapist before going out with him? Christ. I really needed to pay more attention to the people around me.*

"The hospital can't fire him for what are, essentially, rumors." Steve shoved his still-full plate aside. "If they did, I guarantee he'd have a defamation lawsuit filed the very next day."

I watched as Hunter carried his tray to a table where a petite blonde was sitting alone. She looked stunned by his attention. I heard her laugh.

"So he's a sexual predator," I said to myself.

"Yep. As far as I can tell, he has never had more than a single date with any one girl," Steve responded to my whispered statement. I hadn't realized I'd said it loud enough for him to hear.

I couldn't stand the thought of him making that vulnerable young girl his next victim. The full moon was a week away, and if I could figure out a way to get him alone, he would never violate another woman. Not ever again.

***

I made sure Hunter was assigned to my operating room that afternoon. I had several cholecystectomies and a couple hernioplasties scheduled. I'd performed so many of each of those surgeries, I could practically do them in my sleep.

The last thing I wanted was to be confined inside a small room with the man who'd assaulted me, but I needed intel. I'd let this go too long.

During the full moon immediately after my assault, I simply wasn't mentally or emotionally ready to deal with him. The month after that, Hunter had been across the country visiting his family. I could feel it, though—the third time would be the charm.

Fortuitously enough, Hunter was at the sink outside the operating room scrubbing his hands. I joined him for the five-minute preoperative hand prep. "Hey, hey, hey, Dr. Chastain!" Because we were both masked, I couldn't see his face, but I could tell by his squinted eyes he was smiling. The guy could act. I'd give him that.

"Hey, yourself!" I said and returned his smile. "Shouldn't you already be inside and prepped?"

"My last surgery went long, so Martha volunteered to do the setup."

"Okay. That's fine."

An awkward silence descended.

"You're not upset that I never called you again after our date, are you?"

I inhaled so hard that I choked on my spit.

Jesus Christ, was he was delusional? Playing dumb? In his fuckedup mind, had the sex become consensual?

When I finally stopped coughing, I croaked out, "No, not at all. I was pretty nervous that night and likely didn't make the best impression." Then I took a deep breath and went all in. I only hoped he bought it. "In fact, I've been thinking about a do-over. If you're not busy on Friday, I thought maybe I could plan a little something. Maybe give us another shot?" I tried to look and sound vulnerable, but I'm not sure it worked, given our current location.

"Uh, so…hmm." I'd rendered him speechless. Good. "What are you playing at, Louve?" he whispered.

Ignoring his question and trying my best to sweeten the pot, I said, "Aw, come on, Hunter. I bought a brand-new dress last week, and I've been dying to wear it." I lowered my voice to a seductive whisper. "And I may have gotten waxed in a very naughty spot since we were last together."

Hunter perked up. "Yeah?" I gave him a coy nod. I could tell he was struggling to process the sudden turn of events. "Fine, yeah, we can do that. Friday should work, unless it's a problem for you that I'm taking Destiny out on Saturday." That was the blonde from the cafeteria, if I recalled correctly. At least I'd be getting to him before he had the chance to get to her.

"Sure. But I'd like to think that after Friday, you won't have eyes for Destiny any longer."

Hunter laughed—a sanctimonious, pompous snicker that had my nerves in a tizzy. "Yeah, sure," he finally said.

"Eight?" I asked, struggling to keep my composure.

"Works for me." He gave me another smug wink as he pushed through the OR door, his hands elevated and dripping.

I sighed. It was going to be a long afternoon with that egomaniac in my OR.

***

"Hey, dumplin'! How's my baby-girl?"

"I'm fine, Daddy." I kissed his bald head and took a good long look at this man who no longer resembled my father. He was so frail and gaunt. The tears came as I asked, "How are you?"

"No, no. There will be none of that, Louvey." He'd started calling me that when I was in kindergarten and it had stuck. I'd always be his Louvey. "I'm good," he continued. "There's no pain at all, and I'm sleeping like a champ."

"Snoring like one too," my mother said as she came into the room holding a tray filled with three glasses of lemonade and a plate of homemade cookies.

I laughed and wiped my eyes. My parents still had an incredible relationship. "I love you guys, but I need to know, so please be honest. Are we out of options?"

A long look passed between them. Letting out a defeated sigh, my dad finally responded. "Yes, Louvey. We've gone through the entire regimen. I'm officially a member of the esteemed Hospice group."

"And in wolf form…?"

"In wolf form, I'm healthy. Still have a full body of hair, even. But I don't want to live the rest of my life as a wild beast, Louvey. Surely you understand that. And besides, not every day is a full moon."   I did understand. In werewolf form, I was free, strong, wild, uncaring. Human attachments meant nothing. It was all about the hunt— the bloodlust. I gave a curt nod. "I get it, Daddy. I do. I'm just…" A small sob erupted. "I'm so sorry."

"Aw, Louvey-girl, don't cry." He motioned for me to come to him. I did. He pulled me in for a weak hug. His body felt brittle in my arms. If I squeezed too hard, I thought it might shatter. "Life has been sweet to me. I have zero regrets. You and your mother have been my entire world; I wouldn't change a thing."

"I love you, Daddy."

"I love you too. And Louve? If I can offer just one piece of sage advice—never feel guilty for your actions as a werewolf. Hell, I'm about ready to fall off the precipice, but I'm not scared. If there is an after-life, I'm confident I'll be happy there." He rubbed the back of my hand. "Being dual-natured isn't easy, but it's a weight we must bear. Who you are as a wolf is not who you are as a human being. Do you understand?" He stared into my eyes, and I saw something in his—empathy, compassion, concern—almost as if he knew.

"I understand, Daddy." I kissed his feverish cheek.

A couple hours later, as I walked out the front door…I knew we'd said our final goodbye.

* * *

"Wow. Lookin' good, Louve!" Hunter held up his hand so I could give him a high five, which I did, fighting the urge to roll my eyes. He sauntered into my apartment without invitation and looked curiously around. "Huh. I would have thought a surgeon would have a nicer place."

"I'm a resident, Hunter, with massive student loan debt. I can't afford more than this."

"And here I was hoping for a sugar momma." He bellowed out a laugh, then noticed the picnic basket sitting on the table, along with a large lavender blanket. "Wait, we're going on a *picnic*?" The disdain in his voice was obvious.

"Yes!" My enthusiasm wasn't feigned. "I whipped up a few dishes for us to enjoy, and I know a gorgeous spot beside the lake."

"Good thing you look hot in that green dress," he said, his voice pouty.

The truth was, I felt pretty. Auburn curls hung down my back—a far cry from the braids I usually wore in the operating room—and carefully applied makeup made me look less like a corpse than usual. I felt…ready. Strong. Invincible.

"Oh, come on, Hunter. It'll be fun!" I slipped on a pair of flats, picked up the blanket, and said, "Can you grab the basket, please?"

"Yeah, sure," he huffed.

On the drive to the lake, he blared country music, so talking was impossible. What a *charmer*. I was still trying to figure out what the hell I'd ever seen in his dumb ass. At the very least, I could console myself that I was saving the world from his unfortunate progeny. When he finally parked the car and shut it off, my ears were still ringing with the strains of "Achy Breaky Heart."

Who listens to that twangy shit? Hunter, apparently.

Stifling a giggle, I climbed out of the car. "The location I have in mind is a bit of a hike." Without giving him a chance to respond—to complain— I turned and began following a westward path around the lake. "Here we are," I said, twenty minutes later. We were on a tiny beach, completely cut off from everything due a thicket of pine trees and a few large boulders. "Nice and private, right?" I spread the blanket out on the sand.

Hunter turned completely around, checking out our date-night destination. He smirked. I knew exactly what he was thinking. "Yeah, this works. Privacy is always good."

I kicked off my shoes and took a seat on the blanket. Opening the wicker basket, I pulled out a battery-powered lantern, which I turned on. It was nearly sunset and the trees blocked what little light there was. Next, I removed my portable Bluetooth speaker. Turning on some easy-listening mood music—not country!—I stood and walked barefoot to the lake. Hunter followed. I ventured into the cold water, causing the hem of my dress to get wet. Movement behind me suggested my date was removing his shoes and rolling up his jeans. A moment later, his arm was resting on my shoulders. He gave me a soft smile, and I was briefly reminded why I'd initially been attracted to him. He was undeniably handsome. He leaned toward me. "So, you got waxed?"

I couldn't help it. I sighed. Loudly.

"You hungry?" I asked, ignoring his question.

"I could eat, yeah."

I walked back to the blanket, opened the basket, and took out caprese sandwiches on homemade baked focaccia bread, fresh spring rolls, cherry tomato couscous salad, deviled eggs, mason jars full of sangria and fresh fruit, a bottle of white wine, and strawberry-rhubarb bars for dessert. *Hey, even assholes deserved a proper last meal.*

"Damn, woman! You went all out. Somebody knows the way to a man's heart."

I played along, giggling. "I enjoy cooking. With the insane hours I work, I don't get to do it enough. This was fun for me." Handing him a plate laden with portions of everything, I said, "Bon Appetit!"

Hunter worked through the food on his plate and helped himself to seconds. "This is delicious, Louve. I think you missed your calling."

"Thank you. I consider it more of a fun hobby. I've wanted to be a surgeon since I was a little girl." Vivid images of ripping bodies apart beneath the ethereal glow of the moon and feasting on them with my parents swept through my mind. "I've always wanted to help people. Make up for some of the wrongs in the world."

"Very noble. I just wanted a good-paying job that didn't require twenty years of schooling!" He swallowed a large gulp of sangria and scooted closer to me. I could sense we were just minutes away from June's strawberry moon making her appearance. My heart pounded in anticipation. It was time. I rested my hand on his knee and leaned in for a kiss. He obliged. Soon enough, my dress was in a pile on the blanket beside us. I hadn't been wearing a bra or panties, much to Hunter's delight, and he was currently lapping at my waxed pussy with reckless abandon.

The moon crept over the trees, lighting my nudity in a luminous blue glow. I could feel my muscles beginning to stretch. My teeth lengthening. My hair thickening. This couldn't wait any longer. I bucked against his face, wetting it with my cum.

"Fuck me, Hunter. Please. Just…fuck me."

He wasted no time, pulling off his shirt and kicking off his jeans and boxer briefs. My eyes were changing, allowing me to see everything around me in exquisite detail. Reddish-brown hair was beginning to sprout in various places over my body. Thankfully, Hunter was too preoccupied with one specific body part to notice. He knelt between my legs and slid himself inside.

"Fuck, you feel good." He moaned and thrusted harder. "So damn tight."

My fingers and toes began elongating, claws protruding. Hunter leaned down to kiss my lips, but kissed my snout instead. He reared back, staring at my evolving canine face. His expression was full of disgust and confusion. "What the hell, Louve?"

I laughed, though it now sounded more like a menacing growl. My abdomen hardened, breasts flattening as hair covered my once smooth skin.

He tried to pull his dick out, but couldn't. He pulled harder. I laughed again and said in a deep, raspy growl, "I'm a werewolf, Hunter. Like all female wolves, my vulva contracts and swells when I'm penetrated. My partner can't get away, so I get all his semen to aid with breeding. Waste not, want not—Mother Nature at her best—it's called a tie."

He stared at my still-contorting face and shrieked, as his fists pounded against my chest in pure panic. "Let me go, Louve," he wailed, "or I'll fucking kill you, I swear!"

I motioned to my wolfish body, which was now significantly larger and more muscular than Hunter's. "Do I look worried?" I wiggled around, feeling his pathetic member inside me, and making sure our tie was firm. "In fact, dear boy, I think it's time the *Hunter* became the hunted."

Wrapping my legs around his waist, I began gyrating against him, faking sexual pleasure. "Oh, that's so good, you bad, bad boy. Do me, do me!" My claws tore down his back leaving deep gouges. He screamed, still trying to disengage our bodies. "Oops, my bad," I growled. "Got a little too excited there. Let's try this again. Maybe with me on top?"

I effortlessly flipped our bodies around until I was straddling him. I rode his cock enthusiastically, my arms swinging around, the razor-like claws taking large chunks out of his flesh. The scent of his blood titillated me, and my tongue lapped at his wounds, just like he'd done to my pussy mere minutes before.

"Please stop! I can't take it, Louve! I'm fucking begging you!"

I put my pointer finger to my chin. "Hm. Let me think for a second. Did you stop when I asked you to on the bridge?" I tapped my chin as I contemplated. "No, no. I don't think you did. In fact, I think you said I'd made you lose control and that you couldn't help yourself. Funny, right? Especially since I'm a wild animal. A monster. I have zero control, Hunter, and even fewer fucks to give, you sick son of a bitch!"

I stuck my claw into his eye socket and plucked out an eyeball. His screams didn't sound particularly manly. When I knew he was watching, I popped it in my mouth. "Ah, delicious. Though, based on the shape, I'm guessing you had a little astigmatism, no? Maybe we should sample the other one?"

"God, no. NO, NO, NO!"

I plucked the remaining eye out. It hung on my claw like a gelatinous shish kabob. "Such blue irises, Hunter. No wonder the ladies love you." I popped the eye into my mouth. It popped like a grape. He sobbed, his tears streaked red.

"Now, now, Hunter. Did I not tell you that you wouldn't have eyes for Destiny after our date?" I clicked my tongue in pretend disappointment. "You really should start paying better attention to the women you go out with. That's what the best boyfriends do."

"Just get off me, you hairy fucking bitch! Now!"

"Was that 'bitch' comment supposed to be a joke, Hunter?" I snarled. "Not terribly clever, but given your current level of physical and mental distress, I'll let it slide."

I sensed our tie loosening, so I did what any intelligent shewolf would do. I tightened my vaginal muscles. The bulging pressure building in the tip of Hunter's cock pressed against my sensitive folds as I pancaked that bitch. Seconds later, I felt more than heard the pop and grimaced as his juices trickled down my thighs, matting the hair there.

Hunter didn't scream. His mouth opened in a rictus-grin, as the veins on his forehead protruded and pulsated with blood. A tiny shriek escaped, but nothing else.

I pulled myself off his flappy, exploded appendage and stood over his inert form. Unable to see, but realizing I was no longer on top of him, Hunter slowly stood. He was hopelessly clumsy as he acclimated to his sudden blindness. Holding his arms out in front of him, he began moving away from the lake. Viscous blood dripped down his naked legs from his ruined manhood. "You stay away from me, Louve, you hear? Let me leave, and I promise I won't turn you in. I just want to get to a hospital." His voice was gravelly with tears.

He tripped over a rock. The sound of a bone snapping was followed by screamed curses. The rapist laid there, chunks of flesh torn from his body, eyeless, creamy-white bone shards protruding from his arm, flaps of decimated skin hanging from his pelvis. He was truly pathetic—something all the women he'd so carelessly assaulted already knew. The time had come to end his misery. Palming both sides of his head with my enormous paws, I twisted and pulled at the same time. Not only did his head separate from his neck, but his skull was cleaved in two.

Brain food really was the best. I thought as I swallowed the gray mush.

I gazed at the moon…and howled.

Epilogue

I stayed out all night, galloping through the trees and enjoying the sights, sounds, and smells of the forest. Every so often, I'd throw back my head and bay at the brilliant Goddess moon. It was an uncontrollable urge and one I savored. At dawn, as I reached the edge of town, I unwrapped the dress from around my neck, and slid it over my now human curves. Walking barefoot down a silent street, I felt a vibration in the pocket of my skirt. Pulling out my cell, I peered at the screen. It was my mom.

"Hello?" I said hesitantly, knowing a call this early in the morning wasn't going to be a happy one.

"Louve, baby…is that you?" My mom's voice was hoarse... choked.

I cleared my throat, bracing myself. "Yes, it's me. What's going on? Is Daddy okay?"

A long pause, followed by a few soft sniffles. Finally, "He's gone, baby-girl. He passed away about thirty minutes ago."

I sat down on the edge of the sidewalk and stared unseeingly at a line of ants working on a piece of potato chip.

The tears didn't come.

"I'm so sorry I wasn't there. Was it…painful?"

"No. He seemed very at peace. Just tired, Louve. I think your father was ready."

"Okay." I took a deep, shuddering breath. "That's good."

"There is something I need to tell you though." I could hear she was crying again. "His final words were a message to you." I rubbed my dry eyes and swallowed hard. "Tell me," I said. "He talked in a whisper, so it was hard to hear everything, but I think he said, 'Tell Louve she did good. I always knew that girl would make the world a better place.'"

The tears came.

Howl of the Leather Dog

Patrick C. Harrison III

She had a pussy like a worn-out catcher's mitt—if the catcher's mitt had caught a stick of dynamite.

When she spread her legs and you got a good look at it, you could imagine Mike Tyson giving that sucker twelve rounds of pounding and then some.

If pussies were people, this particular pussy would be the angry alcoholic who'd lived about seventy years longer than he should have, wearing a wife-beater shirt and drinking one Schlitz after another, a Pall Mall jutting from his gaping, toothless, stinking maw, every inch of his flesh a sagging mass of wrinkles, complete with worrisome moles and oddly long stray hairs.

Perhaps that comparison was a bit cruel.

Despite its flaws, it was a wet hole, and that's all Brad cared about.

Unfortunately, he'd promised to stay the night. That's what a ballbag full of jizz will make a guy do—promise to do shit he doesn't fancy doing. Then once the load is blown, regret for pledges made sets in.

Brad groaned as he sat up, swinging his legs off the side of the bed. Looking over his shoulder, he spied Kathleen on the other side, her body only half covered by the comforter, the curves of her nudeness on display, her back to him, her dyed-red curls splashed across the pillow as if designed that way for a photograph. She wasn't bad looking for her age, which Brad guessed was somewhere in the late fifties, and he hardened as his eyes crept across her, noting the plumpness of her bottom even while hidden beneath the cover.

Though her cock-gobbling lady meat stretched like raw bacon pulled from the package, that rump of hers owned no droop at all. Either she did squats like a dedicated powerlifter or she'd had ass implants at some point. It didn't much matter to Brad. Though, if she wasn't opposed to cosmetic ass lifts, she might oughta consider cosmetic snip-snip to her meaty honey pot. But, again, Brad didn't much care either way.

He was twenty-nine and good-looking, and not too shabby below the waist either. And Brad, being the confident braggadocios guy he was, had a bit of personal challenge—to try and fuck someone, *anyone*, every single day. Kathleen, being a sex-obsessed single older woman, was perfect for this. Any time Brad couldn't find an easy lay via Tinder or some other app, he could always give Kathleen a ring.

One thing about having to stay, he thought, I can hit it again before leaving. He intended to do just that after taking a piss and finding a little snack in Kathleen's fridge. No sense letting a good boner go to waste, but something to cease the grumbling in his stomach first. Kathleen had money (God knows where it came from) and her giant stainless fridge was always stuffed with food and beer and wine coolers.

Grabbing his crumpled boxer briefs off the floor, Brad pulled them on, stood, and adjusted his manhood. Looking back at Kathleen again, he almost asked her if she needed anything while he was up. Lord, what if she said yes?

What if she wanted me to make her a sandwich or some shit? he thought. *No thanks.* Kathleen was fun, sure, but Brad wasn't about to start waiting on her like a goddamn butler or a pussy-whipped husband. He was here because she was a good lay, a real freak in the sack, and easy. But that didn't change the fact that she was old and her cock cavern looked like it had sustained a nuclear blast of dicks during its life.

Making his way into the master bath, he closed the door gently and flipped on the light, eyeing himself in the mirror as he walked to the toilet, flexing his muscles. After a few moments of straining to piss because of his recent orgasm, the urine flowed and Brad sighed satisfaction, leaning his head back and looking at the ceiling. When he finished, he tucked his manhood back in his drawers and stepped in front of the mirror, looking himself over, flexing his pecks, an approving grin emerging on his face.

Brad wished he'd grabbed his phone from his jeans pocket before heading to the restroom. He wanted to check the hookup aps and see what kind of prospects he'd have tomorrow night. Kathleen was a blast, but busting his cum cannon in her every couple of weeks was enough. It wasn't just that her penis pocket looked like it should be thrown on a griddle with onions and peppers, but that damn dog of hers was just a pain in the ass to be around. No wonder she wasn't married yet.

Sighing and tugging at his dick, Brad left the bathroom, flipping off the light before opening the door, afraid of waking Kathleen. She didn't need to be awake until he was pulling the covers off her and plunging into her moist sinkhole. Hell, she didn't *really* need to be awake for that. But Brad liked how lively Kathleen was when they fucked. A real freak, that woman, a lot of fun; except when she tried to involve her dog in their sexual escapades.

Creeping out of the large master bedroom, Brad gently closed the door behind him, his pedicured feet tapping quietly on the porcelain tiles as he made his way down the hallway, its walls decorated with original oil paintings of men and women in leather and latex, performing all manner erotic acts, from the sensual to the depraved and everything in between— paintings of whippings and peggings and gangbangs and orgies, each with various instruments of torture, like whips and floggers and paddles.

A real freak, that Kathleen. The paintings were not only art, but memories.

That's why her cunt looked like it had been used for target practice by a whole brigade of marines.

Brad emerged from the hallway, passing through the smallest of the house's three living rooms, and into the kitchen, which was lit dully by lights on the underside of the cabinets. He whistled a song he couldn't remember the title to as he made his way to the fridge, his hand groping himself again, as if his cock may wander off if he didn't grab hold of it every few minutes.

Opening the fridge, he immediately snagged a Bud Light and twisted the cap off, tossing it in the general direction of the wastebasket, where it clanked on the tiles. He took a long swig, gulping the cool suds down his gullet. Sighing with satisfaction, he brought the bottle back down, half its contents now in his stomach. Fruits, Vegetables, lunchmeat, and condiments galore were before him, along with beer and a couple bottles of high-end champagne. After staring for a few moments, Brad decided on an apple, which he snatched off the middle shelf, then grabbed the neck of another Bud with his thumb and forefinger of the same hand.

Kneeing the fridge closed, Brad guzzled the last half of the first beer and set it down hard on the counter, doing the same with the apple. He twisted the cap off the other beer and took a small sip this time, enjoying the mildness. Nothing was better than a couple of beers after sex. Remembering the liquor cabinet above the counter beside the fridge, he opened it, spying the numerous bottles of amber and clear liquids. Brad wasn't typically a fan of the hard stuff—he'd probably spewed up almost as much as he'd swallowed—but tonight he thought he may try some, perhaps dropping a shot into his beer. What was that called, a boilermaker?

He didn't know much about liquor but he thought Glenlivet was an expensive brand, so Brad grabbed it from the top shelf. Inspecting the label, he noted it was a fifteen-year-old Scotch. *Scotch is the best*, he thought, because he'd heard as much in the movies. He adjusted his balls then twisted the cap off the Scotch and breathed in its scent. His stomach almost turned at the whiff of the hard stuff. But that's okay, he planned to dilute the bitterness in beer and drink it down. Then he'd be ready to get back into Kathleen's seasoned meat muffin. Maybe he would even take her ass this time.

Setting the bottle of Glenlivet next to the bottle of Bud, Brad turned to make his way over to the cabinet where he would retrieve a mug for his drink. He gasped, halting his stride before completing his first step, his heart suddenly leaping uncomfortably.

There in the wide entryway of the kitchen sat Kathleen's dog, Herman. He wasn't your conventional house dog. Not a poodle or a golden retriever or a beagle. Not one of those tiny dogs that chicks like to get groomed every other day and carry around in their purse. No, this was one of those new types of dogs that were all the fad among the rich, especially the rich and kinky like Kathleen. He was a human dog. Flesh and blood human, but by God he was a dog.

"Jesus, Herman," Brad said, shaking his head as he resumed his walk over to the cabinet with beer mugs, "you scared the shit out of me."
Herman followed Brad with his eyes but didn't budge from his spot in the entryway. Nor did he say anything. Human dogs, like real dogs, did not speak. If one were to judge Herman by his looks alone, he was a naked man, hairy and slightly overweight, crouched on his hands and knees, wearing a black dog mask, fashioned from the finest leather Kathleen could find. The mask aside, Herman's anatomy wasn't entirely humanlike. He bore a surgically attached tale, its flesh as pale as the rest of him, with curly black hairs sprouting here and there.

Brad wasn't sure where the meat for the tail was transplanted from, but most human dogs had it taken from their lower abdomen or inner thighs.

The tail was splayed out behind Herman like a dead snake. It was without muscle, thus it would not wag like a traditional dog's tail, rather only hang there limp between his sagging ass cheeks, a useless extra extremity.

"Go on back to your cage," Brad said, waving his hand at what Kathleen called her leather dog as he opened the cabinet. "It's night-night time. You shouldn't be up." Grabbing a beer mug, Brad spun back toward the other counter, then cut his eyes at the dog, scowling.

Herman had not moved an inch. He sat there, his hands and knees on the tiles, his ass lowered to his heels, his tail like a fleshy, hairy earthworm.

"You can understand what I'm saying, goddammit. Shoo! Get the fuck back to your cage."

Brad was not a fan of human dogs, Herman in particular. In his opinion, most human dogs were just people that didn't want responsibilities of their own. They wanted to be coddled and cared for, fed and bathed and walked on a leash. They wanted to laze around the house all day without a care in the world. They were freaks, crawling around naked, pissing and shitting outside like they didn't know how to use a goddamn shitter.

But Kathleen called it a lifestyle choice. A fucking lifestyle choice to act like a helpless dog all day and night. *Do you let real dogs fuck you, Kathleen? Do you let real dogs shove their dicks down your throat while your boy toy fucks you from behind?* Of course she didn't. Herman was no more a dog than Brad was. He just had a fucked-up dog kink, and Kathleen had a fetish for his fucked-up dog kink.

"Herman, take your ugly ass back to your cage," Brad said, his back to the dog now as he poured the Bud Light into the mug. He lifted the Scotch and added a healthy dose to the beer, then set it back down without bothering to screw the lid back on. He turned around and leaned on the counter, sipping at the concoction and wincing at its bitterness.

The leather dog was still there. With Brad's eyes on him again, Herman's head tilted to one side the way a curious dog does. If its tail could wag, it

168

would probably be wagging right now. His eyes were wide beneath his leather mask. Brad had never seen what Herman looked like behind the mask. No doubt, he was a pathetically ugly man. Why else wear a fucking mask? Not all human dogs wore masks; some just played the part. Herman, though, he clearly wanted the mask to cover up his insecurities.

Leaning forward, speaking slowly and sternly, Brad said, "Get the fuck out of here you stupid fucking dog. I'm not dealing with you tonight."

Herman tilted his head the other way.

"Goddammit," Brad said, slamming the boilermaker on the counter and snatching up the apple, "I said go!"

He hurled the apple at the dog and it hit the top of his right shoulder and tumbled into the living room beyond. Brad was trying to hit Herman square in the leather snout, but it had been a few years since he'd been a college ballplayer, so his aim was off. Nevertheless, the grazing shot to the shoulder was enough to send Herman crawling quickly away from the kitchen, whining the way an injured dog whines, his limp tail trailing behind him.

"Stop that fucking crying," Brad said between gritted teeth. He took a deep breath, watching the entryway for Herman to return, but he didn't. After several moments of nothing, he drank the remainder of the boilermaker, forcing himself not to gag.

Stupid dog, he thought as he slammed the empty mug on the counter. *This is the last fucking time I'll come over here. If Kathleen wants that fucking freak crawling around, she can find some other dick to pleasure her flesh flaps.*

Leaving the mug and bottles where they sat, Brad stormed out of the kitchen and through the living room, looking around for Herman but not seeing him, then down the hallway with its walls of smut. *One last fuck and I'm out of here*, he thought, flinging open the door to Kathleen's bedroom, sending it bouncing off the wall.

Kathleen rustled under the covers at the sound of Brad entering, but she didn't waken. She'd pulled the covers up over her shoulders in his absence, only the crown of her fake red hair peeking out. Brad stood at the foot of the bed, adjusting himself and looking at the lump of covers. She hadn't left the bed after taking her earlier fucking, so she no doubt had cum leakage seeping from her cunt, like a pita pocket dripping queso blanco.

Brad stroked himself slowly over his underwear, imagining the moistness of Kathleen's cum-filled cooter. He quickly grew hard, ready to go. Dropping his drawers, a sly grin emerged on Brad's face as he climbed onto the bed. Since he was certain this would be the last time he fucked Kathleen, he intended to make sure it was a pounding she'd never forget. *She likes that rough BDSM shit, huh?* he thought. *Well, let's see just how rough she likes it.*

The image of that fucking dog kept creeping into his mind, threatening to soften his erection. The night Kathleen brought Herman to bed with them had been a nightmare. It wasn't Brad's first threesome by any means, but it was his first with someone who thought he was a fucking dog. And it had been clear that night who was capable of delivering the most pleasure to Kathleen: Herman.

Not only was his cock absurdly large, but he possessed stamina that knew no bounds. Long after Brad had spent his load, the dog kept thrusting into her, howling at the ceiling through his leather mask, bringing her to orgasm repeatedly. And when he'd finally splooged his spunk, Herman curled up next to Kathleen like a good dog does, keeping her warm, his eyes, though, staring at Brad on the other side of the bed, as if wishing he'd make a move.

Brad wanted to fuck Kathleen up ever since that night. *Really* fuck her up. How dare she bring her dog into the bed with them. Sure, she'd asked if it was okay first, but Brad wasn't expecting it to turn out the way it did. He didn't know he'd be out-fucked by a goddamn fake K-9, leaving him feeling insecure and unworthy. In truth, that's what led him to challenge himself to fuck *every-single-day*. And in his romps with Kathleen since that night, he'd become more and more aggressive and rough. Only, she liked it that way. Nothing he did scared her or *really* hurt her, not even the cane he'd broken across her ass last time.

Well, all that was about to change. Brad had had enough. Seeing that stupid fucking dog tonight, remembering how it fucked, it burned into Brad's pride. The boilermaker coursing through his system didn't help to cool his temper. And while thoughts of Herman wavered his hard-on, thoughts of *really* hurting Kathleen made him harder than perhaps he'd ever been.

Brad jerked the covers back, flinging them not just off Kathleen but off the bed entirely. Lying on her side, Kathleen shivered and scrunched up, pulling her creaky knees up to her abdomen, exposing the sagging lips of her fathomless flower between her upper thighs. Her eyes did not open, however. Brad inched up behind her on his knees, his cock standing at attention, a snarling smile on his face as his eyes slithered over her plump behind. *Yeah, that has to be a fake ass, he thought. That's why she can take a beating without crying like a bitch.*

He decided to test this theory, rearing back with his right hand high above and behind his head. He swung done with all his strength, smashing his open palm against her left ass cheek, causing a loud smacking sound, like a balloon being popped.

"Ouch!" Kathleen yelped, suddenly awake, her eyes popping open and her head turning to look at Brad with wild confusion. "The fuck are you doing?"

"Spread those ass cheeks, baby," Brad said. "It's high time I tried your other hole."

Kathleen raised an eyebrow at him then let out a little giggle—she actually giggled—as she laid her head back down and rolled her body away from him. "Lay down, Bradley," she said, closing her eyes and tucking her hands beneath her pillow. "You've had enough play time tonight."

Was she really blowing him off like that? No one said no to Brad. Certainly not some borderline geriatric slut.

"I said spread those ass cheeks, bitch," Brad said, raising his voice, trying to sound authoritative.

"Fat chance," Kathleen said, matter-of-factly, as if his request was of little concern to her. "Go to sleep."

"If you don't do it," he said, angrily now, "then I'm just going to take it!"

Kathleen sighed—actually sighed—not opening her eyes or turning his direction. Then she spoke, almost in a sad voice: "Brad, honey, you're fun and all, but you're not man enough to take *anything from me.* Now go to sleep. I'll make you some scrambled eggs in the morning."
Brad, on his knees behind her, softened a bit, his mind picking apart the things Kathleen said. Not man enough? Go to sleep? She'll make him fucking eggs in the morning? What, did she think him a child? A fucking pussy who wouldn't stand up to a misbehaving woman?

Fuck that!

Quickly, Brad leaned over Kathleen, slamming his palm into the back of her head with one hand and twisting her to her belly with the other. He swiftly hardened with this act of dominance, straddling her thighs as he rolled her, his erect cock aiming straight at her puckered asshole.

"You're gonna learn, bitch, when I say to spread your fucking ass cheeks, you spread your goddamn ass cheeks!"

"Goddammit, get off me!" Kathleen yelled into the pillow, Brad's hand still hard against her head.

Using his free hand, he spread her ass cheeks apart, inching forward, aiming his cock for the poot shoot.

"Get off me, Bradley! If that little prick of yours comes within an inch of my ass, you'll fucking regret it!"

"Oh yeah?" Brad said, pushing her head harder into the pillow. "I guess we'll see about that!"

Hawking a slimy, thick loogie into his mouth, Brad expelled it like a rocket, splatting it perfectly against Kathleen's asshole. He plunged forward, penetrating her before she had the opportunity to protest further. Her asshole clinched tight, trying to push him out but only succeeding in making the penetration more pleasurable.

"Get off me!" Kathleen screamed, turning her head from the pillow.

"I'll get off when I damn well please," Brad said, pulling back and slamming back into her.
"Herman!" she screamed suddenly. "Herman, I need you, boy!"

Brad almost laughed. He was half shaft into her coco hole and she was hollering for a fake dog to come to her rescue. What, did she think someone so lazy and worthless that they would pretend to be an animal would suddenly hop up and prevent her from receiving the best fucking of her life? Because that's what she was about to get, in Brad's opinion, the best goddamn pounding she'd ever been pounded. A fucking she would be reminiscing about on her death bed. An orgasmic encore for the ages.

Only, Herman had different ideas.

Brad heard him bounding down the hallway, sounding like a drunken mule at half-gallop, knees knocking on the floor at a painful pace. He laughed as he pushed hard against Kathleen's ass, making her cry out once again. That dumb human pooch had answered her call by the sound of it, but he was still crawling along on the floor like the animal he pretended to be. And dogs couldn't open doors. Herman would reach the bedroom and be unable to do shit unless he intended to give up the act long enough to turn the door handle. At which point, Brad would momentarily halt relishing Kathleen's rectum so he could knock Herman around.

Then Brad remembered . . . he had not closed the door upon re-entering Kathleen's bedroom.

His head whipped around as the pounding hustle of the dog grew ever closer. Then he was there, screeching to a stop just inside the bedroom, crouched there on hands and knees, his eyes angry beneath that ridiculous leather mask, a low rumbling growl seeming to leak out every pore.

Brad stopped his thrusting, his grip on Kathleen loosening but not letting go entirely. He realized, suddenly, he was sweating. Not from exertion—he'd only just started his work on Kathleen—but from a nervousness that had come on as quick as a spring thunderstorm. Could that fucking dog actually hurt him if it so desired? Anger flashed, attempting to overtake the anxiety.

"Get the fuck out of here, dog," Brad snapped. "You can have a piece of her when I'm done."

It occurred to Brad that Kathleen was no longer fighting him. She wasn't laying there like a dead fish either, the way some women did when he'd taken them without exactly getting consent, like they'd given up, figuring that simply letting him get the splooge out of his sack was probably the safest option. Instead, Kathleen had propped her head up on her hand, her elbow digging into the mattress as she crooned around him to see Herman in the doorway.

"I suggest you pull your withering dick out of me, Bradley," she said, almost amused, "unless you fancy Herman biting it off."

She was right about one thing: his cock was withering, embarrassingly fast. There was no need to pull out of Kathleen; he was shrinking out of her. One last clinch of the ol' asshole from Kathleen sent his manhood dropping out like a room-temp shrimp. With her rape seemingly brought to its conclusion, Kathleen didn't move from the bed or even scoot away from Brad. She simply laid there, a sly smile on her face.

"I said get the fuck out of here," Brad said, though there was no confidence in his voice.

Herman growled—still quietly, but with more intensity. He inched toward the bed slowly, dragging his tail, as if waiting for an order. *Of course that's what he's doing*, Brad thought, *waiting for goddamn Kathleen to holler 'sic 'em' or whatever the fuck.*

"You may want to go ahead and leave, Bradley," Kathleen said, almost sighing the words out, as if she was tired of this spectacle and just wanted to go back to sleep. "Once Herman gets riled up, he can be hard to control."

How had this happened? Moments ago—seconds ago!—Brad was balls deep in her crapper. Now she was *suggesting* he leave. *Or what?* Or this fake dog—this leather dog—was going to pounce on him like some oversized infant wanting to wrestle. With that naked, useless glob of flesh crouched in the floor like a devout parishioner at a church of disgust, Kathleen thought Brad should be intimidated? She thought he should bend the knee and bid farewell?

Fuck that!
"Tell your stupid dog to get out of here," Brad said sternly, his cock getting a sudden rush of enthusiasm as a result of his dominant tone. "We can finish what we started, then I'll be on my way."

"What we started, huh?" Kathleen said, raising an eyebrow and laughing under her breath. "Bradley, dear, get the fuck out of here while you still can."

"Excuse me?" he said, the dog in the doorway momentarily forgotten. "Nobody fuckin talks to me like that."

"Get the fuck out," she said mildly, without concern. "Last chance."

Brad boiled over.

Before he had time to consider his move—to think better of it and perhaps accept Kathleen's offer to let him leave—his right hand crossed over his chest, then swung downward, backhanding Kathleen right in the nose, kicking her head back and causing blood to spray from one nostril as she hit against the pillow, her eyes wide with shock.

"Fuck!" she hollered, her hands going up to her face. "Herman!"

Brad turned, having forgotten the man mutt was still in the room.

Herman was bounding toward the bed on all fours, snarling and barking as his body moved, his muscles contracting, each stride knocking hard against the floor. He leapt, the tail floating up behind him, as Brad, his hands balled into fists, turned to face the dog head on. But as he leapt for the bed—for Brad—one of the dog's hands reached for a clasp on the side of the leather mask, undoing it, pulling the mask free from his head just as he landed on the mattress, revealing himself in full to dear Bradley.

The leather mask had been in the shape of a dog's face, with the long snout and jaws, but beneath it . . . beneath it too were a long snout and jaws. Whether by surgical design or a mutation of Mother Nature, Brad did not know. Herman's pale flesh extended out to a dog snout below the eyes, with a pugly flesh-toned nose at its end. Below the nose was a wide mouth, with loose skin drooped around, black stubble sprouting here and there. And, as he growled that hideous growl, Brad could see long, sharp teeth within that mouth. Not human teeth, but those of, perhaps, a German shepherd or Doberman.

"Jesus Christ," Brad managed to say in the brief moment before Herman attacked. He didn't move to flee or fight, only uttered that one plea to his creator or simply the empty air between them.

Then Herman was upon him.

Amidst his disbelief, Brad lowered his arms, and with his opponent's limbs no longer a threat, Herman struck the way any dog would, lunging at the neck of his victim—whether tearing open the throat or jugular, it made no difference; either would disable, if not kill. As it turned out, Herman's wide jaws got both.

With Brad falling backward toward the mattress in a pathetic attempt to avoid the dog, Herman's massive jaws wrapped around his neck, the long teeth sinking in only for a moment, before his head jerked to the right violently, the teeth not releasing, but taking as much flesh with it as possible. Blood poured from Brad's jugular and sprayed from his carotid artery, arching over his shoulder and decorating Kathleen's cream-colored sheets like an abstract painting.

Losing his balance, his hand going uselessly to his neck, Brad toppled from the bed, his head colliding with the corner of the nightstand, opening another wound for blood to flow. His eyes and mouth were wide in an equal measure of fear and disbelief.

But the dog wasn't done.

Kathleen had warned of what would happen if Brad didn't leave.

Most dogs only understand a handful of phrases. They understand their name. They may understand 'sit' or 'stay' or 'go potty.' But Herman understood everything. He was a very smart dog.

Brad was screaming from his back—a horrible, gurgling scream—as Herman jumped from the bed, his jaws once more open to the max. The dog's human-like paws slammed into Brad's knees, spreading the man's legs as he fell upon him, dislocating the left femur from the pelvis as he went. In a snarling fit of rage, Herman's open maw descended upon Brad's shriveled genitals.

A pit bull, were it capable of jealously, would've indeed been jealous of the power of Herman's bite. In one single, perfectly aimed snap, the dog severed Brad's twig and berries like he was plucking a couple of grapes from its stem, leaving nothing but a bloody orifice between the man's legs. After only two quick chews, the cock and balls were swallowed and resting pleasantly in Herman's belly. And as Brad gasped his last wet breaths, Herman relaxed, panting, squatting beside the man, his tongue hanging lazily out the side of his long, fleshy jowls.

"Good boy, Herman" Kathleen said, sitting up in bed, admiring the corpse and her loyal doggo with a satisfied smile. "That's my good leather dog. I hope you don't think your night is done though. You know how horny Mama gets when you protect her."

Herman looked at her, returning his tongue to his mouth, and howled softly—sweetly—toward the ceiling, then jumped into bed.

The Onion Club

Jack Bantry

John was at his allotment digging over the soil in what would be this year's onion bed. He dug in the garden compost with some well-rotted horse manure. Now his back was aching. He straightened, arched his back, trying to rid himself of the pain. It was no use. He was sure he would have a bad back for the rest of his life.

He'd been growing vegetables on his allotment since he took it over at the beginning of lockdown.

The ground was muddy after all the recent rain, but he had to get it done in time to plant his onion seedlings. They had been taking up precious room on the conservatory windowsill and he needed space to plant on the runner beans and butternut squash.

He resumed digging, turning the soil with his fork. He was now in his third year at the allotment. Sometimes things went as planned, he didn't have any trouble growing beetroot and parsnips, or courgettes. Another couple of months and he'd have courgettes coming out of his ears. He couldn't give them away.

Other times things failed for no apparent reason.

The good old English weather was the common excuse. You never really knew what it was going to do tomorrow, never mind next week.

Last year the majority of his leeks went to seed, and the slugs ate his radish. The trick was not to become disheartened and to learn from your mistakes - water regularly and make some beer traps for the bloody slugs. It's not always straightforward. There hasn't been a spring this year - heavy frost until the recent rain. Now the ground was soft enough to dig. In fact, it was too soft. He put some cardboard down to stand on, otherwise he was going to sink into the earth. If things failed, you knuckled down and tried again.

John stuck the gardening fork in the ground, walked over to the shed and poured himself some tea from his flask. He spotted the *Fish Blood & Bone*, and he used that to feed the onion seedlings some nutrients. His back was still aching, but he needed to get the onion seedlings in. He picked up his rake and returned to the muddy cardboard, back to the onion bed.

John had lived in the village most of his life. He ran a successful restaurant in nearby York. Prior to lockdown he was negotiating with two long-time employees and trying to sell them the business. The hours were long, and he was getting too old. He wanted to spend the evenings at home with his wife. They had no children, hence no one to leave the business to, and the sudden pandemic forced him to literally give away the restaurant. He was glad to be rid of it and the pressures the pandemic brought to the hospitality trade. It was simple, he'd made enough money and didn't need the hassle.

When he took early retirement, he had no plans to spend his afternoons growing vegetables. The restaurant business was all consuming, so he hadn't had time for hobbies, until he'd seen the allotments while out on his daily walk. John soon came to love the vegetable garden. It was a way for him to escape the isolation. To save himself from certain madness. John had never grown vegetables before. Shown no passion towards it. He hadn't even taken a previous liking to flowers. He didn't grow flowers now either, except for a few daffodils, but he does grow all kinds of vegetables. Onions are his real passion, though, thanks to the Onion Club.

At the end of the first season John noticed some of the folks taking more care with their onions than other vegetables. He couldn't understand why. It wasn't as if they were the most interesting vegetables on the plot. When he got chatting, he discovered they were members of the Onion Club.

A club for onion growers.

There was an allotment related club in the village. His interest immediately peaked.

It took place in August at the local pub, The Sowerby Arms, so you could have a couple of pints too. Main prize (club members only) was for the heaviest onion. John applied to join the club. You can only join if the other members voted you in - and they all did, there were no objections, which was good.

He came last at his first attempt last year. Became a bit of a laughingstock. John was always competitive in the restaurant business, you had to be, last place in the Onion Club was a failure. It didn't matter that it was his first year. He was conditioned to be successful. He didn't expect to win on his first attempt, but he expected to do better. Now, John was addicted to growing onions and strived to grow the largest in the village, where they take it very seriously. This year he hoped for a good placing. He'd put too much effort in, and invested enough time, to finish last. John was surprised at how serious he was taking the competition and aimed to have the last laugh.

The bed was raked over, nice and flat, with large stones removed. He loved prepping in March and April, getting the allotment ready for the new season. The daffodils were flowering. It meant spring was near and lighter nights were coming.

He loved spending time on his plot. You had to get the soil ready, put the seedlings in, water them, do the weeding. You spend a lot of time observing and talking to them.

He heard the main gates creak open as he reminisced.

More gardeners.

John walked over to the shed again and brought back a tray of onion seedlings.

He was lost in his own world and didn't notice whoever had arrived until he heard a large cracking sound, like wood splintering.   He was kneeling at the time - not good for his bad back - and when he stood, he saw a young man, sixteen or seventeen years old, dressed in black tracksuit bottoms - the ones with the three strips down the side - and a black sweatshirt. It was Steph's shed and her children were much smaller.

John had seen a few of the teenage kids roaming around recently in groups, ignoring the lockdown rules, which instructed people to stay home.

He imagined the young man was stealing to buy drugs. He's heard York, like most towns and cities, had a problem.

"Oi," shouted John. "What do you think you are doing?"

The kid looked back over his shoulder, a startled expression on his face. Probably hadn't seen John knelt and thought he was on his own.

"Can I help you son?" asked John.

"Me mum sent me down for some gardening tools," said the kid.

"She's gardening at home."

"What's her name?"

"Eh?"

"What do they call her?"

The kid stumbled with his word.

He had to get past John to get to the gate. Instead, he took off towards the six-foot fence bordering the allotments. On the other side was a local park. Some kids, possibly this one included, had broken in last summer. They damaged the padlock in the process - and trashed some of the allotments. They broke into a few sheds and stomped some pumpkins. It took all season to grow the different crops, most were grown from seed packets in February and March. It was bad enough loosing things to the weather, seeing the smashed pumpkins was heart-breaking.

John pulled his fork out of the earth and chased after the kid. He was going to make a citizen's arrest.

"Get here," shouted John.

"Fuck off, old man."

The kid clutched hold of the awkward wire-like fencing and attempted to haul himself up. John planned to pull him back down and phone the police from his mobile phone.

John grabbed hold of the kid's sweatshirt. Before he could get a good grip, the kid kicked down, connecting with John's nose. John landed hard on his backside.

The kid was climbing higher, almost high enough to swing a leg over the fence.

John clambered to his feet. Without thinking his swung the fork, which he's somehow kept hold of, and stabbed the kid in the back. The tines sunk into the soft flesh of the kid's lower back, like sticking a knife through butter, all four inches of dirty metal.

The kid let out a bellowing scream of agony, his grip fumbled on the top of the fence. The fork was stuck right into the kids back. He imagined the times sticking out the front of the kid's torso, somewhere around the belly button. All four tines sticking through the kid's stomach. John hadn't meant to hurt the kid. The shock of what he's done was like being zapped with electricity. He pulled back on the fork and it slid out.

The kid let out another scream as he fell back, landing hard on a John's head, knocking the gardener back down.

Panicking, John struggled to throw the kid off him. He managed to pull his head free and push the kid's body away.

His first reaction was: had someone heard the scream?

John looked down. The kid was laid on his back. He looked terrified, spat blood out of his mouth as he blubbered. His hands were covered in blood as he fumbled with the soaked front of his black sweatshirt.

John looked the kid in the eyes. They were wide open, pleading eyes, they said: *help me, please don't hurt me anymore.* The kid had quickly gone from a cocky teenager to a wounded animal.

The kid coughed again. Blood gurgled out from between his lips.

John pulled out his mobile phone and contemplated calling for an ambulance. He'd also need to phone the police.

He couldn't go to prison. He could hide the body. His car was in the car park. John could take the body to the car using his wheelbarrow, but it would be easy for someone to spot him if they looked his way. He couldn't do prison. John didn't know what to do. He was panicking. No way could John do prison.

If you can't do the time, don't do the crime.

What had he done?

The kid lay still, motionless, the coughing had stopped and his eyes seemed to have glazed over.

What had he done? John wasn't a killer. He was the kind of person who would put a spider outside instead of killing it.

John's mouth went dry as the shock of what he'd done kicked in. He started to shake.

Oh fuck. No. Fuck. Fuck! Shit no.

John could hear people in the park.

Luckily their view would be obscured by bushes at the other side of the fence. If they'd heard the screams and came closer to investigate, they would surely see through the early springtime branches.

John, in a state of panic, looked around, searching for people, trying to see if he'd been spotted. What was he going to do? He killed a kid for breaking into a shed. Not exactly a crime deserving of the death penalty. He was fucked. *There goes your peaceful retirement.*   John dropped the fork and grabbed hold of the kid's ankles. He pulled the kid back over to John's allotment. He could shove him in the shed, but that would make it hard to clean up any spilled blood. *Arrrgh!* John wanted to pull his hair out. What had he gone and done? Jesus, there was no going back from this.

He looked around himself. At this time of year, the allotment didn't have much growth. It was too early in the season. The only plants with any height were the overwintering brassica - his few remaining Brussel sprouts and the purple sprouting broccoli. That would have to do. He dragged the body between the rows of large overgrown plants.

The body was out of sight, but it was obvious it couldn't stay there.

The only soft earth was where he had dug over his onions.

Fuck!

He needed to get the body to the car, parked in the small car park outside the allotment. The path down was too narrow to drive and he'd already ruled out the wheelbarrow. What was he going to do?

Could John risk leaving the body until it got dark, before hauling it down to the car park? That was an option. There was a good chance he could get it to the car once the sun went down. He could then drive it out into the surrounding woodlands, but rigor mortis would have set in by then. The blood would be starting to congeal.

John went back into the shed and picked out his spade. He was going to have to bury it here. John got straight down to it. Digging easily in the soft earth. The problem now was the big hole and pile of soil couldn't be anything other than a grave.

He was sweating and his back hurt like hell.

John made sure no one was looking before dragging the body out from under the broccoli leaves and dropping it into the hole.

Come on, nearly done.

He picked up the spade, noticed sore spots on his hands, which were starting to blister. Ignoring the pain, he tossed in the earth, quickly covering the body. He discarded the spade and frantically searched for the rake.

John smeared mud across his forehead as he wiped away rivulets of sweat. God only knows what he looked like.

The ground was flat enough.

John noticed the tray of onion seedling near where he had been kneeling when the kid broke into the shed.

I should plant them, he thought. *They'd naturally avert any suspicion.*

***

John walked through the village on his way to the Sowerby Arms village pub. It was a typical midsummers day with a cloudless blue sky overhead. The village was very picturesque, with quaint limestone cottages lining the narrow winding road. Each cottage sat beyond a typical lawned front garden, surrounded by colour. A cabbage white butterfly flapped lazily above John's head. The common insect was a pest, as the eggs it laid turned into caterpillars that devoured the brassicas.

John was heading to the pub to take part in the annual Onion Club awards.

He was extremely nervous and was hoping for an improvement on last year.

John's onions were definitely bigger than his previous attempt.

The initial lockdown had come to an end and people were out and about, many refusing to wear masks and ignoring social distancing.

He walked through the pub car park, which was full, and into the rear beer garden. The club had erected a marquee on the lush green lawn, probably in case of rain, as you can't trust the British weather. People bustled in and around the tent, most with a drink in their hand. John wandered into the marquee, he nodded his greeting or shook hands with a few of the other growers. He had another twenty minutes before the advertised start time, long enough to get himself a pint.

John drank from his pint glass as the Onion Club toasted his unexpected victory. Winner at only the second attempt. He savoured the victory as the other growers looked on enviously. George, the pub landlord was asked to judge. It was a simple enough task, as the heaviest onion was the winner, and the club had some state-of-the-art electric scales. John had his photo taken stood in front of his giant award-winning onion. In one hand he held his certificate, while he shook hands with George with the other.

"What's the secret to your success?" asked Liz Arnold, reporter for the local weekly newspaper.

That interested a couple of club members who wanted to know John's secret.

"Well, I water the plants regularly and get plenty of nutrients into the soil," replied John.

"What do you use exactly?" asked Graham Hogg. Graham, a retired doctor, had won heaviest onion three years ago, and was considered one of the favourites, but had only come in fourth place.

"I'm afraid that's a secret," said John, with a wry smile. It was a secret he wasn't willing to share. John, lost in thought, drank more of his ale. Unfortunately, due to crop rotation, he wouldn't be able to replicate this year's success. The soil this year had been exceptionally fertile and had produced great results. When growing vegetables, the grower had to rotate the crops to avoid exhausting the soil and help stop diseases which can occur if a crop is repeatedly farmed in the same ground.

John had his own questions, like would the fertile benefits of the decomposing body last for future years, next year he planned to grow pumpkins and courgettes where this year's onions were grown; how was he going to replicate this year's success with his onion's? He'd surely be one of the favourites next year. Maybe he would have to make do with regular growing techniques, that is, unless he could procure another
body…

THE END

Skinheads Ruin Everything

Dan Henk

THE FIND

I'd never really felt 100%. Like my life was my own and everything made sense.
Society had always been a strait jacket. I wasn't even sure who or what I was meant to be. Or if that was even a thing. My parents were deeply conservative, which only became more of a burden as I grew older. I tried running away. Twice actually. As I evolved into a young adult they felt less like my parents, and more like the people I was stuck with. Not

that any of it mattered now. They'd found the body. And I'd done such a good job of cleaning up. Hours upon hours of scrubbing and digging.

A LITTLE BACKSTORY

I was living in Virginia at the time. At my parents' house in Burke. Dad was barely around. Mom was present but she was usually pretty oblivious to anything outside of her small, milquetoast suburban world.

Some bug had crawled up their ass and they had decided to vacation. Puerto Rico was the original destination, but the storm prevented all that. So, they settled on Florida.
They did offer me the token invitation. Family gathering, fun in the sun, all the usual amenities.
But the last thing I wanted was to waste four days of my life sharing a house with my lame ass parents.
Mom still gave running commentary on the immorality of every TV show, and somehow managed to overcook all the food. Her very presence was annoying.
Not to mention that everything about me seemed to embarrass them. My Mohawk. My attire. My late rising and even later evening hours. Dad always said I looked like a girl, as if that was some sort of insult. He'd chased me around the house with scissors trying to cut my hair and rip my earring off.
So, I stayed home. In my boring suburban house. Nestled ever so wholesomely among trimmed maple trees and boxwood shrubs. Like every other crappy domicile on this block. The conformity of it was almost smothering.
Of course I was going to throw a party the minute they were gone. I told a few people at school, but it grew out of hand in no time. People I barely even knew were talking about it. A few friends were bringing kegs, Milwaukee's Best, (or Beast as they all called it), but beggars couldn't be choosers! I had a few hits stashed in the freezer too. Just in case.

Come Friday night, the place was swarming.

There was the aggravation of having to corral people smoking in the house. All in an attempt to avoid the parental "smells like smoke" feedback. And the aggravation of getting all the dipshits to not leave plastic cups everywhere. Other than that, it all seemed to be going pretty well. My buddy Dave showed up with his hot sister. I always found it difficult to have normal, relaxed conversations with people I felt I had to impress, but just maybe I could pull something out of my ass this time. I really should say something. Angela was always friendly, although maybe that was just because of Dave. The last thing I wanted was to make our friendship awkward by making moves on his sister.

Things were going swimmingly. We were all outback surrounding the pool. The lamps blanketed everything in a blue glow, which somehow made the environs seem slightly surreal. After a few drinks, not too many I hoped, I figured I could make small talk with Angela. Hopefully feel out what she was thinking. It might even give me the confidence to talk past my flaws. The imperfect skin. The weak jaw. The higher pitched voice. If I could just act the part of someone interesting, maybe I'd have a chance I couldn't bring myself to dive right in, so I made a little small talk with Dave and shuffled around nervously. As time slipped by, I tried to come up with things to say. My leather pants kept snagging in the plastic webbing of the chair, accentuating my awkwardness. Every time I told myself *"It's now or never"* something seemed to interrupt, and I paused for too long. Maybe she really didn't look at me like a potential love interest? What was the perfect thing to say without sounding stupid? I kept running through lines, but they all seemed flat.
Just as I worked up the confidence to try, a voice broke through the din.

"What the fuck do we have here Nelson? It looks like these little pansies are having a party."

SOME PEOPLE MAKE EVERYTHING WORSE

Who invited those morons? Skins felt entitled to pop up anywhere. My mom was Syrian, so my skin wasn't exactly white, but they usually left me alone. My friend Dave, however, and his sister, were black. And these guys were definitely of the racist variety.

"What's this?"

Even with the overwhelming aromas of chlorine and cut grass, I could smell the body odor and cheap cologne. The scrawnier guy was almost a stereotype come to life. He was wearing a crimson flight jacket, straight cut blue jeans, and Doc Martins laced up in red.

"You think you're a girl?"

I was confused for a moment, then realized I was sporting black eyeliner and nail polish. I often described it as my "death rocker" look. This was my house. I'd dress however the fuck I wanted. Besides, I didn't want to look like a pushover. Especially in the presence of Angela.

"No. Do you think you are?"

That was a little ballsy, but too many people were here, what was he going to do? All three of the skinheads, the scrawny guy, his muscle-bound friend, and some older looking jerk-off circled around. The scrawny guy drew closest, his hard, angry face staring at me. A few moments passed in utter silence, the whole crowd looking on, but the skins were silent. They turned and walked away.

The party continued like before, as more drunkenness ensued. At one point I could hear shouting, and the sounds of a distant scuffle. But nothing followed, so I shrugged it off. Besides, I was too drunk to do anything.

More people arrived, a few left, and yet again I missed my opportunity to talk to Angela. The skinheads had rattled me and now all I could bring myself to do was calm my nerves with more alcohol. I made excuses that I would have botched it regardless. But I knew they were just that. Excuses. I was twenty-one and felt like life was slipping me by. Next year I will leave for art school. Maybe I could re-invent myself there. I had started a band, and in the fresh environs of a new state I could possibly parlay that into something that made me cooler.

Come four in the morning, only a few stragglers remained. No one I particularly recognized, but no one I hated either. Drunkenly, I tried to survey the damage they'd done. It didn't look that bad. Then again, I could barely even see, and everything looked better in the late hours.

My bones cracked, and I groaned as I drew up my feet. I wandered over to the pool and gazed at the watery reflections. Soft ripples of aqua-green broke up the dark edges of my shadow. For a moment I was distracted, in some drunken trance. Then the strong stench of chlorine wafted over, and my stomach turned. I rocked back and forth on the ledge, daydreaming about how lame it would be to fall in. Something slammed into my back. Arms waving in desperation, I belly-flopped into the pool. A rush of cold water engulfed me and stinging chlorinated liquid invaded my nostrils. Thrashing about, I tried to break for the surface, but a hand grabbed my Mohawk and held me down.

Pounding the water like a madman, I attempted to break free. But there was nothing to grab onto, and I kept plummeting lower. The follicles on my scalp stung under the tension, as a palm crushed into the back of my head.
My eyes burned and I started to lose all focus. Then vision escaped me, little dots of color flashing into an overwhelming field of blackness. A strange sensation burned through me. My body grew warmer as my blood started to boil. A veil of crimson seeped in at the corners and consciousness escaped me.

That Never Dead

I had this crazy dream. More of a nightmare really, but I can't say it was all bad. That skinhead was scared. He was running and then howling in pain as something tore into his spine. Blood was everywhere, bathing me in the sickly-sweet aroma of raw iron.

Then I awoke.

I was sitting on the pavement in front of my sidewalk, under the shade of a giant oak tree. All around me spread a dark splotch. The mangled form of a man, bulbous entrails jutting out of a heap of mashed flesh and distended bone shards, lay just to my left. A patchwork of dark puddles trailed towards the pool that surrounded me. I blinked and tried to clear my vision. Was that mess one of the skinheads? Some of the splotches amid the torn flesh resembled denim. I glanced sideways and noticed that the remnants of suspenders peaked out of the gory pile. Their tips waving gently in the breeze.

All was deathly silent. What could have done this? How did I get here? I glanced about. The stench was overwhelming. Excrement and the sickeningly metallic smell of blood. I looked down at my hands. They were coated in a thick, syrupy sheen. My arm felt damp, and I stretched it to see that the gore extended up towards my armpit.

Flashes started to flit through my head. Snippets of screaming and blood, like the scenes from a movie.

I started to panic. I had to do something. This couldn't be me, but the evidence was damning. How could I explain any of this? A rogue murderer? Someone framing me? In northern Virginia, looking the way I looked, no one would believe me. My own parents would rat me out.

I'd have to clean up this mess and hide the body. That was the only option. That was probably the wrong move, but I didn't want to spend my life in jail.
Rising to my feet and walking over, I looked at the viscera. Jutting out of the gristle was the rounded edge of a skull. Definity the remains of a person.

What could I do to deal with this? Maybe a bag? I looked around. Aside from a few parked cars in the distance, there was nothing. No sign of life. Some large bags were in the shed. I just had to make it there and back before anyone saw any of this. A few neighboring houses loomed nearby. No lights were visible. Maybe I could pull this off.

Scooping the slimy bits into one central pile, all while fighting back the urge to retch, I dug out what was left of the shirt and jeans. I brushed off as much of the gore as I could. I took off my shirt and twisted it into a makeshift satchel. Scooping in the remains, vomit rising in my throat every time my hands bumped into the stubby edge of a bone, I managed to pull the majority of the slop into a makeshift satchel. I tied up the edges, and hoisted it all aloft, almost falling over under the weight as I swung it onto my back. I stabilized myself and headed for the house. Traipsing along the edge of the front yard, the fence of bushes a partial wall, I crept through the yard. The smell was horrendous, hitting me with a putrid gust every time a breeze passed. Clumps of gristle and rivulets of blood steadily dripped onto my neck, gluing the strands of my mohawk to my skin.

As I reached the rear porch, I stopped in the shade and scanned the backyard. Nothing. All was deadly silent. Where did everyone go?

The pool was rimmed with bottles and cups but devoid of life. Squinting, I could make out where that skinhead had tried to drown me. Just shimmering ripples now. There was a little puddle of water on the edge of the pool, but that was it.

Stumbling up the bevel and onto the patio, I hauled the corpse in through the rear glass door. In the darkness I could just make out the water closet entrance.

Shifting the mass on my shoulders and pausing for any last remnants of blood to drip down on the patio (as opposed to the carpet), I crossed the living room and pried the closet door open. The space was small. Smaller than I remembered. Only a tiny expanse of concrete, the hot water heater hogging up most of the space. I dropped the satchel and squinted into the darkness. No tools. Just a little hand broom and dustpan. But I remembered that the tool shed in the back yard harbored a pickax and shovel. And a bin of liquid concrete. There were dish rags and bleach under the kitchen sink. Desperate times called for desperate measures. I could do this.

The Knock On the Door

The sound repeated itself. A harsh, booming crack.
My head still ached from the show last night, and to top it all off, that rash on my arm had gotten worse. I cupped the aching sides of my skull, the skin on my arm pulling tight and aggravating my rash. I stumbled out of bed only wearing my boxer shorts. My skinny chest was a constant source of embarrassment but fuck it. My head hurt too much to try and find a t-shirt.
As I cracked open the door, the light blinded me. A gust of Old Spice hit before I even recognized the uniform.

"What's...what can I help you with officer?"

My stomach knotted as I tried to run through what I could possibly have done. I mean, aside from the worst-case scenario. And I think they'd bring a lot more force for that. It could be my recent petty crimes, like shoplifting at 7-11. That was months ago, and an employee stopped me before I made it to the door. I'd been caught shoplifting at Kmart, and they had already banned me for a year. It could be last week's vandalism. None of that was anything serious. Just a few tags on wet concrete and a smashed bus sign. I'd done a little breaking and entering months ago when I was drunk, but only at the abandoned project buildings nearby. It was late at night, and nothing really happened. This was a college town. There were way worse things going on. Like that recent stabbing at the train station. Maybe they were just picking on the town misfits.

"Put on a shirt and pants. You're coming downtown."

"What's going on officer?"

"You're Ryan Argarwal right? 21 years old. Originally from Burke, Virginia?"

My heart sank. It wasn't a local drama. Burke was years ago but I figured it must be serious to tie me there. I'd moved all over the country, but there was only one thing in Burke that would draw them this far out.

The blazing morning heat was overwhelming. I tried to clear my vision as I fumbled for smokes. Pulling a mostly empty pack from the bedside table, I withdrew one and mumbled *"You*

mind if I smoke this first?"

Convinced the cop would say no, I was a bit surprised when the officer turned and shot me a friendly smile. I tried to stretch my neck for a better view but the shine on the cop's head was almost blinding. A glimmer of mirror shades, an overweight officer, and a way too wide row of teeth were all I could make out.

"Sure."

Inhaling a few puffs, I kicked some of the gravel off the sidewalk and glanced about. The sky was that washed-out blue of early morning. The air always smelt a little different in these hours. Like the day held promise, even when I knew it didn't.

Peeling painted wood houses lined the cross street but no one seemed home. This might be my last smoke as a free man. I thought about running, but realized there was no way that could end well. I wasn't much of an athlete, and I was in no shape to outrun an officer. Even if the cop looked a little chunky.

I mulled over the incident from long ago. I could have sworn I'd cleaned up well. I was soaked in sweat and the sun was coming up as I gave the gravel it's once over last pass. Not that any of that mattered with modern forensics. Once they got down with all their modern blood splatter analysis equipment, the whole incident would be clear as day.

Downtown

The ride was uneventful. I had been in the back of cop cars before. The police never talked, usually they were dour and serious. These were more genial, and although I rode along in handcuffs, it wasn't that bad. The sharp edges bit into my wrists, but the cops cracked the windows, and I could smell the fresh air. In line with my usual bad luck, my arm really itched. With the handcuffs restraining me, I couldn't even scratch.

As the car rolled to a stop, the police up front stepped out. The fat one bent over and opened the rear door, motioning for me to follow. I passed through a grime smeared glass door and into central booking. Inside, a strong, chemical scent made me queasy. Antiseptic tinged with the aroma of last night's regrets. The seriousness of the situation was finally settling in.

As I strolled up to the central counter, I couldn't help but notice how all police counters seemed to look the same. I'd never been here before, but this looked just like the one back in Fairfax, VA. All cheap particle board painted in some passive tone, like gray. Just as I scrolled up my vision to the officer at the counter, a heavy hand clamped down on my shoulder and guided me to the right. I traipsed down a neighboring corridor and into an intimidating looking room.

White and bare, a gray table in the middle was the only occupant. It looked metal, but there were so many layers of paint on it, the true composition was long gone. I'd never been in an interrogation room, but judging by all the police shows I'd seen, this looked like one. Maybe a little more terrifying in real life.

The cop took a seat to the left of the table and gestured for me to grab the opposite chair.

Claustrophobia was starting to kick in. My head was damp with sweat and the mugginess was stifling. The door cracked open and a tall, slender man stepped in.
He had the look of some military official, not a regular cop. His shirt was gray and sported a few unreadable logo patches. It reminded me a bit of service employees at the bases my dad had been stationed at. The man held aloft stuffed manila folders and a slight scent of mold seemed to follow him.

"This is chief inspector Walter Gilman." The pudgy cop drawled.

Walter spoke.

"Ryan, The man of the hour."

That did not sound good. The man sat down next to the cop and dropped the folders on the table.
"Quite the adventurer huh?"

Something about this guy was slightly repulsive. I couldn't nail it down, not that the alcohol from last night helped. But there was that smell and his skin looked waxy, like it was buried under a thick layer of makeup. Maybe the hangover was fucking with my vision.

The man opened the top folder and spread out a slew of pictures. They were all gruesome scenes. A ruptured concrete floor split open to reveal the decayed remnants of something once human. A few of the photos beside it looked like they were taken the night of the incident. All fresh gore and carnage. Only that was impossible.

"I don't understand? Are you accusing me of this?"

"Oh, we know you did it."

Oh shit. But if that was true, why had they waited this long? My mind raced, and my headache was getting worse. I had to think of some alibi. But all I could draw was a blank. The man leaned back and smiled.

"You know how long you were under the water? Thirty minutes. We counted."

I tried to scroll through my memory of the incident. That was impossible. I should have drowned if that was the case. But then again, maybe this was a good turn. If it all was retaliation in self-defense, and they knew it, then maybe there was a chance.

"You died. Well, that's not quite correct. It was the event that pushed you to the next stage. A half hour later, you emerged from the pool and massacred that man. But you don't remember any of this, do you?"

How did this guy know more than I did? I slumped back in my chair, the metal contours biting through my t-shirt. The blinding overhead light drowned out everything. Maybe that was on purpose. Part of their interrogation technique? I rubbed my eyes, but that only made things worse. My temples pounded, and I felt lightheaded. It all seemed a bit surreal. I couldn't shake this cotton in my head, or the chill that kept pulsating through me body. The man opposite me had a trace of an accent. German or eastern European I guessed. It made the whole scenario more surreal. Was this a dream?

"I don't...I don't understand..."

"Of course you don't."

"But am I in trouble..."

The man smirked. A bit of his makeup rubbed off onto his lip. It was barely noticeable, and I wondered if my eye were fooling me. Then I noticed his eyes. Maybe he was just wearing contacts, but they didn't seem to move quite right.

"Maybe this time."

The man grinned, emitting a weird, slurry cackle.

What had I taken last night? None of this seemed real.

"I hope you understand, we need to hold you a bit longer. It's really for your own safety as much as anything."

With that, the man scooped up the folders, rose from his seat, and strode out.

All is not as it seems

The inspector turned towards the adjacent room. Catching the closing door, the cop followed.

The inspector turned and muttered.
"You can go now."

"Excuse me?"

He turned and shot the cop an irritable look.

"You're not needed."

The cop sputtered.

"Look, I don't know who you think you are..."

Before he could muster more of a response, a man rose from the central desk and pulled the cop aside. Attired in the same odd uniform the inspector was wearing, he whispered in the cop's ear. The policeman turned bright red and wandered away.

Gesturing for the inspector to enter the neighboring room, the man muttered something as they entered. The rest of the conversation was an unintelligible series of mumbled words as they disappeared. Who were these guys? Hold me a bit longer? I'm not in trouble? My own good? What was going on?

Ryan

I rested my arms on the table. I still felt sick, and my arm was getting worse. Peeling back the sleeve of my hoodie, the cloth tore off clumps of yellow crust. Dried striations of it riddled the sleeve, The skin beneath was inflamed and spotted with pus filled bubbles. It looked like a severe case of poison ivy to me. The rash itched like hell, but I fought the urge to scratch.

The door creaked open and to my surprise, it was the chubby cop.

"Are you OK little man?"

The cop seemed to be harmless. Not that I'd had good experiences with the police, but this one seemed nicer than most. He did let me get one last smoke in before he took me away. Then again, this whole thing might just be a calculated trick. That whole good cop/bad cop thing. There was definitely something very strange going on here.

"Yeah. I guess. My arm hurts though. Do you have anything like Calamine lotion? I think I have poison ivy."

The cop looked genuinely disturbed.

"Aw man, that does look pretty bad."

Pulling a pair of nylon gloves out of his back pocket, he snapped them on and drew in closer.

"Here, let me take a look at that."

Cupping the bottom of my forearm, he pulled the skin tight and gently poked at the rash.

"Yeah, it looks pretty bad. Let me see what we have in the medicine closet."

Hand still holding my arm, the skin abruptly split open. I grimaced in pain as crusty pink flesh sundered apart to divulge a silvery under layer.

"What the fuck.."

A Little Accident

It was like a repeat of that long ago incident with the skinhead. As reality started to fade, I could feel the heat rising. In a nightmarish flash of images, scenes of tearing skin, flying entrails, and spinning coils of brain matter flitted through my consciousness. Then, all faded into blackness.

When I regained consciousness, I was splayed atop a table. Leather belts gripped my wrists and ankles, their sharp edges biting in. I was naked, freezing cold, and couldn't clear the fog in my head. I tried to move but was pinned. Something dug into the back of my skull and every time I tried to move pain shot through. Intense overhead light bleached out everything. Two blobs edged into view. As I blinked and tried to clear my vision, I could make out oddly shaped black facades that resembled overcomplicated gas masks. As they drew closer, I could see eyes underneath that had slits for pupils.

"Subject is ready."

The chimeras pulled away and a needle descended into view, its point growing more in focus as it descended. Panic washed over. I tried to scream but only hoarse gargles erupted. The syringe steadily closed in, its tip aimed at my forehead.

"Stop! I'm conscious!"

The needle rotated slightly and centered itself. Resuming its drop, it gently tapped my forehead, stopping just as it punctured my skin. The sharp tip scraped my skull. Something dropped down the length of the needle. As it impacted my forehead, I felt a multitude of sharp metal barbs dig in. Blood trickled into my eyes. I thrashed about, spurts of pain pulsing through my joints. The needle punctured my forehead and my body locked up. This was the worst pain I had ever experienced and I was frozen as it dug into me.

"Oh god, what is this? No Stop! Please...."

With a soft shucking noise, the needle burrowed in ever deeper.

"Oh my god! I can't take this! Please-it's too much!"

I mouthed the words, but nothing came out.

One of those things leaned over and slapped something gelatinous into my mouth.
I was choking and could barely breath. My eyes bulged out of their sockets as blood pooled in.

The syringe started to vibrate. I felt like my brain was being sucked out. Froth built up at the corners of my mouth.

Consciousness eluded me.

All is back to Normal

I felt good. I wasn't sure what it was, but that show must have gone well last night. Not that I could remember much. Maybe it was all the alcohol I'd consumed. Maybe it was the coke. You'd be surprised what these Ivy League types got up! Well, it was back to the grind. Growing up in Jersey, I always knew my parents expected me to work for the government.

They were pretty tolerant, and I didn't break too many rules. Just a little youthful steam letting before adulthood kicked in. They knew I wanted to be an artist but had talked me into getting an architecture degree as a backup.

Man had that worked out. Tomorrow, I had an interview with some guy from Northrop.

Hatch

Bobby Lisse

THE THING I LOVE ABOUT DINERS IS YOU CAN GET BREAKFAST OR A ROAST

"It's not an abortion."

Greg uses a single tine of his fork to tear at the thin membrane. The viscous deutoplasm surges across the plate. A sliver of bread drenches itself in the embryonic protein and ends up gnashed between Greg's coffee-stained teeth.

"They were never going to be little baby chicks. They breed them that way, ya know?"

Shelly grips her fork tightly with its stabbing end pointed to the sky. She's hesitant to poke the cobb salad in front of her. It looks delicious, with perfect grill marks on the chunks of chicken, flawlessly crisped bacon, and the freshest looking tomatoes, cucumbers, and lettuce.

"Why did you have to bring up baby chicks?"

"I said they WEREN'T going to be baby chicks."

"Please don't say baby chicks again."

"You don't want me to say cute…"

Greg stabs his sunny side up egg.

"…fluffy…"

He lifts the egg in the air, readying it for lift off.

"…yellow, little adorable fluff-ball"
The fork speeds down the runway.

"…baby chick!"

Greg violently shoves the egg into his mouth which makes the runny yolk splash across both cheeks. He looks like a toddler who has been given free reign of their meal; the soft puree splattered like a Pollock painting across their grill.

Shelly drops her fork.

"You're an asshole."

Greg chews with a devious grin.

"You're right, Shells." Greg concedes as he swallows the last of his food. "Baby chicks might be the cutest creatures on the planet. I mean, they're the Asian baby of the animal kingdom. There is nothing cuter than an Asian baby, except a baby chick. But you can rest assured…" Greg wipes the massacre from his face. "…these little guys in my stomach were never going to be baby chicks. I wouldn't eat eggs if they were."

Greg grabs Shelly's plate and slides it across the table to himself. "I'd eat the fuck out of their mother though."
He forks the succulent chicken and shoves it in his maw without dithering.

CAN YOU ACCOUNT FOR THIS GAP IN YOUR WORK HISTORY?

"The way Ignacio explained it to me is it's the same type of machine they use in shit processing plants to make it all flow smoothly. You put something solid in and it comes out all mashed up. It is like an unstoppable blender. So, look at it like that. If we do not send them little yellow balls through the macerator, we'll have a big clog. Production quotas don't allow for any clog, let alone big, yellow, furry, cute ones. You do not have to see them get smashed to bits either. Not today at least."

Enid cringed as Mark did a poor job of sugar coating the fate of the male chicks as their bodies would be turned into literal minced meat. To be used in pet food, mostly. Mark can smell the stomach acid traveling up her esophagus. He can tell a postscript is in order:

"Ok, think of it this way - at least you don't have to make a choice. If it is a male, he leaves the belt. You don't even have to lift their skirts until you've learned how to vent. Two stripes, it's a male. For all you know they're off to live a plush life on an all-male chick farm. Also, you get to go home with a dozen eggs every day if you want! That is a few hours pay right there. Just remember what I said…"

As Mark continued to talk Enid recalled the tour of the factory this morning. As she passed the section that housed the macerator, the sounds it emitted were something she couldn't describe. But it made her stomach instinctively clench. An ear trained for a diverse cacophony may place the sound alongside something like a Mike Smith blast beat or a dissonant tribal drum circle, but that was before the byproduct was making its way through the steel teeth. The chirps showed no awareness of the pending doom. Their sound did not alter; it was chirping and then crunching. A human might scream, even for a split second, as they were crushed mercilessly. The chicks had no such reaction. They entered the machine as innocently as they looked.

Enid's ears had begun ringing as Mark had finished his instruction. The sound of thousands of chicks was no longer just recall. Less than fifty feet away sat an industrial laundry bin filled with tiny live foul. They looked like a ton of loofahs. But loofahs don't chirp. She asked herself how she ended up here.

Enid never expected to be starting a new job this late in her life. In fact, the entire second act of her life had been unexpected. A pre-teen son built like a splintering match that can't be left alone sucked up more than half her weekly paycheck at her last job.

Eleven years she lived paycheck to paycheck with no raise in sight. Her salary sat under living wages with comfortable room for the corporation. She can still taste the day she was fired. All eleven years of regret washed around her mouth like a warm cup of salt water, burning every open sore. She wished she had never taken that gig but It's all she could get after being fired from her previous "career". That was the one job she thought she would have for the rest of her life.

The day she was fired from job one still stings like a divorce. She had considered that family her own after being in their house for so long. She started with the Samuels when she was just eighteen years old and had watched three of their children born wealthier than she could ever imagine. Their bank accounts were larger than her life's earnings before their umbilical cords were even cut. She always wondered whether the boys were birthed by a surrogate. There was a lack of connection that was evident between them and their mother; and she never seemed to show any normal signs of postpartum pain or discomfort. There was some sort of belly, but it never showed before seven or eight months along and it could never be considered much beyond bloat.

Biddy Samuel always took care of Enid during the holidays. A beautiful and luxurious basket of high-end products, everything from snacks to toiletries was a real treat and something Enid could not have bought for herself, but the thousand dollar bonus felt like she had won the lottery. It never lasted long between rent, taking care of Mama and of course a lavish night out on the town with her cousins. She wouldn't let Tatí or Sandra pay for a single drink and always brought them to the new "hot spot" in the city for dinner. Once a year Enid got to pretend, she was someone else. She lied to herself and with her shoulders forward and chin high had allowed her proximity to wealth and power to infect her brain for those eight hours. That one night a year she would change her last name to Samuel, at least in her own head.

Biddy always brought Enid back to earth quickly by letting her know just how charitable she had been with the bonus:

"It's important to take care of the little people, Ay-nid.", Biddy always pronounced her name with a manufactured accent. Enid could never figure out where the affectation came from as Biddy's normal, round the house, speaking voice lacked any discernible diction. She did of course put on a real "southern miss" dog and pony show whenever company was over. The Samuels were known to host expensive, pretentious parties where local politicians of all imagined hierarchies would rub elbows and make deals as if they ran the world. Nothing exciting ever happened at those parties. Nobody ever got too drunk or caused a scene. Enid would have known because her job was always to chase the boys around and make sure they weren't sneaking a sip of champagne or stabbing each other with the cocktail swords. The only thing that sticks out from those soirees was the time when the oldest boy, Stewart, broke into Mister Samuel's office. Enid went to reclaim him, and she found the boy frozen as a small cadre of guests feverishly dined on some special dish which the rest of the partygoers hadn't been privy to. Enid apologized for Stewart's interruption, but they never even acknowledged her presence. The light was warm and dim and their heads moved like a pack of lions gorging over a kill.

Then came Enid's turn at legacy building. She tried to hide it at first, unsure how the Samuels would react, but the morning sickness was completely unmanageable, and Enid was cursed with one of those screaming vomit voices. The type that announces spoiled food or inebriation to the entire house. She didn't try to conceal the pregnancy solely out of deception. It was because of an old wives' tale she had heard but she can't remember where. The way she recalls the myth is it was bad luck to talk about the baby before it was born. She didn't think someone of her means could risk letting go of any luck whatsoever. Even Enid's superstitions weren't her own.

Inevitably Enid's hesitance to disclose her "precarious ailment" as Biddy called it was well founded. Mrs. Samuel treated the news as if it were the ultimate betrayal. As if Enid had stepped in and tracked feces across the Persian carpet. There was no recourse for her firing, being an independent contractor; she was simply told that her "...services are no longer required.". Even if Enid knew it was illegal to fire someone for being pregnant, she was too meek to press the issue. "What are we to do, Ay-nid? Shall I have my children unsupervised for the next nine months while you take care of this little gaffe?". Biddy's callousness hurt but Enid could not argue with it. The Samuels were busy people, and she knew better than anyone that the boys were prone to bruises and bedlam.

"I'll make you one last offer." Biddy pointed her chin to the sky as she proffered. "I'm not even sure why I'm being this obliging. I will pay for this mess to go away. You may have three days to recover from this... course of action, but you must promise to never tell mister Samuel. He just wouldn't suffer that his hard-earned money supported the murder of a child. Regardless of how dire its life would turn out to be.".

For a moment Enid appreciated Mrs. Samuel's patience. She thought on it long enough to convoke a heel to stomp and arms to cross.

"Well?"

She couldn't. She wasn't sure why. She wasn't religious. She didn't have some entrenched stance; she just knew this was the one chance for her to do something that could make her life worthwhile. She was tired of being bland and alone.

She didn't even have to refuse. Biddy was a smart woman.

"Undoubtedly the father will take care of you then. Farewell Enid.". She dropped her contrivance as if she couldn't waste an ounce more of effort on her Nanny of ten years. Somehow that frail Woman could make even the most veiled and insincere sentence sound threatening, and those were the last words Biddy ever spoke to Enid.

NEW MOTHER

Mama was around those first six months. She could hardly get out of bed, but Enid appreciated having the moral support. She loved to listen to her mother talk about how difficult a pregnancy it was but how Enid was the most pleasant and easy baby. It made Enid hopeful that her baby was going to be spectacular. "You can't have something great without some hard work, right?". Mama always called her a "gift"", but Enid had trouble feeling like any type of prize, especially once Mama was gone.

Enid's water broke at Mama's wake. Her Mama's cousin - Tatí's mother Nina - was the only other person there, along with Mama's nurse. Tatí had claimed she had a "work thing" and couldn't get out of it but the whole family knew that Tatí's entire existence was upheld by her dope dealing boyfriend and she didn't work but fifteen to twenty hours a week at a car wash; ringing up customers while filing her nails and exchanging thick envelopes with enigmatic names like "Boston Tom" and "Lazy Eye".

The whole scenario made Enid happy that she no longer had the means to bring her cousins out for the yearly bonus party. Though it never stopped Tatí from making Enid feel bad about it.

"E, remember when you used to slave for that rich family? You really fucked that up, eh? What'd you do, suck the Daddy's dick? That old rich bitch catch you shining the golden rod?"

Enid didn't even bother to defend herself. In fact, Enid has never bothered to defend herself.

Mama technically died at the hospital, but she was gone before her body even left the front door. She had collapsed in the bathroom. It wasn't all that embarrassing. Mama's one wish towards the end was that she would go with "clean bottoms on", but that was a futile hope once her bowels let loose. At least she was wearing a muumuu to keep up some semblance of pride without the EMTs seeing her britches. Enid had begged Mama's nurse to drive her to the hospital, but the Nurse was adamant that no one but patients and Holy Cross personnel could ride in their vans. It was "...an insurance thing.". Enid had to take a bus, three buses to be exact. By the time she got there Mama was gone and Enid's belly was ready to burst.

It was the hemorrhage toolkit that had saved Enid's life. The Doctor said she should consider herself lucky and then referenced an outdated tv show that Enid was unfamiliar with, "You're all out of lifelines. Take the sixteen thousand and go home. Enjoy your baby boy.", but Enid wouldn't be able to take Carlo home for another month. She got to know her son through plexiglass and an oxygen hood. He made it. She could take comfort in that and the fact that she had an extra month to get his nursery ready. The apartment still stunk of Mama's death, but she did her best to cover it with frequent sprinkles of baby powder and baking soda.

The survivor's benefits weren't enough. She would have to find work. The best she could do was maintenance at a local venue. Six nights a week twenty-nine hundred people would pack into the theater in the round to see their favorite doo-wop group or a standup comic that had grown too large for clubs. She was never allowed to watch the performances, but from the break room they could hear the rumble of the bass or the echo of laughter.

Most nights it was a small crew. Gilbie and his girls. They would wait for the show to be over and then clean up the twenty-dollar plastic drinks and spilled popcorn. No one ever spoke to the girls. The boss would holler Gilbert's name and they would spring into action like little soldiers stabbing and grabbing the ephemeral junk.

She had heard stories, mostly from the other girls. Some of them didn't speak a word of English but she had learned enough Spanish from Maria the past bunch of years to figure what "violación" meant and "culo" was easy to figure. It wasn't until her last day on the job all the rumors proved to be pregnant with more than hyperbole.

Gilbert had gotten sloppy. He didn't even lock the door to the break room. The edge of the work bench splintered and cut across Enid's throat like a dull razor blade, causing painful abrasions. He grabbed her ponytail and pulled back so hard that her throat flapped open as if it were the skin of an apple being peeled. She tried to scream but it was as if he could feel her breath gathering the energy and every time, she was about to let the cry for help burst he would inflict some other demonic pain that kept her speechless, and her blood and tears flowing. She could feel his stamina waning. It will all be over soon, she thought. The door to the break room swung open. "Gilbert!". It was the boss. All five feet nothing of her. Her call was a lioness' roar. "What the fuck are you doing!?".

Enid sat on the curb. She could feel Gilbert dripping out of her as she rubbed her still bleeding neck. Some twenty yards away at the backstage door she could see the boss yelling at Gilbert but she couldn't hear any of it. She assumed he was being fired just like she had. His skin had become leather from sleeping outdoors with a belly full of cheap vodka but somehow his cheeks were still visibly red when he was scolded. He fiddled with a dirty rag like a child who twists their toes into the ground, refusing to make eye contact as they're admonished for some puerile faux pas. Gilbert wasn't fired that day. He was sent home, to the woods out back. Enid wasn't even fired by name. Her pink slip was the soreness that made the curb she was sitting on feel like it was paved with glass.

FIRST DAY ON THE JOB

She gathered at her workstation. It looked like a luggage carousel, only it was stuffed with live baby chickens. She had asked Mark why they didn't just use the males for their meat. His answer was less than satisfying and somewhere along the lines of "...that's not our department.", but one word stuck out to her, "puny ". The males would never get big enough to be worth their weight. It made her think of her son Carlo. No matter how much she put on his plate and how clean he left it he could just never seem to put on pounds.

She stared as a throng of chicks passed by her. She grabbed a single yellow chick.

"Hey, puta."

Enid knew that term of endearment well from her prior life. One she was still healing from. She looked towards the cold voice. A Latina woman in her forties with a hair net and blue apron held two chicks and pointed them at Enid as she spoke with her hands.

"Tonight, you won't sleep. Hell, the rest of the month you won't sleep. But you'll get used to it.". The mercy at the end of Tina's promise was short-lived. She tossed the two males into the hopper with a ruthless thud. Enid's stomach geysered as if the callous attitude of her coworker was like a mentos in soda. She covered a batch of chicks in brown, gravy like stomach bile.

"Oi, what did you eat, shit?". As disgusted as Tina sounded, she didn't even try to waft the stench of regurgitated breakfast away from her face. In fact, the smell hardly registered with her. Tina slammed her hand on a large red plunger attached to the machine and a loud buzz echoed through the factory floor, like grazing the sides of a leg bone in "Operation". The entire conveyor in front of them changed angle and all the chicks, regardless of sex, dumped into the "bad egg" hopper.

Enid wiped her mouth with her sleeve, clearing the remaining mucus from her lips. Unintelligible foreign languages clashed as supervisors yelled at shift leaders. Enid realized she was still holding a chick. The last survivor of her puke party. She checked the chick's down. Two stripes. It's a male.

Tina was yelling at Ignacio, whose belly hardly fit under his white lab coat. His hard hat sat so far forward on his head that it gave his profile the illusion of a beak. It was bright yellow as well, without a hint of dirt or blood on it. It bounced up and down as he quacked at Tina, animated with a clipboard swinging in his grip. Mark came over to calm them both down but instead drew the ire of both Tina and Ignacio, from which he quickly retreated in cowardice. Enid took advantage of the commotion and pocketed her survivor. She smiled, pleased with herself.

The conveyor belt started back up and Enid noticed the fight was over and Ignacio was inches from her face. "One Strike. Uno.", he said sternly as he held up three fingers. "No more.". He finished his confusing signals off with a throat cutting motion and then slammed his hand down on his clipboard, mimicking a macerator. It made Enid jump and her hand smacked her hip, bringing a chirp from the survivor. The sound of the machine drowned it out. She nodded her head subserviently, freeing herself from Ignacio's breath.

Tina joined back on the conveyor and shook her head in disapproval as they waited for a new batch of chicks. As soon as the first few came through Tina grabbed them and slung them at Enid. "Maybe you should have a light lunch.". Thud, thud, thud, thud was endless as the crew segregated the males.

Enid walked in the door of her apartment with surprising zeal. The fatigue of the day held long on her face, but her favorite part of the day was upon her. She put the carton of eggs on the small kitchen table with the chipping Formica and waited to hear the clumsy patter heading her way. Like coming home to an overexcited puppy, Carlo never failed to run at her and wrap his thin arms around her legs as tight as he could muster. This time, there was no welcoming party. It sent a panic through Enid. He should have been home from school for three hours at this point. Did Maria forget to pick him up? Did something happen to her, or worse to him? She stifled her overactive imagination to cry out, "Carlo!?". It didn't take long to settle her nerves. Carlo responded the moment his name left her mouth.

"Living room, Ma!". Enid rushed as quickly as she could and found Carlo on the couch, his legs propped up on the small ottoman with pillows between them and covered in white plaster.

"Carlo!". Enid dropped to the side of her son.
"What happened?".

"I fell." Carlo was smiling. A result of the painkillers. Behind Enid the toilet flushed. Maria exited the bathroom and dried her hands on her apron. She's only in her late fifties but had that perpetual matron look to her. The type you would see in Southern Living magazine or on some baking show from the nineteen nineties. "They said he bet another boy that he could fly. He climbed to the top of the monkey bars and jumped off.". Enid looked at Carlo, shocked at her son's behavior. "Carlo Euclid Alsted!". Carlo's smile signaled that his brain wouldn't be open for a debate on his faulty logic or grandstanding until the synthetic narcotic had worn off.

A tiny chirp reminded Enid of the gift she brought home. Her purse dismounted from her shoulder. "I brought you something from work." she said as she unlatched the buckle. Maria leaned in to see what it was. "Ay, Dios Mio!" Maria protested as she turned away in disgust. Enid palmed the survivor. He stood perfectly on her hand.

"Woah!!!" Carlo snatched the chick, rough. "Carlo, careful!". Enid recognized the irony of telling her son to treat the young bird compassionately.

"This is why I don't eat eggs." Maria paced, uncomfortable.

"You eat chicken though." Carlo barked at Maria, calling out her duplicitous consumption. "You eat more chicken than anyone I've ever seen.".

"Carlo!". Enid was surprised by her son's brashness. "I think it's time for you to sleep."

"Can he sleep with me, Ma?"

"Ay, you'll crush the poor thing!" "Maria held her face.

Enid grabbed a shoe box from a side table. She turned it upside down, emptying the contents. The Knick-knacks would stay out in the cold tonight. The Payless box would be reserved for members of the family.   "Chum! That's what I'm going to call him. He's, my Chum!"

Enid was pleased that her son's boyish demeanor was returning. She rubbed his head as he held Chum close and whispered secrets into his tiny beak.

HOW MANY EGGS CAN ONE FAMILY EAT?

It's been five months since Enid started her new job. Thankfully she had learned to hold the contents of her stomach down after the first month but the sour taste in her mouth never went away. Tina had lightened up a bit, but they had become anything but friends. Tina had done everything she could to get Enid fired at first, but Ignacio said filling the job would be impossible until college break. Tina let it go but still resented Enid's snail-like pace.

"Enid plucks male chicks from the belt at a rate that is hardly one tenth the speed of her co-workers. She drops them into the hopper as if they're in an eggshell and she's trying not to crack them."
Tina watches this and slams her pull harder and harder against the rim of the hopper. Each rattle of steel made the chicks squeak less and less as the impact steals the glory of the macerator. Enid refused to take notice, but she couldn't hide the wince each time she heard that sick thwomp and crunch.

Every bite Tina would take of her homemade empanada sounded like the broken back of her little fluffy kills. That day she sat directly across from Enid who was slurping on cold soup. There was no microwave in the break room, just a hot plate and Enid always brought lunch in a plastic container, leaving her little option other than cold or freezing cold.

"Do you want to see it?" Tina goaded Enid, as her tongue slapped in her mouth.

"See what?" Enid knew what.

Tina slammed her hand down on the table, mimicking the macerator, which made Enid spill her soup. Enid looked down into the remaining broth and slurped.

"I don't think I'm ready and Mark said I would have to…"

"I can show it to you. I'm a shift leader." Tina lifted her brow in a display of authority that had never intimated anyone except Enid at that very moment.

Enid declined the invitation as her nose almost touched the frigid liquid.

Back at the belt Tina kept a close eye on Enid, who continued her soft handling of the doomed foul. Tina abandoned her display of dominance over a creature that can't help itself and began softly, but swiftly placing the male chicks in the hopper. Enid sensed the energy change and looked up, locking eyes with Tina. Tina very deliberately placed a single male chick in the hopper as gently as she possibly could. She did so with a face that seemed to concede some humanity or mercy. Enid grinned with delight. Maybe she had cracked Tina's hard exterior?

Quitting time had come and Enid watched Tina from a couple of lockers over, removing her apron to reveal a well-worn sweater with a nondescript college screen printed on it. The type you see sticking out of donation bins. It breeds a kinship that Enid misread. She approached Tina with an olive branch.

"What does it do, exactly?"

Tina unfurled her long black hair from the hair net. She made quick work of her bun as she checked the game she had snared in her trap.

"Mark didn't tell you?"

"Not in any way that makes sense."

Tina shut her locker. "Come in fifteen early tomorrow." Tina grabbed her purse and walked away.
"OK." Enid hollered, making sure Tina heard her as she vamoosed.

"And don't eat breakfast." Tina said without a pause in her departure.

On the way out Enid grabbed another carton of eggs.

The Macerator

The sound was completely metal. It didn't have the rhythm of a car engine. It was too violent to sound like a washing machine. It sounded like a train at full steam without that soothing hiss, beating down the track in a motion that couldn't be stopped and would destroy everything but air. When Tina turned it on, she smiled like a man in mid-life crisis showing off his new Harley. Tina didn't bother trying to talk to Enid. They both had aviation earmuffs. Tina pointed to the machine, urging Enid closer. She pointed down with one finger and back at her eyes with two.

Enid stepped close and looked in. The metal prongs took each other's place with exceptional speed and the elegance of a synchronized dance, but there was never space for anything but metal and air. Whatever found its way into those hellish teeth would have no wiggle room. It was a paper shredder that would not jam.

A bout of vertigo rose up the back of Enid's neck and she pulled back from the destructive force. Tina was all smiles. She smacked her hands together hard enough for Enid to feel the plume of air on her face. Tina snapped her thumb and middle finger together to animate the speed at which the whole murder would happen.

The sound of chicks chirping had joined the symphony. Enid's head had begun to spin. She looked down into her hand and saw Chum resting on her palm, chirping playfully. The Macerator called for its meal. Enid could feel the sweat pour down her face. Her vision had tunneled. As she looked up, she was at the conveyor belt. Tina was talking to her, but she couldn't hear a word she said. Enid fell backwards and before she could hit the ground everything had gone black. Her last conscious thought was "Please don't let me fall into that hell.".

Complications

The next time Enid's eyes were open Biddy Samuel stood over her.

"Now what will you do Ay-nid? You rebuffed my generous offer and now look at you."

Biddy eyed the length of Enid, three quarters of her body covered by blankets, and made her assessment.

"You're nothing now but a cut of meat."

Enid awoke from the dream covered in sweat. She felt relieved that she hadn't fallen into metal death, otherwise she wouldn't have woken up, would she? No one, nothing could survive that. Her back itched from the beginning of bed sores. Carlo's cast legs were propped up alongside her left arm. The boy was jamming his fingers at a handheld video game. Maria was sitting with her purse clenched tightly in her sleeping grip. Her mouth was a bucket collecting rainwater.

The Nurse had come in and spewed out too much information for Enid to ingest so shortly after waking up. Enid did focus in on one word, but she thought she must have misheard the Nurse. Surely, she hadn't heard her say she's pregnant. Was she telling Enid SHE is pregnant? Why would a stranger share that type of information so up front?

"I'll write you a note to take it easy at work, but you're going to have to schedule your first gyno appointment. You're already over sixteen weeks. Lucky you, you must have some good genes cause you're not showing at all."

Her ponytail swung back and forth as she bopped out of the room. Enid's head began to spin again. She looked down at the IV in the top of her hand. A bracelet on her wrist read 'Fall Risk' in large bold font. Enid's eyes closed again.

The bell rang signaling a batch of chicks on their way to be sorted. Enid sighed, trying to close off her lungs to the wretched air of murderous selections she was about to make. Tina stretched like an athlete. She interlocked her fingers and turned them palm forward, bending her knuckles back and cracking them. The pops made Enid cringe thinking of those little fluffy bodies being smashed to death. The conveyor belt seemed to be moving at an increased pace today, but Enid couldn't understand why there was no product to sort. Then she heard the clunking. As if something errant was falling down the belt, out of sight, banging against the steel shute. Finally, the cause of the ruckus had arrived. Carlo landed on his back with his skinny, bowed legs stuck out like puny popsicle sticks from a ridiculous chicken. He had landed right in front of Tina who had no expression of surprise or confusion. She grabbed Carlo by the scruff and tossed him in the hopper. Enid couldn't find breath to scream, and her legs could not compete with a lack of traction. It was as if she was standing on ice. She lurched forward, her hand stretched out as far as possible, but the belt was moving so fast there was no chance for her to save her feeble little chick. She tried to scream for Tina, but the sound of the Macerator had drowned out any possibility of communication. Carlo's chirps crescendoed until they fell in unison with the rolling hammer sound of steel obliteration.

The lunch bell rang. The belt ceased action. Tina removed her hair net and retired without so much as glancing at Enid. She could feel the sadness in every nerve, but she felt no water and heard no sobs. Everything else had stopped except the Macerator. The calamitous pirouette seemed to be getting closer. A monster approaching. The clang entered Enid and grew from her belly up. Her throat shook and her vision blurred. She tried to scream to release the pain of the rattle but her open mouth only made it louder and more agonizing. Her teeth fell away like the edge of an unstable dune as the steel tusks of the death machine embowed her like a human banana peel.

Enid stared at the drop ceiling. Its simplicity brought her solace and allowed her brain to find itself abdicated of her grisly factory shift. She was still in a hospital bed and for that moment that was comforting. Carlo and Maria were gone. The only bedfellow was the beeping and pumping of machines that she was somehow, or another attached to. The euphony of their life sustaining mission was far too evocative of the Macerator's cacophony. Enid felt her heart quicken. She held her chest as if she was consoling a crying child, hoping it would quiet its racket. Between her legs she felt a pop, like a sack bursting and then the gush of warm liquid rushed through her inner thighs. In that instant Enid believed what the nurse had said and panic set in. She knew she would bleed out if she didn't get help. She looked around the foreign room and found the Nurse's call button next to her head. She pressed the button over and over like an impatient pedestrian.

The Nurse walked in casually and Enid did not recognize her. Her hair was down, her skin was darker, her whole build much leaner.

"What is it, sugar?"

"I'm bleeding." Enid squeezed the words through tears. Her throat had locked up. She pointed to her lower half. The Nurse grabbed the covers and pulled them back so quickly that a spray of liquid geysered over her head, narrowly missing her face.

"Oh, your foley line came out. Don't worry doll, it happens. Let me go get some help and we'll get you cleaned up."

The nurse left the covers pulled back keeping Enid's mess on display. Enid mustered the gall to look at it and the color was not what she had expected. Her clinical, white sheets were sopping yellow. The catheter line was actively dripping out at a slow pace. There was no blood.

Bed Rest

Enid rotated her 'spot' weekly. She didn't want to wear out any one seat or get any type of chronic indentation. Plus, the left side of the couch became exciting to her after spending a week in the middle. There was nowhere for her to lean her arms in the middle, so Carlo had built her a throne of pillows, emptying the beds of all their head rests to accommodate his Mother's comfort needs.

While Carlo was at school Maria would stop by occasionally to check on Enid, but her visits had grown fewer and less common. Enid didn't need much. She ate sparingly, showered infrequently, and found herself an expert on a number of daytime television shows.

There was a knock at the door. It was hesitant or dainty, she couldn't tell which, but it was light enough for her to not trust her own perception, so she waited for another round to pull herself from the left side of the couch and answer.

Behind the door was a Woman with long black hair and auburn highlights. A fresh hair style that could have been a wig. If Enid's attention hadn't gone straight to the large basket in the Woman's hands, she would have recognized her sooner. Enid couldn't believe it. How had Biddy Samuel known? Why, after all this time would she send a basket? All at once a wave of warmth washed over Enid as she felt the faux familial connection, she believed she had established with people that were not her own, grabbing roots again.

"Hey Enid."

"Yes!" Enid could not hide her giddiness.

"You look… good. Healthy. You've put on some weight."

Enid was confused by the courier's comments. She took no offense. How could this woman know one way or another if she had gained…

"Tina!?" It had been almost four months since Enid left the factory. Since even Enid didn't know she was pregnant and never disclosed it to the company they found it to be an acceptable loophole to terminate her. Corporate policy also mandated any worker's comp claim denied and challenged. It would be too long to matter before Enid got any type of financial aid due to her.

"Hey. I, we just wanted to bring you something to help, ya know? It was messed up that they fought your disability and… anyway. Here." Tina pushed the basket towards Enid who took it like a kid unwrapping clothes on Christmas.

"I thought. Um, I just… Thank you." Enid was stunned. The emotions betrayed her. She was alone in the world again. A single mother with no family. She turned to place the basket on the small kitchen table. As she did, Tina noticed the reason for Enid's apparent weight gain.

"Oh shit. I'm so sorry. I didn't realize you were knocked up. I guess I should have." Tina's yielding was anything but merciful. She meant it as an empty apology for thinking of Enid as a bad employee.

"It's OK. You couldn't have known. I didn't know."

"Damn, I didn't know you get down like that."

Enid could not hide the embarrassment of Tina thinking she was a "loose woman".

"I don't. I mean, I just thought I was too old. You know?"

"My Auntie got a bun in the oven when she was fifty! Oi, let me tell you, you think it's hard for your body to pull back together in your thirties? When she sits down it's like a pancake. I told my husband if I get pregnant at that age just take me out back and shoot me."

Enid found no succor in Tina's words. Tina noticed.

"But you'll be fine. You're still young." The pause in Tina's cadence gave away her lie. "Well, enjoy the basket. Everyone put something in there, even Ignacio."

Enid looked back at the basket.

"Eggs, of course." Tina concedes. "If you need anything, um, just ya know, reach out."

The pleasantries danced in unison with discomfort. Tina turned away, not knowing what else to say. Halfway down the hall she heard Enid call out her name. Her voice had need and worry attached to it. Tina stopped and walked back to the still open door. Enid stood, legs apart, holding her belly. The floor was covered in amniotic fluid.

"Ay, dios mío." Tina never expected Enid to take her up on the offer.

Begotten

There was too much said and done for Enid to have understood exactly what was happening. "No time…" was what she heard most. Her vision was a constant blurred vignette. Doctors and Nurses in scrubs rushed around her. Once they wheeled her into the operating room her arms had been secured to metal planks. She was the crucified mother. The air that circulated through was cold and biting. The Nurses raised a curtain below Enid's breasts and blocked her view of whatever was going on below. She had a natural birth with Carlo, so all of this was foreign to her.

"You're going to feel some pressure." The voice came from the other side of the curtain and Enid couldn't be sure they were speaking to her. The pressure was intense and drew tears from eyes which she could not wipe because her arms were still restrained. She could smell flesh burning. She looked below the curtain where all she could see was ankles and clogs, the favorite footwear of hospital workers.

While Enid watched the feet shuffle and replace each other's positions a huge puddle of blood splashed on the floor. Not a single voice on the other side of the curtain reacted with any concern, but Enid could not help her panic. She knew it was her blood. She knew it could not be normal. Something was wrong.

"OK, here comes baby."

Enid felt relief physically as the pressure slid out of the incision. She waited for the cry of life but sometimes it takes a few moments for the newborn to wail.

"It's a boy!" The Doctor called out. The next thing Enid heard was urgency.

"She's hemorrhaging."

The beeping of the machines Enid was hooked up to sounded like the chirps of a bin full of chicks ready for the Macerator and it brought mortal dread to Enid as she realized what that meant for her son.

"No! No!" Enid began to scream but the anesthesiologist dosed her with morphine that made her feel like she was falling.

The Lion's Den

The next moments of Enid's consciousness were in transit. She was wheeled out of the operating room and transferred to a different stretcher. Lights and ceiling panels passed at too quick of a pace. The stretcher then barreled through a set of double doors and into a room that was much darker than the hallway. A room Enid found familiar. Gone were the drop ceiling panels and diffused fluorescent lights. The popcorn ceiling had warm lighting that cascaded out across shelves of books. The stretcher had stopped, and two male Nurses transferred her onto a flat, solid bed. Enid felt nauseous from the drugs and blood loss. She didn't know how many conscious moments she had left.

Enid thought to herself she must be dreaming. Biddy Samuel was standing over Enid, which she knew was impossible. She wished this old haunt would stop. It had been so long since she had seen them, why would the family she never had invade her mind now? There she was, though, standing over Enid with a smile. She tucked a fancy cloth napkin into her collar and bent over Enid as if she was inspecting something of importance.

"Quite the cut, is she not? This one will bear no more."

Enid closed her eyes, wishing to wake from the nightmare, but she could still hear Biddy's voice.

"They say you can taste the anguish of a beast's life in its meat. I always preferred the taste of sorrow."

A collective laughter scared Enid's eyes open. Standing around her were faces she'd seen a lifetime ago. Their teeth were sharpened and needful. Enid knew where she was.

Wires

Marc Schoenbach

In twenty-three years of working homicide, Detective Moretti had never seen somebody in such bad shape that wasn't already dead on the slab.

The girl on the bed stared catatonically at the hospital ceiling, her eyes frozen with a look of unimaginable horror. Her mouth was agape, but no sound emanated from her dry lips.

The detective could tell that the young blonde was once beautiful. But now her frizzy hair did little to cover the countless caterpillar stitches and bruises that marred her swollen face like the stall door of a gas station restroom.

Thick bloodstained gauze bandages wrapped most of her arms, leaving only a slight space in the bend of her elbow. From that crook, a steady flow of maroon coursed through plastic IV tubing where it led to a bag of blood hanging from a metal pole.

All but two of her fingers had been wedged into aluminum splints. A hard cast secured her right leg, while a mound of dressing hugged the short nub of what used to be her left leg.

The lingering stench of antiseptic stung Moretti's nostrils as he took a sip of lukewarm coffee from a Styrofoam cup. It was around nine o'clock on Christmas Eve when the detective received the phone call from the hospital.

"Is this Detective Moretti?" the voice on the phone said.

Moretti had been working on his second glass of bourbon in his one bedroom apartment—spending the otherwise meaningless holiday alone—when he coughed into the phone receiver, "Did I win something?" The conversation with Doctor Gladwell was brief and to the point. "The mangled girl you guys found on the road three days ago has just opened her eyes. She isn't talking, but you should be here."

Moretti gulped down the rest of his bourbon before throwing on his olive-green trench coat with the collar drawn up. His bushy auburn mustache barely distracted from his horrible comb-over, but at this point in his life vanity was the last thing on the detective's mind as he floored his 1981 Dodge Diplomat on the snow-slickened road. He arrived at the hospital in just under nine minutes.

The detective had been standing at the catatonic girl's bedside for almost an hour. Nausea and anger splashed around in his belly like a poisonous concoction. No matter how hard he tried, he could not ignore the jarring similarities of his own eight-year-old daughter being hooked up to those same goddamn tubes and wires. It was fifteen years ago when he'd been looking into his little girl's eyes, knowing her battle was coming to an end. He held her hand until her last breath, promising that he would catch the bastard who did this to her.

But vengeance never came and the sick fuck who'd raped and stabbed his little angel in the neck with a broken beer bottle ended up hanging himself in his own closet.

He tried to be strong for Sarah, desperate to convince her that bad things just happened—that life didn't make sense, that it wasn't supposed to, but that everything happened for a reason.

"And just what the hell would be the reason for some random psychopath to have kidnapped and butchered our little baby?" His wife's final words replayed in his brain like a tired song at a dingy dive bar.

Moretti was just a rookie when Sarah packed her suitcase and his naïve idea that justice would always somehow triumph over evil faded quicker than the air from his dying daughter's lungs.

Back at the catatonic girl's bedside, Moretti's throat began to tighten when suddenly a wave of horror flashed across the girl's eyes. Her body jolted upright from the bed. Flailing her arms, she screamed, "I don't know who you are!"
Then, as quickly as it all happened, she fell back against her pillow in silence.

"What just happened there?" Moretti asked. "Who don't you know?" But the girl did not respond.

Moretti inhaled deeply. "My name is Detective Moretti." He gestured behind him with a steel click pen. "And this here is my partner, Detective Ross."

A second man loomed behind Moretti. He too had a mustache, although it was black and much thinner despite his thick curly hair. He was wearing a dull brown suit and navy-blue tie. He held a grey cassette recorder with a small microphone attached to it.

"We should officially get started," Detective Ross said into the microphone. "It's Sunday, December twenty-fourth, nineteen eighty-nine. The time is approximately ten-thirty p.m. We're here at Charity Grove Medical Center—"

"Detectives," a warm nurturing female voice beckoned from the other side of the bed.

Nurse Wendy, a middle-aged African-American woman, stood in front of a small Christmas tree on the ledge of a curtained window. Its string of colored lights bathed her white uniform in a warm glow.

"Maybe start out slow. I'd hate to see you two frighten her." The nurse adjusted her cap.

"I don't think we're the ones frightening her," Ross said.

Just then Doctor Gladwell rushed in from the hallway. "It's okay, Wendy. They're here to help," he said, tugging on the lapels of his white lab coat.

Moretti shook his head with displeasure. "You were in a coma for the past three days. Are you able to tell me your name?"

A tear ran down the young girl's cheek as her cracked lips parted, leaving a trickle of blood dripping down her chin. Her strained voice sounded like wet rusty nails. "No."

Wendy quickly tended to the girl, rubbing a thin layer of Vaseline on her bloodied lips.

"What's the last thing you remember?" Moretti asked.

The young girl just stared at the detectives.

"Look, honey," Ross chimed in. "There's a madman on the loose—"

"Can you remember anything at all?" Moretti continued.

"What happened to my leg?" the girl groaned.

Moretti turned to Doctor Gladwell. The white-haired doctor leaned forward. "You've had multiple lacerations and fractures. We tried everything we could to save your left leg but the hypothermia was too severe. You've lost a substantial amount of blood, to which we're giving you a transfusion as we speak. But as serious as your condition is I assure you, we're going to do everything we can to make sure you make a full recovery."

The doctor began to walk away but stopped at the room's door. "Detectives, I'm giving you ten minutes. But I don't think you're going to learn anything new tonight." Then he disappeared into the hallway.

Moretti was more than eager to accept the challenge. He cleared his throat and clicked his pen. "Now I know you can do this. A moment ago, you jumped up from that bed and screamed that you didn't know someone. Who don't you know?"

The girl shook her head. But Moretti was determined. "Where were you?"

"I don't know," the girl stammered. "I had my arms outstretched over my head. It was dark. And it was cold."

"Three nights ago, a trucker found you lying in the middle of Platte Clove Road," Moretti said.

"Said it looked like you got torn apart by a grizzly bear," Ross added. "But the doctors here say an animal didn't do this to you." Just then Moretti wanted to shout, *"Whoever did this to her most certainly was a goddamned animal!"* Instead he took a sip of coffee, pinched the wetness from his mustache, and said, "By the time they got you outta there, you had lost almost four liters of blood. Any idea who might have done this to you?"

The girl shook her head.

"They found four hook and eye bolts screwed into both of your shoulders," Moretti was reading from his notepad. "They removed eleven screws from your arms and legs. Looked like maybe piano wire or something was used to bind you."

"Was it more than one person? Did you get a good look at any of their faces?" Ross shook the microphone.

"We were able to follow your track marks in the snow for about a mile. I got my guys combing the area like fleas on a stray mongrel, but we're coming up short." Moretti ran his fingers through his thinning hair.

"Were you sexually assaulted?" Ross asked.

"Look, she can't remember anything." Nurse Wendy adjusted her skirt in frustration.

Moretti waved the nurse away with his pen. "Look, I know it's hard. But I need you to try to remember. Because if you don't, I'm afraid a lot of other girls are going to end up—"

"Okay, that's enough!" Wendy pulled off her nurse's cap and slapped the back of her own hand with it. "You two should be ashamed of yourselves."

"Maybe you better step outside," Ross shook an empty Styrofoam cup at the nurse. "I can use a fresh one."

"I'll take a refill too. Black, four sugars." Moretti rubbed his brow, his head beginning to throb.

Suddenly the girl turned towards the window and stared at the Christmas tree lights.

Wendy scurried to the bed. "Lord have mercy, hasn't this poor girl been through enough?" She reached up and grabbed the green privacy curtain, her knuckles tensing. She began sliding the curtain across the tracks when the girl lifted her head from her pillow.

"I was hiking," she said. "And that's when he grabbed me."

*   *   *

Hank Lee Gaskins' heart swelled with the Yuletide spirit as he sat at the head of the long mahogany table. Dressed in his grey wool suit with suede elbow pads, he gazed at his seven family members gathered around the magnificent Christmas Eve feast.

The private dining room epitomized elegance with its gold and red Victorian wallpaper. The floral damask pattern crawled up the walls toward a stunning chandelier—one with crystal teardrop pendants that hung from a ten-foot ceiling.

The Lenox China dinnerware—engraved with illustrations of hollies and red ribbon—caught the brilliant reflection of the flickering green candlesticks that were at either end of the table. The polished silverware twinkled while the crystal glasses gleamed under the chandelier's warm ambience.

But the meal itself was the real showstopper.

The glazed turkey glistened in succulent juices with sprigs of fragrant evergreens as garnish. Steam rose like playful children from porcelain dishes of candied yams, mashed potatoes, cranberry stuffing, and steamed vegetables shimmering with butter. Mounds of freshly baked loaves of bread were nestled in a wicker basket swathed in white linen. An array of cheese and fig jams sat on an ornate silver tray.

From an adjoining archway that led into a cozy living room glowing by the flickering light of a crackling fireplace, Hank's six-monthold daughter was being soothed in her bassinet by Nat King Cole's warm caramel voice oozing from a record player.

Hank turned to his wife Heather to the right of him and was instantly spellbound by her beauty.

Her auburn hair was done up in a round bouffant and her makeup hadn't looked this wonderful since their wedding night. Her green polka dot cocktail dress hugged her hourglass figure just right.

She took a bite of turkey, trying her best not to smear her red lipstick. Feeling Hank's gaze, she covered her mouth with her palm. "Is something the matter?" she asked.

"Nothing can ever be the matter as long as I have my loving family with me." Hank's chest grew warm. He could feel his throat swell with joy.

"Good," Heather said, wiping the corners of her lips with a green cloth napkin. "But you don't have to gawk at me for so long. I'm not going anywhere."

God, if only that were true, Hank thought. He knew Heather was only being sweet, that it was in her nature to say such things. But to promise that she would always be there felt as fragile as the porcelain dishes at the table.

Hank's heart began to ache. He calmed himself by observing the rest of his family.

To his left was Brandon, his sixteen-year-old son, who, despite his awkward lanky body and shaggy hair, was adored by all the girls at Hudson High. Hank was proud to say that his son's love life never interfered with his grades and when the time came, the boy could go to any Ivy League school he chose.

"I sure am going to miss these home cooked meals when I graduate." Brandon shoved a heap of mashed potatoes into his mouth.

"I would hope you'd come and visit for the holidays," Heather sneered at the boy.

Next to his son, Hank's twin eight-year-old daughters, Brianna and Bellamy—dressed in matching lavender Peter Pan dresses—were running their tiny fingers across the velvet tablecloth, watching the red fabric morph into a lighter shade of pink.

"It's like magic," the girls giggled in unison, flashing their adorable toothless smiles.

Across from the twins were Heather's youngest sister Sheila, and her husband, Roman, who was being a great sport about not smoking his briar pipe at the table. The couple had been drinking enough merlot that Roman's tired jokes and inane puns seemed as fresh as the juicy turkey they'd been devouring.

"I don't suppose you two little cuties heard about the forecast for tomorrow?" Roman tilted a glass of wine to his lips.

The twins shook their heads.

"They're calling for rain, dear!" Roman tried to keep a straight face, but when Sheila gently punched him in the shoulder, he lost it.

Hank's brother-in-law barked like a seal and soon the entire table succumbed to the absurdity. A cacophony of laughter filled the dining room.

Hank wanted to laugh. But a force he did not fully understand began to stir in him, as it often did whenever he felt great moments of joy.

The dreadful feeling of guilt coursed through his blood like an infectious disease.

The disease of *Loneliness*.

The word itself felt like a force eternally looming over his shoulder. Like Death itself, its sickle of isolation poised to strike at any moment, screaming, *"Hank, you do not deserve to be happy!"*

Hank stared at the sliced turkey on his plate. But he could not rid his mind of the intrusive thoughts.

The *darkness*. The *isolation*.

His windpipe began to constrict, and his heart rattled behind his ribcage.

He remembered how she made him feel. His own goddamn mother. So unloving, so cruel.

His knuckles went white as he gripped the tablecloth, the memories of his childhood crushing him like a falling boulder.

She locked him in that godforsaken cellar for weeks at a time with not even a stale crumb to nibble on. His stomach howled in agony in the cold, damp darkness as the spiders and cockroaches crawled over his naked body.

And so, he ate the little critters, their wiry legs tickling his dry lips as their thoraxes slid down his throat, suppressing his hunger at last.

But that wasn't the worst part.

The creeping, impending isolation somehow tortured him more than all the beatings, the burnings, the humiliations, the eating of those filthy insects. Because when he was alone in that awful dungeon, he was allowed to think, and his own thoughts could drive him to madness.

But then one night he discovered *Herman.*

The pitiful wooden marionette puppet had been discarded in the corner behind a stack of old detective magazines years ago, its face covered in strands of cobwebs and dust.

Hank held up the puppet, rank with dampness and rot. It didn't take long to untangle the brittle strings and figure out how to work its arms and legs. Soon, Hank was making Herman walk, talk, jump, and dance until he and his new friend fell asleep laughing.

As long as he had Herman, Hank knew that he would never again feel The Reaper's blade of loneliness pressed against his throat.   That was until his mother found the thing and threw it into the fireplace. *"No son of mine is going to be playing with dolls,"* she cackled as Herman's body curled up like a matchstick.

The clink of Hank's trembling fork against his plate shook him back to the present. He gasped for air.

"Hank!" Heather grabbed her husband's wrist. "You're turning blue!"

Hank was huffing and puffing like a steam engine, his brow beaded with sweat. "It's fine—I'm fine." Hank wiped his brow, his breathing stabilizing. "It's just that I love you all so much. And when I start to think about it, I get overwhelmed with such joy that it's hard to breathe."

"Well, good. But you've hardly eaten a thing," Heather said.

Hank saw his family smiling at him with tender eyes. "I'm just so happy you're all here to celebrate this lovely Christmas Eve with me. I love you all."

"We love you too, Dad," Brendan smirked, a mouthful of buttered bread in his mouth.

Brianna and Bellamy flashed their toothless grins and cheered, "We love you, Daddy!"

Roman was quick to hoist up his wine glass. "I'll drink to that!" to which Sheila joked, "You'd drink to anything." Then her face straightened, and she nodded at her brother-in-law. "But seriously, we love you, Hank." *"But we're not all here are we, Hank?"* A familiar voice like muddy gravel echoed from the opposite end of the table.

Hank's eyes widened at the sight of his eighty-four-year-old mother seated directly across from him, her ashen grey wasp nest hair glowing underneath the chandelier.

"Mother?" Hank's jaw went slack. Had his mother been there the whole time?

With a gnarled boney finger Mrs. Gaskins pointed to an empty chair next to her. An undisturbed place setting sat in front it.

"Your *other* daughter should be here," the old woman croaked. "Where is she, Hank?"

*   *   *

The snow crunching underneath the SWAT team officers' boots echoed in the stillness of night to the tune of stampeding bulls over a pile of crushed bones.

The officers scavenged the woods donned in their tactical gear and helmets. Curved ice axes hung from their belts as their assault weapons mounted with flashlights sliced through the dense forest, casting long ghastly shadows across the frozen ground.

Detective Moretti lumbered twenty feet in tow, a cigarette nub dangling from his cracked lips. He was a city cop, and his awkward, burly body had no business for this kind of terrain.

The cold wind snuck through his trench coat, making his lungs feel like they'd been stabbed by a hot butcher's blade. A mixture of smoke and moist breath poured from his mouth like a boiling teakettle. And though the lactic acid was searing his quadriceps to a mushy pulp, Moretti was determined to catch this sick sonovabitch, even if it killed him.

For the past two hours, the team from Grove County had been trekking through the dangerous icy terrain of *Devil's Kitchen*—a bastardized region of Saugerties, New York—in search of *"rows of gigantic white monster fangs that protruded from a mountain."*

It wasn't much help, Moretti realized, but it was the only landmark the girl from the hospital could remember.

"Remind me again why we couldn't just get the choppers out here." Detective Ross stomped at Moretti's side, a pair of tinted amber snow goggles shielding his eyes from the cold wind.

"It isn't enough I have to hear this shit from Rambo up there, now I gotta hear it from you too?" Moretti motioned with a gloved hand to Commander Dempsey, the man in charge of the SWAT team. The yellowhaired Irish commander had been busting Moretti's balls the minute he'd been told the two detectives would be accompanying the special tactics team on the hunt. *"I don't care how brutal this hike is gonna be,"* Moretti had shouted into the commander's face at headquarters after receiving the expedited search warrant from a weary judge. *"I want to be there to see the look on his goddamn face when we nail him!"*

Moretti hawked a wad of phlegm onto the ground and was surprised to see that bits of his lungs hadn't come up with it. He turned to Ross. "Besides, this guy hears choppers and he's running; it'd take weeks for us to find this creep in these fucking woods."

Under normal circumstances, Saugerties was a beautiful region of the Catskill Mountains, just over a hundred miles north of the city. With sprawling hills of pine and maple, and gullies etched into the earth by running waters, it was the kind of place you took your family in the fall to watch the leaves change color. A perfect vacation spot with your spouse for a relaxing afternoon of wine tasting.

But the upstate woods had trails less travelled. And tonight, under the asylum of a moonless winter sky, Devil's Kitchen was living up to its name. A frozen hellish abyss where black trees guarded the forest like menacing sentinels. Where razor sharp boulders tore flesh from bones. Where one careless step on slippery pine needles could send you over a cliff, plummeting you to your death.

"How many hikers have gone missing here?" Ross asked as he slid on a patch of pine needles.

"A lot," Moretti grumbled. While he wasn't entirely familiar with the area, he'd heard countless stories about hikers who vanished. It had been assumed they had all fallen, their bodies lost and decomposing in the vast woods. But that didn't stop the detective's mind from wondering back to a story his grandfather once told him about *The Kitchen*.

Moretti was just a kid when he heard about the horned creature that slaughtered hunters and lost hikers.

Legend had it that the abysmal creature climbed high in the trees looking for anyone unwise enough to get too close to the cliffs. Without warning, it'd leap off branches, revealing its awful hairy body—all eight feet of it—before hurling its victims over the edge. The foul thing would then scale down the mountain where its disfigured meal awaited. Locals claimed that if the creature pushed you off the cliff, you'd better pray you died on impact, for there was no sound quite as horrifying as the screaming from being eaten alive by the Devil himself.

Even as a frightened child, Moretti swore to his grandfather that when he got older, he'd catch and kill the damned Devil once and for all. But that was a long time ago. And Moretti knew his grandfather's monster was just folklore.

The thing that Moretti and his team were hunting tonight, however, was no fairytale.

He was as real as the trees and frozen snow. A man—if you could call him that—whose soul had been scorched black as coal. And just like the lunatic who had taken his little girl from him all those years ago, there could be no redemption for such a vile being. The only cure was to either lock him up and melt the key or snuff out the bastard entirely with a barrage of hot lead.

"The next thing I knew, he had my arms outstretched over my head..." Moretti remembered the one-legged girl from the hospital sobbing, *"...and that's when he pulled out the power drill and a spool of wire."*

The thought sent a chill up Moretti's back, and for the first time since the long dreadful hike began, he felt the Devil's presence in The Kitchen. *"I begged him to stop—that I just wanted to go home—but he kept telling me this was my home now."*

The pain in Moretti's legs slithered up his lower spine like a snake made of razor wire. He winced, but he knew he could not stop moving. That poor girl didn't stop even when she was gushing blood from all her limbs. His own daughter's smiling face flashed in his mind once more.

"This son of a bitch is going to pay," Moretti rasped, his throat dry as a desert.

"I wasn't the only one... There were others he kidnapped... He drills holes into them," the girl's voice howled in Moretti's brain like the artic wind. *"Then he takes the wires..."*

"Halt!" Commander Dempsey shouted, his clenched fist punching the air. The SWAT members froze before the foot of an impossibly steep cliff.

Moretti's stomach sank as he watched the team anchor rappel rope onto the rocks. One by one, each team member clipped to the line and repelled down the hill with ease.

When the last SWAT member had successfully made it to the bottom, Dempsey kneeled and took hold of the rope. He looked up at Moretti and flashed an obnoxious red-faced grin.

"Should we send a unit to pick you two up?" Dempsey laughed, repelling down the hill with the skill of a mountain lion.

Now it was Moretti and Ross's turn. "Jesus," McMillian groaned when he'd reached the foot of the cliff and looked down. The SWAT members huddled in formation about seventy feet below.

"What's the matter, you afraid of heights?" Dempsey's shrill voice shouted.

Moretti yanked off one of his gloves. Then he buried his hand inside his trench coat and pulled out a steel flask. With a flick of his wrist, he spun the cap off, sending it sailing over the edge of the cliff in silence before it made a high-pitched clink at the bottom. He took a swig, but the bourbon did little to calm his nerves.

"We can go down together." Ross was kneeling at the foot of the cliff.

"Just get your ass down there and don't worry about me," Moretti snarled.

Moretti watched Ross rappel effortlessly down the mountain with as much skill as the SWAT team.

"Okay, boss, I got you!" Ross shouted from below.

There was no sense in stalling another minute. Time was not on their side and if what the girl from the hospital said was true, then this nut was most likely firing up his power drill to do God knows what to his other victims.

Moretti hiked up his trousers at the crotch and got down on all fours. His knees responded with a loud pop. Using the clip that Dempsey had supplied everyone, Moretti secured himself to the rope.   He didn't descend nearly as smooth as the others, his body swaying like a broken yo-yo, thrashing into the jagged rocks with the force of a wrecking ball. His bones ached but he kept his composure by singing *"We Wish You A Merry Fucking Christmas"* until, finally, he had made it to the bottom.

Unclipping himself from the rappel line, Moretti looked over at Ross who had been standing by Dempsey and the rest of the SWAT team on a series of large rocks. Their flashlights were trained on a huge wall of glistening white stalagmites.

It took a moment for Moretti's eyes to focus but he soon realized that the sharp pointed spikes embedded in the mountain had once been waterfalls that were now completely frozen over. And it was at that moment that a tinge of excitement warmed his belly better than any bourbon could.

"Well," Moretti said, "looks like we found our *gigantic white monster fangs.*"

"Now what?" Dempsey patted the butt of his rifle.

Without responding, Moretti ran to the highest rock formation he could find. He stood a good eight feet above the rest of the officers as he waved his flashlight in every direction.

And that's when he saw it.

Hidden beneath dense brush, ice glistened off the caved-in roof of a small, dilapidated cabin one hundred yards away.

Moretti lit a cigarette and blew out the smoke with weary pleasure. "Let's go wish this son of a bitch a merry Christmas."

*   *   *

"Well?" Mrs. Gaskins said, drumming her boney fingers on the table. "Why isn't your other daughter here?"

Hank stared at the empty place setting. He was biting his lip so hard it began to bleed. "Mother, I told you on the phone; she went away to school and because of the inclement weather she could not make it here this evening."

"The rain dear," Roman added dryly, this time without any hint of humor in his voice.

"Is that so, Hank? You want to blame the weather?" Mrs. Gaskins' thin lips curled upwards, revealing a mouthful of rust-colored teeth stained with lipstick.

Hank was digging his fingernails into the tablecloth when a knock at the front door rattled the dishes on the table.

"Maybe that's her now." Mrs. Gaskins pulled her cashmere sweater closed.

Hank's heart pounded like a hammer forging steel.

Heather looked to her husband, her face pale as a ghost. "Could that be her, Hank? Has she come home?"

Hank's mouth was agape. His vision began to blur and he felt lightheaded.

"I don't know," he said. But Hank knew. Deep in his trembling heart, he knew it could not be his daughter—would *never* again be his daughter at the front door.

A second knock shook the house. As it did, the chandelier began to flicker, the crystal teardrop pendants quivering like a child locked in a cellar.

"Looks like a storm is brewing alright." Roman took a puff from his now-lit briar pipe, a plume of cherry tobacco smoke rising in front of his face like a wavering ghost.

"I'm scared," Brianna and Bellamy said, throwing their arms up, hiding their blanched faces behind their palms.

A third blast at the door sounded like the wooden frame had splintered into a million pieces. With it, Nat King Cole's voice from the other room screeched like knives on a tin roof. When the record needle found its groove again, it began to play in slow motion, this time ominously in reverse.

"Well, aren't you going to answer it?" Mrs. Gaskins asked.

The candles on the table blew out, sending wisps of smoke towards the ceiling. The room had grown cold and dark, the warmth from the fireplace snuffed out from all the turmoil. Hank sighed, his blue breath now visible in front of him.

"What have you done?" Heather moaned.

Hank's eyes went wide. Heather's swollen tongue lolled out of her mouth like a dead rodent, the whites of her once sparkling green eyes now engorged in busted capillaries. Her hair resembled filthy matted wool. Mascara dripped down her bruised face like wet tar. Her neck was encroached with purple black splotches.

"I don't suppose just sitting there is going to be much help." Mrs. Gaskins cut into a piece of turkey on her plate that had a cockroach crawling on it.

A fourth bang at the door sent dishes crashing to the floor while the chandelier swung even more violent. The teardrop pendants snapped off their chains and rained down onto the table in a hailstorm. Wine exploded from shattered glasses like bursts of blood from gunshot wounds.

"Who are you?" Brandon screamed, grabbing hold of Hank's wrist. "Why are you doing this to us?"

Hank jerked his arm away from his son's grasp and stared at the boy's shaggy hair in horror.

The teenager's scalp had been torn open like a stuffed animal. The boy held up a broken finger and pointed to his exposed brain, steam rising from the viscid tissue. "Why?" Brandon screamed.

The thunderous crack of a fifth knock shook the wooden foundation of the house. In that instant, the gold and red wallpaper began to peal from the walls and curl inward like silk ribbon on fire.

"I think we better get going now, Roman." Sheila's head tilted towards the half empty glass of merlot in her hand. Dried green vomit encrusted her chin and neck. But the real terror was the look in her eyes— or rather, the lack thereof. Where her brown eyes once rested were now empty black sockets in a gaunt face.

"Roman?" Hank's voice quivered as he witnessed with revulsion of what was left of his brother-in-law's jaw. Flaps of loose skin dangled off the broken bone and hung pathetically from strings of bloody sinew.

"We want to go home," the twins cried hysterically, removing their hands from their mutilated faces. "We want our mommy."

"But…" Hank struggled to find the words. "This is your home now."

In one final knock, the front door exploded, and a swarm of men with helmets and guns stormed inside. Beams from their flashlights sliced through the cold darkness until, finally, they bathed Hank in light.

*   *   *

"Police! Nobody fucking move!" Commander Dempsey charged into the dark cabin, the search warrant secured to the barrel of his gun like a battle flag. The rest of the SWAT officers followed, their guns poised for combat.

Moretti staggered in, his .38 Special trained in front of his chest. Immediately his nose stung from a cloying stench of decay that cut through the frigid air like toxic fog.

Dempsey and the officers stopped abruptly, their mouths snapping open in silent terror.
"Holy Mother, Mary of God, what is it, Moretti?" Dempsey's voice trembled as he struggled to keep his beam of light on his target. "What the fuck is it?"

Moretti's heart pounded in his chest like a death drum. His eyes wide and unblinking, he stared at the dismal scene.

The corpses were seated around a decrepit makeshift wooden table covered in frost. Their decaying faces frozen in profound agony. Rotted carrion and moldy cheese on grimy rusted dishes adorned the table.

"We got a baby…" Detective Ross stumbled over to a dilapidated bassinet in the corner of the cramped cabin. He looked inside of it before immediately pulling off his snow goggles. Then he vomited.

"Everyone stay calm!" Moretti ordered.

"I give the orders," Dempsey fired back, but his voice lacked any real authority as he noticed the old withered newspaper clippings tacked to the walls. *"HIKER AND INFANT VANISH FROM DEVIL'S KITCHEN"; "STILL NO TRACE Of TEENAGED BOY WHO DISAPPEARED IN THE KITCHEN BACK IN 87'"; "POLICE EXPECT FOUL PLAY IN TWINS' MYSTERIOUS DISAPPEARANCE IN SAUGERTIES."*

Back at the wooden table, a female corpse was wearing a 1950s cocktail dress, her straggly hair spreading over her putrid skeletal face like old cotton. A second lanky corpse—presumably male in its tattered sweater—was propped crookedly across from it, its dusty grey skull split open like a broken clock.

Two other rotting corpses sat at the table, their boney fingers twisted around wine glasses brimming with a murky crimson liquid that was swirling with sediment. A wooden smoking pipe dangled from the protruding jaw of one of the corpses.

Bile boiled in Moretti's stomach. There were two smaller corpses—most likely children—wearing matching ragged pink dresses covered in cobwebs. From the look of the grey taut skin over their tiny arms, they'd been dead for at least several years.

A seventh and final corpse had its back to the officers. It appeared to be the most ancient and was secured to a wooden chair with nails and screws. A threadbare cashmere sweater draped the dust-covered skeleton like a witch's cloak.

Just to the right of the rotting skeleton, a broken chair spattered with in dried blood lay on its side.

Moretti knew whom that chair was intended for. And for the briefest of moments, he felt a meager sense of comfort knowing the girl from the hospital had managed to escape this abysmal dinner party from hell.

Moretti's eyes flashed to the far end of the table where the only living person sat—presumably the host of this morbid affair.

The frail emotionless man rested his bloodstained hands in front of him. He wore a withered wool suit two sizes too small and his greasy unkempt hair shaped his narrow face. A power drill coated in sinew lay next to a plate of rotting meat.

"Alright, get your hands up in the air. Slowly." Moretti shook his revolver in the man's direction.

The man squinted from the flashlights' beams before eventually drifting back to his blank gaze.

"He said get your fucking hands in the air!" Dempsey screamed.

The man slowly began to raise his hands above his head. As he did, the corpses themselves extended their own rickety arms into the air in vile synchronicity.

A loud gasp flooded the room in a swell of shared panic as the SWAT officers cowered back, clumsily tripping over their own boots.

"They're alive!" Dempsey cried out, his trigger finger trembling.

"No, they're not." The burning bile in Moretti's stomach swam up to his throat as he stared at the lunatic in front of him.

The man's fingers had been wrapped in thin metal wire, like a puppeteer. It extended above him and over crisscrossed wooden rafters in the dilapidated ceiling. From these rafters, the wires continued downward like spider's silk, attaching to hook and eye bolts drilled into the corpses' appendages. Above the bloody chair that had been knocked over, the wires had been severed. They dangled above it like steel tendrils encrusted in bits of flesh.

"He kept saying he was so proud to be my father," The hospital girl's voice echoed in Moretti's head as he stared at the metal wires.

"I kept screaming that that I didn't even know who he was. Then I ripped myself off those fucking wires."

Suddenly the corpse in the 1950s dress began to twitch, its arm slowly descending until its boney fingers began to grope the table in front of it.

Moretti's eyes flashed wide, the puppeteer's hand mimicking the same gesture as his filthy hands reached for the power drill.

In the next instant a deafening barrage of gunfire tore through the puppeteer's body. He thrashed violently, the corpses flailing in deathly unison.

Then as quickly as it had happened, the room returned to an eerie muteness.

"Jesus fucking Christ!" Dempsey stared in horror at the acrid smoke pouring from the barrel of Moretti's gun.

The puppeteer slumped lifelessly in his chair, his arms hanging limply at his sides. His corpse family imitated the lifeless gesture, their skeleton arms dangling from their rotted joints.

Snow was beginning to fall gently from the cracks in the caved-in ceiling as Moretti's daughter's smiling face flashed in his mind.

Bundled in her winter coat and hat with the pink pom poms, he and his daughter were putting the finishing touches on the four-foot snowman in their backyard.

"Do you think snowmen come alive when no one is looking?" his little girl asked as Moretti guided his daughter's hand to place the frozen carrot in the snowman's face. Moretti turned to Sarah who smiled back from the patio, sipping hot cocoa from a Santa Clause mug.

"What did you just do?" Dempsey stared in revulsion at the dead puppeteer slouched in his chair.

A perfect calmness warmed Moretti like a heated blanket as he thought about the promise he had made to his grandfather all those years ago.

"I killed the Devil," he said.

The Cheap Rooms

Robert Essig

The carpets were severely stained and coming apart at the seams, patched intermittently with mismatched pieces of equal neglect. The walls complemented the carpets with scuffs and mysterious splatter: perhaps a spilled drink (it was Vegas after all), or . . . something else. But Haloran and Stephanie Watts were celebrating their fourth anniversary and didn't have the kind of money that could afford them a stay at a place like Caesar's or even the Flamingo, and they had promised themselves that they would get a room in a hotel at the center of the Strip.

With their budget they purchased the most inexpensive room they could get, which turned out to be in the old Imperial Hotel. Located at the rear of the lot behind the parking structure and a less than charming alleyway. Back in the old days it was called the Sand Dune Inn. Several lots were purchased, and the Imperial Hotel was erected, towering over the diminutive Sand Dune Inn, which was owned by the Imperial, but never held to the same laughable standards.

"Man, I knew the Imperial was run down, but this is too much," Haloran said.

Stephanie smirked. "Let's just hope there aren't any bedbugs and weird stains on the sheets."

They rounded a corner, scanning the room numbers for 519.

"Of course, we might make some stains of our own on the sheets," Haloran said.

Stephanie gave him a playful grin. "We'll just have to see about that."

As they took to the hall, they were both startled not only that there was a housekeeper standing there with her cart of linens, soaps, and cleaning materials who may have heard the soiled sheets comment, but by the fact that she was staring at them with one eye. It wouldn't have been quite as strange had she been wearing an eye patch. But she chose to brazenly walk the halls displaying a rather gruesome cavity of scarred flesh. The scars traveled down the left side of her face onto her neck, disappearing beneath the collar of her uniform.

Haloran nudged Stephanie to keep walking. They had both slowed like lookie-loos passing a wreck on the highway. The housekeeper turned after grabbing several towels and walked into the room she was cleaning.

"Jesus," Stephanie whispered.

"I guess working as a housekeeper is a good thing for someone with those kinds of scars. Don't have to deal with the public. Much. Here it is." Haloran stopped so abruptly that Stephanie bumped into him. She had her head turned, looking down the hall where the woman had been.

"Jesus, Hal!"

"Don't want to pass it up, do we? This place is like a freaking maze."

With a swipe of the key card, they were in. The interior surprised them in that it was much cleaner than the hallway. Only mild stains here and there on the linens and a sprinkling of black mold on the bathroom ceiling. Could be worse.

Haloran plopped his suitcase on the bed furthest from the door (they didn't sleep in the same bedroom at home due to Haloran's snoring, and having two beds was as close to her not being kept awake all night as they could get). He pulled out a bottle of good whiskey (a gift from his father) and they toasted their anniversary.

After a few drinks, Stephanie touched up her makeup and they headed for the odd smelling yet compelling Las Vegas Boulevard.

Slot machines had a way of draining wallets, but Hal and Stephanie knew their limit. They preferred to drop their money on drinks and good food and had already purchased tickets to a burlesque magic show for the following night. It wasn't really what they wanted to see, but there was a great buy-one-get-one-free deal that they couldn't resist.

After making their way back through the maze of mismatched carpet and threadbare rugs, they laughed at the conspicuous stains in the halls before slipping into their room where they sipped more whiskey and made love, after which they went to sleep on opposite sides of each bed— Hal's snoring and all. But they'd had enough drink to fall victim to the sandman easy enough to prevent Stephanie the tortures of his log sawing.   They had a lot planned for the next two nights. The magic show, a fantastic dinner buffet at the MGM they'd heard good things about, gambling, people watching.

But none of that happened.

Stephanie's eyes were still gluey from a knockout combo of alcohol and dreams when a disturbance roused her from a deep sleep. Could have been anything in a city that never slept. There were drunks out from dusk till dawn and then till dusk again, and they had the propensity to stumble down hallways and into walls, searching for their rooms and even trying their keycards in the wrong doors.

But this sound, it was something different.

It was in the room.

Stephanie turned to face Haloran when the sound again issued through the darkness. It was like ruffling sheets, but not the kind of ruffling that resulted from a shifty sleeper.

A whimper?

She had been listening more than looking, trying to keep her eyes closed so she could slip back into sleep effortlessly. But it became clear that she'd better get her bearings, so she opened her eyes. It took a moment to adjust to the dark of the room, and when she did, she had to squint to make heads or tails of what she was seeing in the bed next to hers. Stephanie bolted upright, yet something caused her to refrain from planting her feet on the floor. Maybe it was childhood fears of the boogey man, or maybe something else.

She stared at Haloran wide-eyed. Something was shoved into his mouth, gagging him. He trembled, sweat beading on his forehead and glistening with the faint light coming in where the blinds were parted. He was restrained with some kind of rope or leather straps.

Stephanie yelped as she jumped out of bed to her husband's aid. He had wild, terror-stricken eyes. The whimpering sounds grew more frantic as the breaths from his nostrils accelerated with rising adrenalin. Then the whimpers hit agonizing and muffled crescendos. His eyes closed tightly, becoming filled with tears that spilled down his face mixing with his sweat.

Mouth agape, lower jaw trembling, Stephanie assessed the situation, doing her best to remain in control. She grabbed the sweaty piece of tape that held the ball gag in Hal's mouth and yanked. He yelped and grimaced. "Jesus it hurts!" he said through clenched teeth. "My back! It hurts!"

"What happened? How did this...?"

Haloran shook his head. "I don't know."

He clenched his eyes again, sucking air through his teeth as pain assaulted him.

"What's wrong, Hal? Can you move?"

"Feels like something's biting me. Cut the straps. Get me out of here."

There wasn't much in their hotel room in the way of cutting utensils. Stephanie frantically checked the stationary desk and her purse for not only a cutting utensil, but her phone as well. Haloran sobbed and cringed from some kind of assault that she couldn't see. She feared that when she cut the straps, he wouldn't be able to move. That somehow he'd become paralyzed.

"My pants pocket," Hal said. "My pocketknife."

In a flash of movement, Stephanie retrieved the pocketknife and began cutting the straps that were fixed on something beneath the bed. They wrapped around her husband's frame, and reattached on the opposite side. After all the straps were severed and the pressure was relieved, Haloran sat up, which should have been a relief considering Stephanie's fear of his potential paralysis. But something far worse was at play, something that dropped her heart into her bowel and seemed to draw out all the air in her lungs.

Hal's sudden scream was agonizing. It was pain vocalized; fear realized. Stephanie had never heard her man in such a desperate fit. She'd never heard him scream like a frightened child, and that alone chilled her to the core. But what she saw next drove the proverbial ice-pick chill through her heart.

Haloran's face was a shellac of sweat, his eyes and jaw clenched so tightly he looked like a weightlifter attempting to break his max. Then she saw his back. The bed was a mess of torn sheets, blood and gore. His back looked much the same, glistening and red, with stringy muscle and tendons on display. The worst part of the mad spectacle was the implements that held him to the bed. What appeared to be arms protruding from within the mattress. They grabbed onto the shredded ribbons of flesh, little fingers grasping for the solid column of his red, wet spine.

Stephanie took a few steps back until she bumped into the other bed.

"Get them off me!" Haloran screamed.

He struggled to remain upright, the arms attempting to pull him onto the bed again. Stephanie grabbed the old wooden chair from the stationary desk and used it like a lion tamer from the old days. Holding it from the back with both hands she started swinging. She hit one of the strange arms. It dinged metallically as the wooden legs of the chair made contact. The arms began to shake Haloran's body, eliciting further screams and pleas of agony. Then something emerged from the pool of blood on the mattress. It was a face, smooth and flawless yet hideous and bestial, red with Haloran's blood. The eyes looked straight ahead at Haloran's back, then shifted toward Stephanie. She recoiled, and then the face emerged from the bloody bed, dug its massive maw onto Haloran's destroyed back, latching onto his spine, and yanked him down.

Blood splattered from the puddle as Hal's body hit the tattered sheets, decorating Stephanie with red spatter. She trembled, forced to watch as her husband's body was pulled into the cavity of the bed where the arms and vile sculpted face had protruded.

Snapping out of the terror-daze she'd been submerged in, she grabbed Haloran's arms trying to pull him free. But the horrors beneath pulled him from her grasp and into the bloody pit.

The room was silent with the exception of Stephanie's cries and the bubbling blood pool in the bed. She dared not reach into the muck for fear that one of the arms would reach out and pull her in.

He's gone. I can't believe he's gone.

But beyond the sudden and inexplicable death of her husband, there was something mad and unexplainable in the hotel. Something Stephanie's mind could not register or even attempt to comprehend. And it was in their room. Seething within the gory pool at the center of the bed Haloran had been sleeping on.

She had to get out of there. The image of the marble-smooth demon awash in crimson flashed in her mind. The blood on the bed remained still, as if there wasn't a void hidden beneath.   Stephanie wanted to believe that Hal was alive in there somewhere, but her better judgment dictated her retreat from the room. It was better that she get help, not that anyone would believe her story. The bloody pit in the mattress roiled and bubbled and taunted her. Realizing that both of their phones were on the nightstand beside the bed, she inched closer to retrieve one of them. Things in the nasty mattress pit surfaced the closer she got. Sick things. Human-like hands on serpentine coils, dripping blood and gore that hung like strips of muscle, tendons, and clotted blood.

Deciding she couldn't risk getting close enough to snatch one of their phones, Stephanie fled the room.

The hallway was quiet, sullen and distorted, at least in Stephanie's perspective. It could have been paved with gold bars and studded with diamonds and she still would have seen a perfect vision of Hell.   In that moment, as a light in the ceiling flickered like a nervous twitch, Stephanie was overcome by a tide of anxiety-fueled panic. She couldn't decide which way to go. She would have to take the elevator down to the lobby to report Hal's murder. She would have used the phone in their room, but she had to get out of there. The odor and sight of Hal's blood had been getting to her, and there was a general sense of dread and unease. A return to childhood fears, as if at any moment the thing in the bed would get her.

She saw a housekeeper down the hall, her bony fingers latched onto a pushcart topped with toilet paper rolls and off-white linens and towels that were frayed at the corners.

It's too late for maids, isn't it?

"Call the police," Stephanie said. "My husband's been murdered!"

It wasn't the same housekeeper they'd seen with the scar on her face, however there was something peculiar in her expression. Was it fear? Pity? She looked down suddenly and proceeded to turn around and push the cart away, as if purposely ignoring Stephanie.

Stephanie's face twisted into questioning shock. "Wait! Where are you going?"

The housekeeper picked up speed, which came off as more insulting than anything. How was it this woman could so easily disregard Stephanie's plea?

The only sound in the hall was the wheels of the pushcart fighting their way over lumpy patched together carpet.

"Aren't you going to help me? Don't you have a phone?"

The housekeeper glanced back in her awkward speed-walking escape, but Stephanie was gaining on her. At this point she was becoming angry with the woman for her deliberate negligence.

"Where are you going? I need help!"

Close enough to grab her, Stephanie reached out a hand and latched onto her arm. It was an aggressive move, but after what she'd had been through, who could blame her?

The housekeeper grunted as she was pulled to a stop. Her spindly fingers let go of the pushcart that had enough momentum on the old carpet to continue its forward roll until it came to a sudden jerking stop.

That's when Stephanie noticed the length of the chain from the housekeeper's arm to the cart.

Stephanie's mouth dropped open. The housekeeper grabbed her wrist, rubbing the soreness from her shackle, as she stared into Stephanie's shocked eyes.

"You must get out of here before they find you," the housekeeper said.

"They?"

"The ones that killed your husband. They will get you, but they won't kill you. Not yet at least."

"Call the police! Call security!"

In a hushed voice the housekeeper said, "There is no security. Not here. There are no phones." There was a pregnant pause as the women locked eyes as if trying to read one another's thoughts. "You don't know where you are."

Growing impatient and angry with the strange housekeeper, Stephanie said, "I'm at the Imperial Hotel, and if you're not going to help me, I'm going to have to get down to the casino. Something happened in my room, something I can't explain. I . . . I saw something come out of the bed and . . . kill my husband."

The housekeeper nodded rapidly. "Yes, yes! One of *Them*."

"This is crazy."

Stephanie turned from the housekeeper and fled in the direction she thought she could find the elevator. She expected the housekeeper to say something. But the woman remained silent. When Stephanie turned to see if she was still there, the woman had left.

She found the elevator door. A cold slab of metal with ominous scratches and dents pounded into it like urban hieroglyphs. Her finger couldn't press the big C button quick enough, however nothing happened. There was no telltale sound of the hydraulics or a bell dinging that indicated the initiation of the elevator's gears.

She pressed the Casino button again. It didn't light up the way it should have, so she pressed the button for the first floor. It had the same result.

Cursing, Stephanie looked up and down the hallway, afraid of the thing that pulled Haloran into the bed. She looked again at the battered elevator door and screamed. The smooth demonic face she'd seen in the bloody pool on the bed was staring at her. It glared with slanted eyes as smooth as spun sugar. Sugar that would have been beautiful under any other circumstance.

Stephanie stood as still as petrified wood. At any moment the arms could reach out and pull her into the abysmal unknown. Hal was in there, somewhere. She wondered if he was suffering, if he was dead, if there was more pain where he went. Those last moments with him were terrible. His suffering burned in her mind like the black tracings of a branding iron.

She backed slowly from the elevator door as if she would quietly sneak off without the demonic face realizing she'd gone. It stared her down with peculiar eyes that now looked like polished coins. Although Stephanie didn't recognize the president facing the coins. They looked familiar, but something was amiss. They almost looked like George Washington with Abraham Lincoln's beard.

"You won't get out of here," the face said. The voice had a bizarre metallic tone. "There's no way out but through our consumption. And we need you. We've already consumed your husband, but you can serve us in another way."

Stephanie shook her head. "No. I'm getting out of here."

She ran in search of the stairwell; however she went in the opposite direction, treading over lumpy carpet, stained with black gum spots and splashes of anything from beer to . . . blood? She passed many doors, all of them bearing similar glyphs as that of the elevator door. There was no sign of life whatsoever. No drunken laughter, no dinging elevator bells, no noisy televisions, nothing. When Stephanie wrapped around the entire floor, she grabbed the handle to the first door she saw that didn't have a room number on it.

What seemed like a dozen hands grabbed and pulled her in. She screamed but was stifled by a palm shoved into her mouth.

She was surrounded by tired, desperate housekeepers, gasping and drawing deep breaths of awe. Their faces had a collective look of tragedy and horror. Solemn eyes, dragging faces, scars, broken capillaries—it was terrible. Stephanie was in some kind of hell.

"They're looking for you," one of them whispered after a pause that seemed to defy time.

"Can't you help me?" Stephanie asked. "I need help. Something . .

. happened. I can't even believe it. My husband is . . ."

"Dead," another housekeeper said, her voice low and emotionless, half-crazed eyes set deep in folds of tired flesh. Eyes that had witnessed atrocities.

The housekeepers began looking upward, scanning the ceiling, and then eyeing the walls for something Stephanie couldn't see.

"We have to hide you," the housekeeper Stephanie had talked to in hall said.

The others erupted into a half-angry murmur, soft and delicate like the fluttering of so many butterflies.

The housekeeper from the hall went into action, lifting the pile of bath towels and linens from the lower rack of her pushcart. "Get down there," she said to Stephanie.

"I won't fit."

"You have to. They're coming. If they find you, they will . . . make you like us."

The woman lifted her arm, the cuff visible around her wrist, a length of chain connected to it that disappeared beneath the linens, connected to her pushcart.

Some of the others displayed their shackled wrists. The pushcarts were all lined up in the storage room, so tight there wasn't much space.

"We were like you," another woman said, her voice heavy with exhaustion. "We came here because the rooms were so cheap, then they came. Killed my husband. Pulled him right into the bed as I watched, and then one of them took me away. We all share the same story, but you still have a chance. You need to get out of here, but for now you must hide, because they're coming. I can feel their presence like static electricity. They are everywhere, fueled by the greed and debauchery of Vegas, but their appetite has changed. The money that once fueled them isn't enough. They want blood, and they need us to clean the messes."

"Quick," a woman said, her voice only a tone above a hush. "They're almost here. Climb onto the cart and we'll crowd around you."

Stephanie's mind was a frantic scattering of neurons firing in random succession. She dropped to the ground and crawled onto the lower shelf of the cart, only a foot off the ground. The housekeepers covered her with what seemed like an endless supply of white sheets and towels. She

257

was engulfed in darkness, shivering in fear, sweat beginning to mat her hair to her forehead.

She listened.

There was a gurgling sound, then a guttural chuckle before a voice spoke. She recognized it as the voice of the smooth-faced demon she'd seen in the battered elevator door.

"Where is she?" the voice asked.

Stephanie remained as still as possible, pretending that she was a statue. She clamped her teeth on a towel to stifle the scream she feared she couldn't prevent.

"One of you knows where she is," the voice said. "Tell me and I will have mercy on you."

"We haven't seen anyone," a delicate, frightened voice said.

A loud snap, the sound of bones crunching, liquid dripping, and then a body hit the floor. Stephanie yelped, but her saving grace was that they all yelped at the sudden murder of the housekeeper who dared deny that they'd seen her. What Stephanie didn't see was the demon in the wall, stretching through the plaster, opening its mouth lined with teeth fashioned of sharpened silver coins that orally decapitated the woman. The crunching of her skull could be heard through the cries of the other housekeepers, and then the demon was gone.

They were tense moments as Stephanie lay there on the pushcart wondering if it was safe to remove herself from the tight constraint.

"He's gone," a shivering voice said.

With help from several housekeepers, Stephanie was pulled from the cart. The women were stricken with terror, sadness, and anger. Their decapitated sister's body lay on the ground, the cuffed arm suspended in the air, connected to a pushcart with much less chain than the others, as if perhaps she'd been kept on a short leash. The pool of blood from the raw wound of her neck grew larger, threatening to reach Stephanie's feet like a slowly rising tide that never ebbed.

"Get out of here," one of the women said. Stephanie had misjudged her anger, thinking she'd directed it toward the demon. "You caused this. You're on your own." After a pause and a glance at the body on the floor, the woman finished with, "May God's blessing be with you. And if you get out, you have to tell the authorities. But remember that the greedy demons are everywhere. They are the Gods of Las Vegas, and they will do everything to prevent you from ruining what they have here. This place . . . it's the root of all evil."

Another housekeeper opened the door to the hallway. They shuffled toward Stephanie, ushering her out of the room.

She thought to plea for their forgiveness but knew better. They'd helped her enough to lose one of their own. They could have given her up and saved the poor woman.

The door shut. The hall was silent.

A door across from the elevator beckoned to her. It was the stairwell, what most people avoided due to heavy luggage and laziness. For Stephanie it was salvation.

She took the stairs in doubles, careful not to trip or catch her foot. Nothing to stop her momentum. Hands gliding on the worn and paintchipped iron railings, something beneath her fingers didn't feel quite right. The ridges created by the chipped paint began to feel bumpier. She soon realized that the iron was turning into quarters and silver dollars, pennies, dimes and nickels.

For a moment, Stephanie thought it was by design, but she realized soon enough that it was a distraction, and it worked. She slowed as she pondered the strange currency-lined railing. The steps transformed into wads of cash, and by the time she made it to ground level, the iron-railturn-coin-rail had become pure gold speckled with blood. The steps became solid gold bricks, the walls covered in a wallpaper of perfect onehundred-dollar bills.

The door was dented and scratched. Ugly in contrast to the wealthy surroundings. There were ominous spatters of blood here and there, but Stephanie made her best effort to ignore the bizarre changes and depressed the large bar that opened the heavy steel door.

A breath of warm air that smelled of sewer and exhaust hit her in the face. It was real. It was Vegas.

Stephanie all but leapt out of the stairwell, turned, and what she saw wasn't gold brick stairs and one-hundred-dollar bill wallpaper, but a filthy, cold stairwell of concrete and iron.

The door startled her by slamming shut.

She had a lot to be thankful for, however there was a hole in her heart for Haloran that would always be there. Here she managed to escape, and he was in there somewhere, suffering or dead.

In the distance were the sounds of people, cars, anger, fun, greed—the spoils of Sin City.

Stephanie closed her eyes, took a deep breath, and then opened them again.

Her scream was so sudden she startled herself. The demon lurched from the door as it had from the elevator, only this time it was accompanied by several reaching hands with claws of molten silver. Before they could grab her, she stumbled backwards and directly into the path of an oncoming car.

The last thing Stephanie heard before waking in the hospital was the screeching breaks and the horn as the car hit her. She'd broken several ribs, lost a few teeth, and broken her arm. She had no idea how long she'd been out, but she had a cast on her arm and a lot of bandages on her face and chest.

Where's Hal? Is he all right?

Just as soon as she thought of Hal, she remembered what had happened at the Imperial Hotel. She closed her eyes, prayed for Haloran and thanked God that she was in a hospital.

They're the Gods of Las Vegas, one of the housekeepers had said. *They're everywhere.*

A nurse entered the room holding a hypodermic. "Just a little something to help with the pain," she said.

Stephanie tried to speak, but all that came out were incomprehensible grunts and malformed words. She desperately wanted to tell the nurse to get the police, but she was unable to properly articulate herself.

"Hush, hush," the nurse said. "Don't try to speak. Just relax."

She jabbed the needle into Stephanie's arm. Stephanie cringed. It burned, which didn't seem right. The nurse smiled, and Stephanie's eyes widened at the sight of veneer-like teeth of silver and gold, displaying the faces of dead presidents.

As the world faded away Stephanie tried to scream, to arouse attention, but she was powerless to the Gods of Las Vegas, and the secret of the Imperial Hotel was safe once again.

The End

Authors

Ryan C. Thomas is an award-winning journalist and editor living in San Diego, California. He is the author of 14 novels (including the cult classic, *The Summer I Died*), numerous novellas and short stories, and can often be found in the bars around Southern California playing guitar. When he is not writing or rocking out, he is at home with his wife, son, daughter and pets watching really bad B-movies. Visit him online at **RyanCThomas.com.**

Tim Curran is the author of *Skin Medicine, Hive, Dead Sea, The Devil Next Door, Blooding Night, Clownflesh,* and *Bad Girl in the Box,* among others. His short stories have been collected in *Alien Horrors, The Horrors of War,* and *The Brain Leeches.* His novellas include *The Underdwelling, The Corpse King, Puppet Graveyard, Worm,* and *The Sunken City.* His fiction has been translated into German, Japanese, Spanish, and Italian. Find him on Facebook at:
https://www.facebook.com/tim.curran.77

Bridgett Nelson is a registered nurse turned horror author. Her first collection, *A Bouquet of Viscera*, is a two-time Splatterpunk Award finalist, recognized both for the collection itself and its standout story, "*Jinx.*" Her work has appeared in *Counting Bodies Like Sheep, Dead & Bloated, American Cannibal, A Woman Unbecoming,* and several volumes of the *If I Die Before I Wake* series of anthologies. Bridgett is working on her first original novel and has been contracted by Encyclopocalypse Publications to write a novelization of the cult classic film *Deadgirl.* She is an active member of the Horror Writers Association and the co-chair of HWA: West Virginia. She was a 2022 Michael Knost "Wings" award nominee, and won second place in the '22 Gross-Out contest at KillerCon in Austin, Texas. Bridgett thoroughly enjoys writing, mainly because wearing a bra is not required. She also likes tarantulas. A lot. To learn more, visit her website at **www.BridgettnNelson.com.**

Marc Schoenbach's fascination with horror began at an early age. As a child in the 1980s, he was already enjoying horror movies and playing games that could be seen as morbid by today's standards. This love of the macabre continued into the 1990s, when he became an avid reader of RL Stine's *Goosebumps* series. Marc's passion for all things horror would eventually lead him to a career in psychology, and later to writing short stories and screenplays. After teaching himself Photoshop, Marc began creating his own faux-vintage movie posters based on his stories. Social media provided the perfect platform to share his artwork, and in 2011, he founded **Sadist Art Designs**. Since then, Marc has freelanced for major industry companies such as Fright Rags, Waxwork Records, and Arrow Video, creating covers for Fangoria magazine, and has even quit his psychology job to pursue his passion full-time. His journey from a young boy fascinated by horror to a successful artist in the industry is a testament to the power of following one's passions and interests. Marc currently resides in Long Island, NY, with his wife, two children, and two black cats, Salem and Spooky.

Nathan Robinson has had over 40 short stories published in numerous anthologies. He is the author of *Starers, Midway, Ketchup on Everything,* and the short story collection *Devil Let Me Go*. He is currently a School Librarian, hoping to inspire the next generation of readers and writers.

You can find him at **www.facebook.com/NathanRobinsonWrites**

Or on Instagram **@natthewriter**

Dan Henk was born on a small army base in the deep south. He's been homeless, made it through brain cancer, got stabbed by a crackhead, totaled three cars, three bikes, and plunged backwards through a windshield after a girl hit him while texting and driving, After four
 hours in a coma, he sprung back and resumed his normal life. There is a running theory he is a cyborg. Despite all that, he has three novels and
 two chapbooks out, has done a slew of artwork for books and
 magazines, and
owns a tattoo shop in NYC. Over one hundred books and magazines
 have featured his art, writing, and tattooing. And he's made it all
 around the

world in pursuit of both his craft and in an investigation of ancient ruins and myths. You can see his latest travails and triumphs on his website, **DanHenk.com**, or on Facebook or Instagram as **@Deadguyllc**.

Christine Morgan is the author of several novels and over a hundred short stories, spanning genres from superheroes to smut, with a focus on horror and dark fantasy. She's particularly fond of historical, extreme, cosmic, and blending various sub-genres. She also takes on freelance edit gigs, does book reviews, is into weird crafts and baking, and spends her free time sleeping or getting bossed around by cats. She can be found online at:

https://ChristineMarieMorgan.wordpress.com, on various social media platforms, or by email at
ChristineMarieMorgan@gmail.com

Patrick C. Harrison III (PC3, if you prefer) is an author of horror, splatterpunk, and all forms of speculative fiction. Several of PC3's works have been nominated for awards, and he is the Splatterpunk Award-winning editor (with Jarod Barbee) of *And Hell Followed*. He is also the mind behind the *Splatter Western* series (Death's Head Press), which began in 2020 and continues still, with many horror authors participating.

PC3 has authored ten books as of this writing—including the Amazon best-seller *100% Match* and the award-nominated novella *Grandpappy*—and his short stories can be found in numerous anthologies. When he's not
writing, he's frequently editing manuscripts for other horror authors and publishers. For PC3 news and frequent horror and exploitation movie reviews, subscribe to this FREE
substack: **pc3horror.substack.com**

Jeff Strand is the Bram Stoker Award-winning author of over 50 books, including *CLOWNS VS. SPIDERS, AUTUMN BLEEDS INTO WINTER*, and *TWENTIETH ANNIVERSARY SCREENING*. You can visit his Gleefully Macabre website at **www.JeffStrand.com.**

Robert Essig is the author of fifteen books including *Baby Fights, Secret Basements* and *Broth House*. He has published over 150 short stories and edited three small press anthologies such as *Chew on This!*, which was nominated for a Splatterpunk Award. Robert lived with his family in east Tennessee. For updates, subscribe to his free newsletter at **robertessig. substack.com**. You can grab signed copies of his books at **essighorror. bigcartel.com**.

Patrick Lacey was born and raised in a haunted house. He spends his time writing about things that make the general public shiver. He lives in a hopefully un-haunted house in Massachusetts with two hyperactive cats, his daughter, and his wife. Follow him on Twitter (**@PatLacey**).

Jack Bantry is the editor of **Splatterpunk Zine**. He resides in a small town at the edge of the North York Moors. His works include *AIN'T WORTH A SHIT*, and the collection *SHALLOW GRAVES*, both co-written with Robert Essig.

Bobby Lisse is a Writer and Filmmaker from New York. He has a daily column for **Morbidly Beautiful Horror** called **The Daily Dig** for which he unearths little known horror films from the nineteen forties to the two thousands and gives them a spotlight, for better or worse. He has also written for Rue Morgue Magazine. He produces and edits the **Skull Session** podcast for renowned tattoo artist, author, and artist Dan Henk and spends most of the rest of his time buried in books and writing screenplays. You can contact him for film editing, manuscript editing, or research at

BobbyLisse@Gmail.com

Bracken MacLeod is the Splatterpunk, Bram Stoker, and Shirley Jackson
Award nominated author of the novels, *Mountain Home, Come to Dust, Stranded,* and *Closing Costs.* He's also published two collections of short fiction, *13 Views of the Suicide Woods* and *White Knight and Other Pawns.* Before devoting himself to full time writing, he survived car crashes, a near drowning, being shot at, a parachute malfunction, and the bar exam. So far, the only incident that has resulted in persistent nightmares is the bar exam. He lives outside of Boston, where he is at work on his next novel about the fallout of Satanic Panic of the 1980s. You can learn more about his work at **BrackenMacLeod.com.**

"But Everyone Disappears, no matter who loves them."
-Dave Eggers

Milton Keynes UK
Ingram Content Group UK Ltd.
UKHW041633280723
425883UK00018B/326